Books by Jude Deveraux

The Velvet Promise   *Wishes*
Highland Velvet   *Mountain Laurel*
Velvet Song   *The Duchess*
Velvet Angel   *Eternity*
Sweetbriar   *Sweet Liar*
Counterfeit Lady   *The Invitation*
Lost Lady   *Remembrance*
River Lady   *The Heiress*
Twin of Fire   *Legend*
Twin of Ice   *An Angel for Emily*
The Temptress   *The Blessing*
The Raider   *High Tide*
The Princess   *Temptation*
The Awakening   *The Summerhouse*
The Maiden   *The Mulberry Tree*
The Taming   *Forever…*
The Conquest   *Wild Orchids*
A Knight in Shining Armor   *Forever and Always*

Jude Deveraux

※※※

Forever and Always

DOUBLEDAY LARGE PRINT HOME LIBRARY EDITION

POCKET BOOKS

New York   London   Toronto   Sydney   Singapore

This Large Print Edition, prepared especially for Doubleday Large Print Home Library, contains the complete, unabridged text of the original Publisher's Edition.

 POCKET BOOKS, a division of Simon & Schuster, Inc. 1230 Avenue of the Americas, New York, NY 10020

ISBN: 0-7394-3725-9

Front cover illustration by Lisa Litwack
Photo credit: Alain Daussin/Getty Images

Manufactured in the United States of America

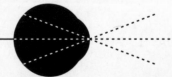

This Large Print Book carries the
Seal of Approval of N.A.V.H.

DARCI ✂

✂ Chapter One

He was lying. I didn't know how much or about what, but I was sure he was lying.

Also, he was acting. More than that, he was playing the character he portrayed on TV, the shy, likable, brilliant detective, Paul Travis. The gorgeous-but-doesn't-know-it Paul Travis. He was dipping his head down and glancing up at me as though he expected me to swoon over the sheer beauty of him, but I wasn't even close. When you're married to a man like Adam Montgomery, other men don't compare.

I sat down across from him and began concentrating to try to force him to stop acting and tell me the truth.

This wasn't what I wanted to be doing but my mother had sent me a letter. It was the first letter I'd ever received from her so of course it had an impact on me. It said, "You owe me." Stuck in the letter was a photo of the actor, Lincoln Aimes.

The letter puzzled me for days. Of course I knew what she meant: You owe me for saving your life, so pay me back. But what did she want me to do with the beautiful black actor?

Was my mother asking me to do what I could to get the man to be her next lover? That didn't make sense because my mother certainly didn't need anyone's help in getting a man, even a man much younger than she was.

After I received the letter and photo, I got on the Internet and ordered the DVDs of the first four seasons of Lincoln Aimes's TV show, *Missing.* The character Paul Travis didn't appear until the sixth show of the first season and then only in a small role, but he was such a hit that they asked him to become a leading character. At least that's what the brochure that came with the DVDs said. When I searched the Internet I read that the actor had had problems finding roles that cast him as anything other than a body and a face.

Poor guy, I thought. We should all have such problems.

It seemed that Lincoln Aimes wanted to play meaty parts. You know, something like a society outcast, the guy who was given bad parents and poverty, but manages to rise above that and become the first American president with no scandal attached to him.

Instead, casting agents took one look at Lincoln Aimes's perfect face, his perfect body, and cast him . . . well, as a sort of dumb blond. With honey-colored skin.

I read that Lincoln Aimes took a few roles, none of which he liked, then was out of work for a couple of years. I guess he got hungry because he finally accepted a small part on the hit detective series *Missing,* which each week looked for a missing person. After just one appearance, he became one of the three main characters.

What made the role work was that, in a way, it made fun of Lincoln Aimes's exceptional beauty. When the cast was working on a case, the character of Paul Travis was all business. He unraveled clues, was great at sizing people up, and had a real knack for putting himself into the mind of a missing person.

What he didn't know was that behind his back, everyone was talking about how gorgeous he was. It was a running joke throughout the show. The other characters constantly used him for such things as getting the angry woman in records to put their requests on the top of the pile. Paul Travis, or just Travis, as everyone called him, would hand the woman the request, speak to her in a businesslike way, then walk away. The camera would show her sighing and saying, "Yes, Travis," then immediately feeding the info into the computer. The next second she'd take the head off some ugly guy who complained that he'd been waiting for the same information for three days.

The whole premise was hokey and bordered on the ridiculous, but it enlivened a show that was like too many others already on TV. It was fun to see witnesses do double takes when they saw Travis. And it was fun to tune in each week to see what the writers came up with to show off Lincoln Aimes's beauty.

Yes, it was a good show, and I, like most of America, watched it regularly. Of course no one believed a person could be so good-looking and not know it, but it was a nice thought. It made the viewer smile when Travis said in wonder, "That man offered me a job as a male stripper. Weird, huh?" We viewers chuckled with the characters in the show. And each week we tuned in to see if maybe they were going to tell us something about Travis's personal life—but they never did. We saw other characters' wives, husbands, apartments, kids. But never anything at all about Travis's personal life. If it didn't happen to him at work, it was never shown.

So now the actor who played Paul Travis was sitting in my living room, looking at me shyly, as though he thought I'd believe he was who he played. But he was lying to me.

I stared at him hard and concentrated, and was soon rewarded with seeing him raise his head and look at me straight-on, with no head-ducking.

"Your mother said you could help me find my son." He had to take a deep breath to get the words to come out, and I could feel that he was very nervous. About what? I wondered.

As for the child, I wondered about that.

From what I knew of the actor, he wasn't married, never had been, and had no kids.

Of course he had a girlfriend: Alanna Talbert, the darling of the screen, "the woman most men wanted to have an affair with," as some poll said. She was tall, thin, had cheekbones that could cut glass, and was as perfect physically as Lincoln Aimes was. She, too, was African-American.

"I didn't know you had a son," I said as I stalled for time. I wanted to know how much my mother had told him about me.

"Neither did I," he said, then gave me another look in the character of Paul Travis.

"You want to cut that out and tell me what it is you want?" I snapped at him.

He blinked at me a few times and I could feel his consternation. Obviously, he wasn't used to being spoken to like that by a heterosexual woman. The truth was, I have certain, well, abilities that make me able to see . . . I hate to say that I can see "inside" a person, but I guess that's what happens. I can't read minds but I do have very, very strong intuition. And right now my intuition said that this man thought he could talk me into doing anything he wanted.

Maybe if I gave him an itty-bitty bit of a

headache he'd stop posing, I thought. Maybe he'd tell me what he wanted, I could say no, then he'd go away. I wanted to get back to doing what I did every day, which was lie on the couch in my bedroom and concentrate on my missing husband.

"I—" he began, then stopped as he got up to walk around the living room. It was a pretty room, done in peaches, yellows, and blues. Until a year ago, it was the happiest room on earth.

He looked back at me and I could feel that he'd released some of the hostility I'd sensed when I first met him, but I could still tell he thought I was someone not quite trustworthy. I couldn't very well hold that against him, could I? Not after what that . . . that man had written about me. The whole world called me the Hillbilly Honey. I was the laughingstock of America. Until my husband and his sister disappeared, that is. Then I became the most hated person in America. People believed I'd murdered my husband to collect his inherited money. I told everyone, the police, the reporters, all of them, that I knew in my heart that my husband and sister-in-law were still alive, but no one listened to me.

So now here I was, alone, hiding from the world, and this man was asking me to help him find his son.

And I knew that he was either lying or hiding something big.

LINC ⟨⟨

She didn't look the way I thought she would. I expected her to be larger, more menacing. I expected to see something in her eyes that would show me the woman all of America was talking about.

I'd first heard of Darci Montgomery from Alanna. She'd tossed a thin paperback book down on the floor and said, "That poor kid." This surprised me, as Alanna didn't usually feel sympathy for people. Any sympathy Alanna had went to herself.

I picked up the book and looked at it. *How to Snare a Billionaire* was the title. I'd been so busy arguing with the producers of *Missing* that I was probably the only person on earth who hadn't read the book. I'd spent weeks talking, yelling, and even begging the producers to stop with the Travis-is-beautiful crap. I said the whole thing lowered the tone of the show. *CSI* didn't need such a gimmick and neither did *Law and Order,* so why did *we* have to have it? Their answer was that if you take away the jokes about Travis's beauty all you have left is a second rate *Law and Order.* I came up with some different jokes they could use. How about a really stupid rookie cop? They couldn't get rid of him because he was the commissioner's nephew. How about a female cop who's a stripper at night? How about a genius kid who helps solve the crimes?

One by one they shot my ideas down. Stupid brings in a stupid audience who'd not like the highly technical investigation we do on the show. Showing a woman stripper would get us taken off the network. They could show naked men, but women had to keep their clothes on. As for kids, go talk to Disney.

So, anyway, I was late reading the book that had all of America talking. It seems that some kid, a journalism major, had conned his way inside the elusive, wealthy Mont-

gomery family enough that he was invited
to join the family for a couple of weeks during the summer. He admitted in the introduction of his resulting book that his plan
had been to write a tell-all about them. He
wanted to sneak around and listen to fights,
get the servants talking and find out about
scandals. He wanted to report on extrava-
gances that middle-class Americans could
only dream about.

But after three days with the Montgomerys in their big marble mansion in Colorado, he was ready to go home. All he had
to report was that they were a nice bunch of
people. Yeah, they were wealthy and they
had servants, but their servants were
treated well and paid very well. Try as he
might, he couldn't get one of them to say
anything bad about their employers.

The Montgomery kids were polite and
considerate—and they didn't own cell
phones or receive Jaguars for their six-
teenth birthdays.

It wasn't until the fourth day that the
writer began to see the possibility of a story.
He'd already read about the great tragedy
of the Montgomery family, when a child had

been kidnapped and later his parents had disappeared. The child, Adam Montgomery, had been found wandering in the woods in Connecticut, so ill he nearly died, and later he remembered nothing of his ordeal. His parents were never found.

The writer stayed because this Adam Montgomery was arriving and he wanted to see if the man had been affected by his childhood trauma.

The minute Adam Montgomery and his family stepped out of the car that had picked them up at the airport, the writer knew he had a story. His nose began to itch and his ears started tingling.

Adam Montgomery was a tall, distinguished-looking man, a young Charlton Heston. Beside him was his petite wife. She was very pretty, with wide-set eyes and short strawberry-blonde hair, but she had a way of staring at people that was decidedly odd.

With her were two little girls who he thought were hers, but one was her niece. Two more people got out of the car. One was a tall, elegant woman who looked downright fierce. When one of the Montgomery women reached out to touch her, the tall woman jumped back, not allowing anyone to get too near her. She backed against a man who was inches shorter than she was, but from the way he put his arm around her waist, he seemed ready to fight for her.

Days of lethargy left the writer and he decided to forget about going back to his girlfriend and to stay to see what he could find out about this odd-looking group.

What he found out was not what he expected. Yes, the story of the tall woman, Boadicea, having been held captive all her life was interesting, but all the Montgomerys were so protective they would tell him nothing. And they were just as protective of Adam's young wife. Try as he might, the writer could get nothing out of any of them, but he knew there was a story there.

It took days of work, but he finally found a man who'd once worked for the Montgomerys and had been fired for pilfering who was willing to talk—for a price. It seems that, besides stealing, the man had been good at listening at doors. He said that all the Montgomerys teased Darci about money and the writer had wanted to know why.

What the writer heard so dumbfounded him that he could hardly speak. It seemed that Adam had been told by a psychic that he had a sister who was being held by a witch in a coven in Connecticut. The witch had a magic mirror but it could only be read by a virgin.

By the time the writer had been told this part, his mouth was hanging open in shock. Laughing, the man told how Adam had been attracted to the young virgin the psychic had helped him find, but he knew he couldn't touch her or she wouldn't be able to read the mirror.

In his book, the writer told the story of how Adam Montgomery had staved off the many sexual advances of the young woman as he heroically tried to find his sister. The book described Darci's obsession with money. There were silly scenes like the time that Darci, malnourished all her life, made a racket with a candy machine as Adam was trying to search the underground tunnels where the witch was said to be hiding.

By the end of the book, the reader felt that Adam Montgomery was a saint who had single-handedly, in spite of all Darci Monroe could do to thwart him, rescued his sister and saved several children who had been missing for months. The kicker was that on the last page, the reader learned that Adam had married Darci.

Of course the Montgomerys sued and the book was taken off the stands. But that just made people more anxious to read it and almost immediately it was available in its entirety, for free, on the Internet. The Montgomerys' attorneys made sure that what money the writer received from the book went to pay lawyers' fees, but that didn't matter. He wrote three other books in quick succession and they sold millions based on his name.

I read the book about a year after it came out. Alanna's copy was old and dog-eared, passed from one hand to another. Like everyone else who'd read it, I had a hard time understanding it. Why in the world had a man like Montgomery married a dingbat like Darci Monroe? In the midst of their adventures did he take her virginity and, like some hero of old, feel he had to marry her? They'd had a daughter soon after they were married. Was the pregnancy why he married her?

Not long after the book came out, Adam and his sister, Boadicea, got on a small airplane, with Adam piloting, and were never heard from again. They had left a flight plan but it was soon discovered that Adam had not followed his charted course. His plane had been seen by the control tower at an airport two hundred miles in the opposite direction, but when the spotter tried to contact them, there was no answer.

About three days after the disappearance, a tabloid printed a full front sheet photo of Darci laughing, a drink in her hand. The headlines said that Adam's widow would inherit nearly a billion dollars. The implication was that party-girl Darci had had a hand in her husband's disappearance.

Once again the Montgomerys sued, but the tabloid had been smart. They hadn't accused Darci of anything. That the photo had been taken before Adam disappeared was not their fault, they said; it was the only one they had. In the end, the paper agreed to publish a retraction, not in the back but on the front page.

The next issue of the paper wrote, "We

apologize. She inherits only two hundred million, and this photo was taken before he flew away forever." The photo had been reprinted, uncropped, this time showing that Darci had been dancing with a man who was not her husband.

Sometime during all of this, Darci was dubbed the Hillbilly Honey, and it was the general consensus of the world that she'd killed her husband for the money.

None of this had touched my life. During the day I was fighting with my producers to change my role, and during the night I was fighting with Alanna. I wanted a couple of kids; she wanted to do four films a year.

Two weeks ago Jerlene Monroe was a guest on *Missing.* Of course I'd seen her work. She'd seduced Russell Crowe in one of those extravagant epics he got to star in because he was white and had that voice. Sorry. My role envy is showing. He got those parts because he deserved them. Great actor.

Anyway, Jerlene Monroe was to do a guest shot with us and we were all foaming at the mouth to get to meet her. Every critic alive had agreed (now there's a cover story!) that Jerlene had stolen the movie she'd been in with Crowe. When Crowe had to kill her in order to save the world from her treachery, the audience cried right along with him.

None of us could figure out why she agreed to do a TV show, so as we gathered around her, it was one of the questions we asked. "I promised someone," she murmured in that silken voice of hers.

It was hard to believe, but she was more beautiful in person than on screen. One thing you soon find out in this business is that an actress without makeup is pretty ordinary-looking. She'll show up for work with frizzy hair jammed under a baseball cap, skin like a teenager's after a grease-eating spree, and wearing ratty old jeans and a T-shirt. You look at her and think, She made how much on her last film?

But not Jerlene. She arrived looking like little girls thought movie stars should look. She never lorded it over anyone, never demanded anything, but we all ran to do whatever she even hinted that she wanted. She smiled dazzlingly at the cameraman, said nothing, just smiled. The SOB made her look better than he'd ever made any of us look.

On the show, Jerlene played the wife of a rich man who'd been murdered, and at the end, we found out she did it. The script, like all the others, had us handcuffing her and leading her away. You know, we were smart and she was dumb.

On the second day of shooting, Jerlene said, "What a shame to incarcerate her. Her husband so very much deserved to die." She didn't complain, just voiced that one opinion and the next second the director was head-to-head with the writer.

The script was completely rewritten; Jerlene's role got bigger. The new story was that she got together with three of her husband's discarded mistresses and together they killed him. They alibied each other. We cops knew Jerlene had done it, but as we uncovered disgusting facts about the man, we were ready to kill him ourselves.

Toward the end of shooting, Jerlene said, "Perhaps it would help the story if I were to enjoy one of the men."

We were all dumbstruck. What did that mean? "Enjoy"? Have sex? With one of us? The entire male cast (and two women) stood up straighter, eyes wide. Silently, we were shouting Me! Me! Me!

"Perhaps him," Jerlene said and pointed to Ralph Boone. Short, old, beer-bellied, chain-smoking Ralph? He'd had one triple bypass and when Jerlene pointed at him he started coughing so hard we thought he'd be back in the hospital by evening.

Politely, the director said, "How about Linc?"

She didn't look at me, just turned away and said, "Perhaps."

She was acting, but then I soon learned that Jerlene Monroe was always acting. In her mind, she was always on camera.

We didn't have an affair for real. Not because I wasn't willing to but because she said no. Sexily, prettily, she said no. I was fighting a lot with Alanna then and she punished me by withholding sex. The result of having two women tell me no was that Jerlene and I played some pretty hot sex scenes. So hot, so realistic, that that show and Jerlene's performance were considered Emmy material. I'm ashamed to say that I told people I thought I should be nominated, too. Ralph, my costar, said, "Everyone could see you weren't acting. Not for a minute."

One thing good about my skin color is that it's hard to see when I blush.

Anyway, because of our on-screen affair I ended up spending some time with Jerlene. Okay, so I admit it. I told her we needed to rehearse in her dressing room—which was bigger than mine and had been freshly painted just for her.

It was during the first day I was alone with Jerlene that the Best Boy knocked on the door and handed me a letter. He said it was from my agent, which surprised me. When had Barney learned to write?

I opened it. "Your kid's missing," it read.

For a moment I just sat there looking at the note and couldn't think what it meant. My kid? I don't have a kid. Slowly, I remembered. Oh yeah. Connor. Or was his name Conan? She'd named him something to do with Schwarzenegger. That woman loved movies—which had caused the whole thing in the first place.

When Jerlene took the letter out of my hand, I didn't protest. She read it and for the first time I saw a genuine expression cross her beautiful face. "Your child," she whispered, horror in her voice. She loves her daughter! I thought in surprise.

Of course I, like the rest of America, knew that Jerlene Monroe was the mother of the Hillbilly Honey, but the knowledge only fed the mystery of the woman. How could someone as elegant as Jerlene have given birth to such a greedy little golddigger as Darci Montgomery? And risk her life to save her?!

At the end of the book all of America had read, Adam Montgomery had worked with some of his Montgomery cousins, Jerlene, and a man from her hometown to rescue Darci and the children. They'd arrived just in time, killed the bad guys, and taken an unconscious Darci to the hospital.

In other words, Darci's qualification of virginity to read some mirror that didn't exist hadn't been needed. Adam Montgomery's sleuthing and bravery had found and saved his sister, then he'd had to risk his life again to save dingbat Darci.

The book had shown Jerlene to be a true-life heroine, risking her own life to save a daughter who had done nothing but cause a lot of people a lot of trouble.

"Tell me everything," Jerlene said in that voice that came from deep within her throat.

Who could resist an entreaty like that? Certainly not me, so I told her my big secret about a job I'd once had when I was desperate for money and the result of it. Yes, I had a son but I'd never met him or his mother. All I knew of the kid was his age, seven, his name, Connor, I think, and I had a photo of him with his mother. My son had sandy hair and hazel eyes. His coloring was more like his mother's—blond, blue-eyed—but slap a little pancake on the kid and he'd look just like me at that age.

After I told Jerlene about how I came to have a kid, I used my cell to call my agent Barney. Since I'd just signed a new contract, he didn't have much time for me. When I was up for renewal, I was his best friend.

Anyway, Barney told me that my son and his mother were missing, and the private investigator he'd hired to keep track of them had told him a couple of weeks ago. He'd been waiting for a ransom note to appear, but since one hadn't, he hadn't thought to pass the info on to me before now.

"So why write me a letter? Why not just call and tell me?" I asked.

"Letter? I don't even send my mother letters. Why would I send you a letter? Look, kid, I told you, so I gotta go."

I hung up, stared at Jerlene for a moment, then looked at the letter again. There was nothing on it to indicate it was from my agent and now that I looked at the paper, I saw that it was top quality, not something Barney would shell out for.

Jerlene didn't have to ask me to tell her anything, I just did. When I'd finished, she said, "Stay here," then went outside. She returned minutes later and said that a short, fat man smoking a cigar had given the letter to the Best Boy and said it was from my agent. Jerlene said no one else on the set had seen the man.

I didn't know what to think about the odd letter, much less what to do about it—if anything. Jerlene advised me to wait a few days to see if anything else happened. I think she meant that I was to wait to see if a ransom note arrived.

Of course I'd pay it. I had to. The kid was my own flesh and blood.

I waited, but I was jittery and jumped at everything. I lucked out because in the season's final episode of *Missing,* Travis was being stalked by some woman who had the hots for him. When someone dropped a stack of papers I jumped half a foot. When the woman sneaked up behind me and held a gun to my throat, I sweated for real. When I asked her not to kill me—which wasn't in the script—I wasn't acting. I was thinking about my kid out there somewhere, being held by some madman all because he had a famous father. Me. I was causing some cute little kid to be tortured.

I was aware that everyone on the set was looking at me weirdly, but my head was too full of my own thoughts to try to understand what was going on. Jerlene's episode had finished so she'd gone back to her house in Malibu to look at the many scripts she'd been offered. She'd told me to call her if I heard anything.

Two seconds after the last show wrapped I called her. I had heard nothing. She told me to come to her house and I went. I missed the season's big wrap party but I was too nervous to care.

Jerlene plied me with booze and a lot of food, none of which she touched. She told me that she'd been thinking and wondered if maybe my child had been taken randomly rather than because he was my son.

That made me feel worse. A kid who wasn't taken for ransom would have been taken for . . . for other reasons. I drained my bourbon and poured myself another.

"I want to know everything you know about the child and the mother," Jerlene said.

I was a little worse for wear by then, what with the tension of the last week and four double bourbons. "Her name is Lisa Henderson and the boy's name is Conan or Connor—he would be seven now. She's a movie buff. Loves them. She—"

"How does she support herself?" Jerlene asked impatiently.

"I don't know. I can't remember. My agent had a PI check her out and they sent me reports. She never seems to have a job for long. She's worked in department stores, as a receptionist, as a bus driver, as a—" I smiled in memory. "She broke her arm one time so she got a job on the telephone. You ready for this? As a psychic. You know, over the Internet. She was called Crystal Spirit or something like that and she told people what they wanted to hear."

When I saw Jerlene's face turn white, I remembered what I'd read about her part in the witch-thing in Connecticut. Her daughter had been kidnapped by a so-called witch. Not one of the modern-day "good" witches, but like the scary ones in fairy tales. No one knew the full story of what happened that night, but when it was over, four people were dead. Had Jerlene had to kill someone to save her daughter?

"Look," I said, "the woman wasn't psychic any more than I am. She just needed a job that she could do while her arm healed."

That's when she told me I had to go to her daughter and that her daughter would help me find my son.

After that I was dismissed. As regally as though she were a queen and I her subject, I was dismissed. She pushed a button by the phone on a side table and instantly a tough-looking man appeared. "Virgil," she said, "would you please drive Mr. Aimes home?"

I was in no condition to protest, so I let the man pull me up and lead me out to my car. He drove. The next morning I awoke in my own bed, fully dressed, with a hangover.

By afternoon, I was feeling better and I began to think the whole thing was a dream—or at least I told myself it was.

There was no way on earth I was going to contact the Hillbilly Honey and ask for help. The woman probably killed her husband and sister-in-law for the money she'd get. No, thank you. I didn't want to be involved with her.

I probably would have dropped everything, and even forgotten all about my son if two things hadn't happened. I'd done a good job of rationalizing everything, telling myself that the boy's mother had probably taken the kid away from wherever they were to go to another job. I promised myself I'd look into it when I returned from Scotland with Alanna, and if the mystery hadn't been cleared up by then, I'd— I wasn't sure what I'd do, but I swore I'd figure it out.

Meanwhile, I was working with a travel agent—a guy so exclusive he had an unlisted number—to plan six weeks alone in the Scottish Highlands with the woman I loved.

Alanna had made five films back to back, each one in a different tropical climate. We'd hardly seen each other in the last year. Between my schedule and hers, it was nearly impossible to get together. Every time I talked to her, she'd cry and say she missed me and that she was very tired. And hot. She said she was sick of hot climates and all she wanted to do was rest some-where cool and private. "I want to go some-where where no one knows me, where the two of us can be alone together," she said over and over.

Fool that I am, I believed her. I secretly rented a castle in the cool, remote, private Highlands. It would be just us, a house-keeper-cook, an old man who kept the fires lit, another man who looked after the 200 acres of woodland, and a whole bunch of funny-looking cows.

I presented the package to Alanna over candlelight and champagne. She looked at me like I was crazy and said she was leav-ing the next day for Key West to do a movie with Denzel Washington.

I'm not prone to violence but I nearly lost it that night. Loudly, I told her I'd turned down two movie offers so I could spend those six weeks with her. That both scripts portrayed me as handsome but dumb was something she didn't need to know. I told her she meant more to me than any movie in the world and she ought to feel the same about me.

Coolly, Alanna said, "How long do you think I'll look like this? When you're sixty you'll be offered roles as a leading man, with some twenty-year-old falling in love with you. When I'm thirty-five they'll be asking me to play Denzel's mother."

She had a point.

But I didn't like it. I had completely cleared my schedule for six weeks so I could go to Scotland with the woman I loved. So now what was I to do? Call my agent and grovel? He'd yelled at me that I was a fool to turn down big screen work during the series hiatus, but I'd said— I'd rather not think of what I said. Not since the king of England abdicated for a woman had anyone gushed so much.

That was the first thing that happened. The second thing was that Jerlene sent the man named Virgil to my house with a thick packet. I thanked him—while praying I'd never meet him on a dark street—and took the package. Instinct told me I'd better pour myself a drink before looking inside, so I did.

Jerlene had hired a private investigator to find out about the woman who'd had my child. I skipped through most of the first pages because I'd seen them before. Lisa Henderson, mother of my son, had had two to three different jobs each year since my son had been born. She'd lived in four states.

"Tough life," I muttered. My son had been dragged around all his little life. I'd been right in ignoring that note about my son being missing. Lisa had obviously moved yet again.

"Wonder where she is now?" I asked aloud as I sipped my bourbon.

The last page nearly made my heart stop. It was a newspaper clipping. There was a photo of a car that had smashed into a tree and a picture of my son's mother. She was pretty in a bland way, with long, straight blonde hair and big blue eyes.

Picking the clipping up, I looked at the photo and thought she should have had better lighting.

I knew I was putting off reading the article. I took a deep drink of the bourbon, then read. Weeks ago, Lisa Henderson's car had run into a tree, and she'd been killed instantly.

Stapled to the article was a second clipping, this one about funeral services, so I read it, too.

Between the two articles, there was quite a bit about Lisa Henderson—at least about her life at the time of her death. I was surprised to see that she'd been an active member of a church and had served on several committees. Since she left no money behind, her funeral had been paid for by the church and her coworkers. "She will be missed," was to be carved on her tombstone.

Okay, so what about my son? What was to happen to him? And why had I missed the mention of him? I reread both articles. The obituary said Lisa had left behind "no known relatives."

I read the clippings another time, then I went back and read every word on every page. Nowhere in any of it was a mention of my son. Puzzled, I went to the safe in my bedroom to remove the file my agent had sent me years ago.

Nearly eight years ago, Lisa Henderson had been working in a cryo clinic in Los Angeles. I'd been a starving actor and, well, I'd earned some money by "donating," well, sperm. My name was anonymous to the people who used it, but those of us who gave had to agree that if a kid resulted, at eighteen he/she could have our names.

I loved this idea; it appealed to my sense of drama. By the time the kid was eighteen I planned to be a bigger star than Mel Gibson. I loved to imagine the thrill the kid would get when he was told who his father was.

When my name was becoming known, one day, laughing, I'd told my agent Barney that someday some kid was going to get the surprise of his life, then I'd explained why. Barney hadn't laughed; he'd gone ballistic. He started calling people who called people. The result was that all my frozen semen was destroyed and number 28176 was taken off the books.

However, Barney told me that one of the women who worked at the clinic had seen me in a bit part in a movie and recognized my name. "She had your kid!" Barney bellowed at me.

I was kind of pleased and wondered what the child looked like, but Barney ranted on and on about lawsuits and what she could someday demand and how this could someday hurt me bad. "Real bad." He said some unpleasant things about why couldn't I have taken up sheep rather than paper cups, but I didn't listen to him.

A month later Barney sent me a file about Lisa Henderson and every year since then he'd added a page or two. I'd put every paper in the safe I'd built into each house I'd owned in the last six years.

But now, when I reached for the file, it wasn't there. I knew I hadn't removed that file. The last time Barney'd sent me new pages I'd barely glanced at them before shoving them inside the leather folder I kept all those papers in. The folder even had a lock on it.

I emptied everything out of the safe. There were some deeds, last year's tax returns, the engagement ring I'd planned to give Alanna in Scotland, but no file on Lisa Henderson and my son.

I sat down on the bed, trying to figure this out. Did someone break into my safe and take the papers? No, of course not. What kind of thief would take papers and leave a $25,000 ring?

Wait a minute, I thought. Barney probably had copies. The man was terrified someone was going to cheat him out of a penny so he made sure he had a copy of everything.

As I picked up the phone by my bed, my cell rang. It was Alanna.

"Change your mind about Scotland?" I said. I didn't want her knowing I was still upset about the canceled trip. Plus, she had no idea about my having a child and I didn't want her to know.

"You haven't heard," she said flatly.

Neither have you, I wanted to say, but I played it cool. "About what?"

"Barney's dead. His office caught fire and he went up with it. Sorry. I'll call you later."

I was left with a dead phone in my hand. As I said, sympathy was not one of Alanna's strong points. After she read the book about Darci Montgomery, when she'd said, "That poor kid," she'd meant it was a shame that Darci had been caught.

I didn't think about what I was doing when I pushed the button to call Jerlene. She answered on the second ring. I was respectful. I didn't ask how a scatterbrained, maybe-killer like her daughter could help find someone. I just said, "How do I go about getting your daughter's help?"

After I put down the phone, I went to the gym. Maybe a long, hard workout would calm the jitters I felt. I knew, as well as I'd ever known anything in my life, that Barney had been murdered and all his files burned because of me and my illegitimate son. And I knew that Lisa Henderson had been killed for the same reason.

Three hours later I felt better. I checked the messages on my cell. Jerlene's lovely voice gave me an address in Virginia and said I was to go there tomorrow at three, that her daughter would meet me. Again she said that her daughter would find my son.

I didn't want to think anymore. I just called my personal assistant, told her to look after things until I got back, then I booked a flight to Virginia. I did it myself because I didn't want anyone to know where I was going. I tossed some clothes into a bag, then I went to a hotel. My own home didn't feel safe anymore.

The next day I was ushered into a very pretty living room and I met Darci Montgomery for the first time. I still wasn't sure why I was there or what I wanted from her, but I did know I needed to be cautious. I planned to tell her as little as possible and to gloss over the bad parts.

After all, what could the woman do? Read minds?

DARCI ⦂⟶

⟵⦂ *Chapter Three*

Lincoln Aimes's mind was harder to persuade than most people's were, but then
since that book came out, people put up
barriers against me. They'd made up their
minds about me and I knew that nothing I
could say—or do—would sway them.

Few people knew the truth of what had
happened in that tunnel full of witches in
Camwell, Connecticut, and I knew it was
better that they thought what they did. It
was better for people to think that my husband and his cousins had been the ones to
kill the witch and her cohorts. People thinking my mother had rescued me certainly
hadn't hurt her career any.

Yes, it was better for people to think what
they did than to know the truth of my in-

volvement in those deaths. If they knew the truth, I wouldn't just be laughed at or spit on as happened to me the last time I left the grounds, they'd probably light torches and drag me out of the house and— I didn't want to think about that.

However horrible destroying the witches had been, the best part of my life had come out of it. I'd found my father and he'd married Boadicea, the sister of the man who was to become my husband. Bo and I'd had babies at nearly the same time.

For a while my life had been wonderful because we were a family. Perhaps we were a little strange, since my father was a world-renowned expert on psychics, my sister-in-law had been raised in captivity, my husband had gone through unspeakable horror as a child, my daughter and niece had the power to make things fly around, and I—I was the strangest of them all.

We weren't unusual to each other, though, and we had great love among us. They had protected me from the outside world, loved me, and they'd known the truth about what happened in Connecticut. That had made everything all right.

But they weren't here now. Over a year ago, my husband had come to me and I could feel he was very excited about something, but I was, yet again, between nannies so I was taking care of the girls by myself. I'd volunteered for this after I found Bo showing the three-year-olds how to shoot a crossbow. Being raised by a truly evil woman had caused Bo to have some gaps in her mothering skills. We'd had to give up fairy tales in our house because Boadicea knew the true stories. (She told the girls the sister of the witch from Hansel and Gretel was alive and living on East 23rd Street in NYC. And, yes, she too ate children.)

Anyway, that day Adam was very excited and I was distracted because my daughter and my niece were making their stuffed toys dance on the ceiling. I just said, "See you later," when he said he had to go somewhere. I didn't know until hours later that Boadicea had gone with him.

That night, alone in my bed, I awoke suddenly and knew that something was wrong. You see, I have the ability to talk to my husband in my head. He can hear me and in return I can sense him. This used to annoy him because I always knew where he was and, for the most part, what he was doing. It was the ultimate invasion of privacy. And my husband had always been a very private man.

When the connection between Adam and me became . . . not broken, but strained, I awoke in fear and ran to my father's bedroom. His bed was empty, and hadn't been slept in.

I knew that he was, as always, in his study, locked away with that blasted Mirror of Nostradamus, his "souvenir" from the witch. He was always studying it and writing about what he saw. I figured Boadicea was with him, as she often was, asleep on the couch.

I gave a quick knock on the study door, but when there was no answer, I got the key from inside the vase on the hall table and opened the door. As soon as I saw my father slumped at the big, carved desk, I knew that something was wrong. When I saw that Boadicea wasn't in the room, I knew that she was with my husband— wherever he was.

I woke my father and minutes later the house was ablaze with light and policemen. A few hours later, Montgomerys and Taggerts, my husband's family, started arriving from all over the country in planes, helicopters, cars and boats.

Somewhere in the confusion, my father pulled me into the study and leaned against the door. "The mirror is gone."

That hit me so hard I had to sit down. If both Adam and his sister were gone and the Mirror of Nostradamus as well, then there was evil involved. True evil, not just some kidnapper who wanted ransom money. I could have handled a kidnapper.

When I started shaking, my father held me. After a while, Michael Taggert came into the room. He was my husband's cousin and one of the few people who knew the truth of what had happened in Connecticut—and knew the truth about me. He knew what I could do with my mind and what I had done—all that I allowed anyone to know, that is.

Michael held my hands, looked into my eyes, and asked me to tell him what I felt. I loved Mike for that. With most people, if they find out I can intuit things about them, they're scared to death. They have nasty little secrets they don't want anyone to see. But not Mike. He didn't care what I saw; he had nothing he was ashamed for people to know about him.

I told him I felt that Adam and Bo were alive, but they were trapped in some way, and I couldn't figure out how. Underwater? In a cave? In an evil-protected place?

A search was launched, millions spent, but Adam and Boadicea's plane was never found.

During the first months, I hardly slept. Adam's cousins took care of the girls. Adam, Dad, Bo and I had worked hard to hide from people, including relatives, what the girls could do. But we'd underestimated the Montgomery-Taggert clan. They laughed at the girls' antics and shielded them from the public.

I concentrated day and night on trying to find where Adam and Boadicea were, but I knew someone was hiding them—and hiding them in a magical way that made it impossible for me to find them.

After they'd been missing for three months, I awoke at two A.M. and knew that something had happened. My heart was racing, the blood pounded in my ears, but at first I couldn't figure out what I was feeling. I had to force myself to be calm and concentrate.

After a while I realized it was the mirror. The mirror was no longer with Adam and Boadicea. It had become separated from them and it was . . . it was traveling. I could almost see it. Desert. Sand. Camels. Trucks.

I ran to wake my father, but he was at his computer in his study. He missed his wife so much that he rarely slept. Quickly, I told him what I'd felt.

"If we find the mirror it could lead us to them," he said, then had me go over everything I'd seen in my vision. By late that afternoon he was on a plane to the Middle East to begin his search for the mirror.

It was after he left and I was alone in the house with two children and a couple of employees—search headquarters for Adam and Boadicea had been moved to the family home in Colorado—that I first heard how I was being accused of having done something to the plane. It was said that I wanted to get rid of my rich husband and my sister-in-law so I could have the money I so dearly loved.

Once again, Michael Taggert came to my

rescue. He fired the people who worked for me because they'd made sure I saw the tabloids, and he begged me to go to Colorado with him. But I couldn't. I couldn't leave the place where I felt close to Adam. I told Mike I wanted to stay in Virginia and raise the girls and do what I could to find Adam and Bo. I said that my father and I were in daily contact, and I promised that if he found anything I'd call in the reinforcements of all the Montgomerys and Taggerts.

I meant every word I said, but I soon found out how impossible it was to do. The first time I took the girls to see a movie, a woman spit on me. I had to grab my daughter in one arm and my niece in the other for fear they'd try—and succeed—in turning the woman upside down and shaking her.

For a few months after that one of the Montgomery cousins lived with us and took the children back and forth to their nursery school, but after there were "accidents" in the classroom that I knew the girls had caused, I removed them from the school.

Finally, Susan Montgomery, the woman who'd raised my husband after his parents disappeared, flew to Virginia to talk to me.

She suggested the children go to Colorado, and until the girls learned to "control themselves"—she was so polite—they'd be homeschooled.

I protested that I could arrange that in Virginia.

All Susan did was look at me and I saw myself through her eyes. I was a mess. When I wasn't putting myself in a trance as I tried to locate Adam and Bo, I was crying. I'd had a lonely childhood, then I'd found a man who loved me, a father who loved me, and a sister-in-law who needed masses of love. Added to this were two little girls who were love personified.

Yet in one day I'd lost it all.

I sent my niece and daughter to Colorado to be with their relatives. The children needed some laughter in their lives. Since their father's disappearance, there'd been nothing but tears in our house.

That had been months ago. I'd flown—privately, on the Montgomery jet—to Colorado several times and had spent a lot of time with the girls, but I'd always returned to Virginia to continue trying to use my mind to locate Adam and Boadicea.

I talked to my father every day that he

could get to a phone. He'd been tracking the mirror for months now. It had been close to him several times but it had always eluded him.

As for me, I'd stopped crying every minute I wasn't in a trance and was now at the stage where I just plain missed my husband. I didn't go out, was never seen in public, because I couldn't bear what was thought of me. Reporters still camped at the end of the driveway and now and then the alarm system would go off because someone had come over the wall.

Now, after all these months, my mother had written me that I owed her and she wanted me to help some actor. I wanted to tell her I couldn't leave my search for Adam, but I'd come to realize that whoever—whatever—was holding him was in control. All my concentrating of the last months hadn't made a dent in the field around them. I was beginning to think that Adam and Bo were asleep. If Bo were here, she'd probably tell me the truth behind the Sleeping Beauty story. No doubt Ms. Beauty's descendants were now living in Minnesota.

The thought of Bo made tears come to

my eyes, so I looked away from Lincoln Aimes. "I don't think I can help you," I said.

"That's what I thought, too," he said as he stood up. "If you could find people you'd find your husband, wouldn't you? Unless—"

When he broke off, I looked back at him to see what he'd meant by that. I knew he'd just been stating facts as he knew them, but his embarrassment filled the room.

"I didn't mean . . ." he began. "I just meant that, how could *you* help? With the Montgomery money? But then—"

When he realized he was making things worse, he shut up. What interested me was that my mother had not told this man anything about me. I'd never told anyone, not even Adam, the details of what had happened inside that room with the witch and her henchmen, but my mother had been there and she'd seen the results, and she could have told a lot. But she hadn't.

Lincoln Aimes was standing; I was sitting. He was over six feet and over two hundred pounds, while I am five-two and under a hundred pounds. I guess he should have been intimidating, but he wasn't. I could sense that he was a good guy. He'd missed

out on some love in his life but I didn't feel
any violence in him. Unless of course he
was a powerful warlock and was able to
block me from seeing his true self, as had
happened to me in Connecticut. Somehow,
I didn't think so.

True, he doubted me, but he'd hidden in
the back seat of the gardener's car to get to
me so he deserved something.

"Here," I said, handing him a pad of paper and a pencil. "Write down some things
you've lost over the years."

He tried to conceal his smirk but I felt it. I
didn't mind. After what I'd been through in
my life, a smirk was almost a caress.

He handed me a list of five items, some
of them from his childhood.

Four of them were easy. "Your father
stepped on the ring and broke it so your
mother threw it away."

"My parents lied to me?" he said in such
shock that at first I wasn't sure if he was
kidding or not. When he gave me that famous grin I almost smiled back.

"Next," he said, his eyes twinkling, proud
of himself for having nearly made me smile.

There was milk money stolen by some kid
with a scar over his left eye.

"I thought he was the one but I could never prove it."

A shirt stolen by a fellow actor, a watch that dropped off his wrist while rowboating. It was still at the bottom of a lake.

The fifth item was serious and I could feel the man waiting for my answer. The paper fairly vibrated in my hand. "This has been destroyed. The . . . What is it? It's a folder but it's more than that. It's leather with a lock on it. The papers in it and the folder were burned."

I looked at him hard because I realized that someone would have killed him to get those papers. In my mind's eye, I saw him asleep and I saw a thin person dressed in black as he or she opened a safe and took the papers.

"What was the combination to your safe?"

He blinked a couple of times that I knew about the safe, but before he could say it out loud, I "heard" it. "Your Social Security number. Not very smart using that number, was it?"

He didn't answer, just sat there and stared at me. After a moment he picked up the big manila envelope he'd brought with him, but he didn't hand it to me. "I read that book about you," he said, "but it never hinted that you could . . . do things. It said you were more interested in candy bars than in finding Adam Montgomery's sister."

I knew he was opening the way for me to tell him the truth behind what had happened in Connecticut, but I had no inclination to do so. The man was impressed that I could tell him about a ring he'd had when he was a kid. If he knew even ten percent about what I could do, he'd probably run for the door. "You have a child?" I asked him. I was sure that envelope he was clutching had photos and mementos, and I truly hoped I didn't have to tell him his child was no longer living.

"Oh yeah, sure," he said, still staring at me in that way I hate, as though I were a freak.

He handed me the envelope; I opened it and removed the papers, but I didn't feel what he wanted me to.

I could feel that the kid who'd made the photocopies was angry at his girlfriend—but, most of all, I could feel my mother.

"My mother sent you these papers?"

"Yes."

For a moment I closed my eyes. Jerlene Monroe and I didn't socialize with each other. We never had, not even when I was a child. I'd never been to a movie or the circus or even to an ice cream parlor with her. But, as had been reported, she'd risked her life for me. I knew from the paper I held that she was well and enjoying her fame immensely.

"No child," I said. "I don't feel any child in this."

"Look at the clippings in the back."

There were two newspaper clippings, but my mother's touch was so strong on them that I had difficulty feeling anything else. I looked hard at the woman's photo. The woman was youngish and simple. I couldn't feel anything complicated in her mind or her life.

"Simple," I said. "Uncomplicated. She likes to make people feel good."

He was looking at me so eagerly, sitting on the edge of the sofa, that I couldn't help but be affected. The truth is, when I'd done this before, it had always been with someone I loved present. As a child, anything "weird and strange" I could do, I kept to myself. My husband was the first person I'd openly talked to about my so-called "power." When my father and Adam's sister came into my life, I was fairly open with them. My father had spent a lot of time with me, trying to find out what I could do, but he was only interested in the big stuff. After all, he knew I'd used my mind to kill four people, so he wasn't interested in my picking up a photo and telling about the person.

But this beautiful actor was. I could feel his excitement, feel that he thought what I was doing was marvelous and magnificent. If he only knew . . .

"No children," I said. "This woman never had a child."

At that, he fell back against the sofa. "Yes she did. She had my child."

I could tell that he'd lost faith in me. "Maybe that's why she was killed," I said.

He sat upright again. "Killed? As in murdered?"

"Yes. Someone did something to the brakes. I think you'll find that this tree is at the bottom of a curve on a steep hill. Her death was well planned."

"Why?" he whispered.

"I don't know. Someone wanted something from her death but I don't know what." I handed the folder full of papers back to him. I'd seen all I could. I wanted him to leave so I could go back to— To what? He and I were alone in the house. Since I'd known he was coming, I'd sent the housekeeper and the two gardeners home. I didn't want them oohing and aahing over Lincoln Aimes.

He didn't take the hint so I started to use what I'd always called my True Persuasion to make him leave. But I stopped before I'd started. Okay, so I knew he was lying to me—or maybe he was just leaving out a lot—but, still, he seemed genuinely upset about this child who didn't seem to exist.

Instead of making him leave, I asked him to stay for dinner, only I didn't use words. I sent the thought to him that he was very hungry and that he wanted to cook something in my kitchen. Heaven knew that I couldn't cook and I certainly couldn't leave the house. If those reporters out there saw me with Lincoln Aimes it'd be all over the papers tomorrow.

When I heard his stomach growl, I allowed myself a little smile. I'm good, I thought, then I started putting it into his head that he wanted to tell me everything about this child from the beginning.

An hour later, Linc, as he told me to call him, and I were sitting at the marble-topped counter in the kitchen eating huge bowls of spaghetti, garlic bread, and salad. Beside us strawberries and those little round short-cakes were thawing.

"Every word," I said as I twirled pasta around my fork. I hadn't eaten much since Adam disappeared and as a result my spinal column was the biggest thing on my body.

It took him nearly an hour to tell me all of it. He didn't know it but I was working on him the whole time to make him tell me more and more.

I must say that, all in all, it was an interesting story. The problem was that it had huge blanks in it, missing pieces.

As a starving actor he'd been a sperm donor to a cryo bank and some woman who worked there had seen Lincoln Aimes in a movie so she'd— What? Stolen the sperm and performed a do-it-yourself job?

Linc didn't know the details. All he knew was what his agent had found out, that Lisa Henderson had given birth to Lincoln

Aimes's child and they'd spent seven years moving all over the country.

"And now your agent's dead?" I asked as I started on my second bowl of pasta. He'd eaten only one. Wimp.

"And so is Lisa Henderson. I had papers that had lots of information about her and my son, such as which schools he went to, but all the papers were taken."

"Out of your safe in the night while you slept. Good thing you didn't wake up because the thief would have killed you." From the way he paused with his glass at his lips, I knew I'd shocked him. "Didn't I tell you that part?"

"Uh, no, you didn't." He narrowed his eyes at me. "What else didn't you tell me?"

"That your girlfriend—"

"I do not want to hear that one!"

I couldn't help it but I actually smiled— and he smiled back.

Getting up, he ladled half-frozen strawberries onto the cold little cakes. He wasn't any better at cooking than I was. "Okay, so now what do I do? Forget about it all? Am I to think this woman did not have my child because now I don't have any proof that a child lived with her? Besides, if a kid did live with her, I'm not sure it was mine. Or is mine. If he ever existed, that is."

"You don't have anything that could be connected to the child?"

"Just his picture."

At that I looked at him in astonishment. He had dark skin but I could see the flush rising up his face.

In the next second he was running and I was on his heels. I knew he was going after his jacket that I'd hung in the hall closet. He didn't know his way around my big, sprawling house. It had once been a farmhouse but had been added on to repeatedly so it was a maze of rooms. Sometimes the girls tricked the nanny into thinking— Oh well, best not think of them or I'd start crying again.

I took a shortcut through a glassed-in porch and reached the entrance foyer before he did and had his wallet out of his jacket pocket in an instant. Wow! What I could feel from holding his wallet! I didn't like his girlfriend at all. Wonder if he knew she was sleeping with another man—or was it two men? Linc liked his mother okay, but he'd like to drop an anvil on his father's head. Figuratively, that is. Linc hated only one person, but I couldn't quite see why.

With a jolt that ran through my entire body, I saw that if I helped Linc, I'd come closer to finding my husband. I couldn't see how yet, but as much as I'd ever known anything, I knew I *needed* to help Lincoln Aimes.

But how could I? I thought. How could I leave this house and go out . . . there?

"Do you mind?" he said coldly as he grabbed the wallet out of my hands.

I smiled at him but he didn't smile back. Obviously, he knew what I'd been doing. It wasn't easy for me to keep from asking him who it was he hated and why, but when he handed me the photo of a woman and a child, I gave it my attention.

"This isn't the woman who was killed. This is a photo of the child's mother and yes, you're the child's father, and both of them are alive."

"Where?"

"Don't know."

"What do you mean you don't know?"

Here we go again, I thought. I threw up my hands and went back to the kitchen, Linc close behind me, talking all the way.

"I've already seen you do psychic things so why can't you tell me where they are? And why was this woman's photo and obituary in the paper if she isn't dead? Don't you think those people would know who she was? They took up a collection for a tombstone because they liked her so much."

"You want some more strawberries?"

"Why aren't you answering me?"

I turned on him. "It's always more, isn't it?" I said, anger coming to the surface. In the last year I'd run through the gamut of emotions and wallowed in all of them, but the one emotion I'd not allowed myself was anger. Truthfully, I was afraid that if I got really, really angry, I'd be like Stephen King's *Carrie* and bring a few houses down.

But now this man—this stranger—was angry at *me!* It was too much.

I slammed the refrigerator door and advanced on him. "More! That's all anyone wants from me! I told you all I know but you want me to tell you more! Don't you think that if I had the power to pinpoint where missing children are that I'd be doing it? Wouldn't I be sitting in a police station twenty-four-seven and going over pictures

and saying, 'This one was taken by his father,' and 'This one is at the bottom of a
lake. His mother killed him'?"

When Linc bent over, his hands to his
temples, I knew he was in pain and that I
was causing it, but I couldn't stop myself.
"My father was always pushing me to see
more, do more. Boadicea expected me to
be like that horrid mirror and see the future.
Only my husband—oh God."

I said the last because a big drop of
blood had fallen from Linc's nose onto the
tile floor. Instantly, my anger left me and I
ran to get a tea towel and soak it in cold
water.

"I'm so sorry," I said, holding out the
towel to him.

He didn't take it but sat down on a stool
and put his head back. I wanted to put the
towel to his nose, but when I couldn't reach
him, I grabbed one of the girls' toy boxes,
pushed it beside him, stood on it, then
pressed the cold towel to his nose. "I'm so
sorry," I kept saying over and over. "I didn't
do it on purpose. Really, I didn't. I try never
to get angry, but sometimes I can't help it."

Linc pulled the towel away enough to
look at me with one eye. "If you hadn't

stopped I think my head would have exploded."

I think he meant to be funny but he conjured up some pretty horrible memories for
me. A few years ago I was led into a room
by four people and only one of us came out
alive. I got down off the toy box and began
to clean up the kitchen. As I worked, I used
my mind to soothe Linc and to heal the rup-
tured veins in his nose. I knew he had a
headache so I quieted that, too.

After a while there wasn't anything more
to do to the kitchen so I looked at him. He
was staring at me but it wasn't as though
he thought I was a freak. Nor did he look as
though he wanted to go running to the reporters outside and tell them all about me.

"I suggest we go to the living room, share
a bottle of wine, and talk. I have a proposi-
tion for you," he said. Quietly, I followed
him.

LINC 🙢

🙢 *Chapter Four*

Of course people like her didn't exist. Not outside books and movies, that is. No one could actually make a person's nose bleed—or head explode. Of course not!

If they could . . . My mind whirled with the possibilities. She could home in on dictators and kill them. No need for wars. She could make millions as a hit man. She could take out Russell Crowe so I could get his roles.

Well, anyway, I'm sure there were uses for the ability to kill people with your mind. Like maybe witches. As I walked behind her skinny little body into the living room, I saw a lot in a short time. All those ridiculous things she'd done while searching for a witch were because she knew and felt so much. She could make sexual advances to a man because she wasn't worried about losing her virginity. Who needed some old mirror when you had a mind like hers?

As for Jerlene and the others saving Darci's life, I had a strong hunch who had killed that witch and her three followers. Fight evil with evil as the saying goes, or, in this case, witchcraft with witchcraft. The thought made me want to cross myself.

But my hands were full of wine bottle and glasses so I couldn't do anything until I put them on the coffee table—and then it might have seemed that I was crossing myself because I was in the presence of evil, so I didn't.

So now what do I do? I thought as I slowly poured the wine.

Part of me wanted to run away, fast and far. I'd wondered why Jerlene had no photos of her daughter in her house or her dressing room. And I'd wondered why I'd never seen them together in person or in print. I guess Jerlene was afraid/squeamish/put off by a daughter who could . . . do what Darci was able to do.

I handed Darci her glass of wine, took mine, and sat down across from her. I had no idea what to say. "Don't hurt me no mo'!" came to mind.

"So what can you do besides kill and maim?" I heard myself say, then tightened in preparation for another blast.

Darci relaxed. "I've only done that . . . that nosebleed thing once before, when Adam made me angry. I never did it again and I can tell you that he and I had some major fights. But I never again used my mind against him. I wouldn't have now but I've had so many awful things happen and . . . and . . ."

She looked down at her wineglass and I was afraid she was going to cry. She didn't have on eye makeup so she might. Alanna never cried if she was in makeup.

"If you get mad again," I said, "I know this guy I can call. You can blast him till his head explodes. You—"

"The man you hate?"

I knew where she'd found that out: my wallet. When I got there, she was caressing it like it was a sex object, sticking her fingers in and around the leather, all while her eyes were half closed, and she had a tiny smile on her face. She was either having an erotic experience or I'd been away from

Alanna so long I was seeing what I thought about night and day.

"Tell me something, Darci, if you get closer to someone or something, can you see and feel more?"

Instantly, I saw that she knew where I was headed. Okay, so I'm an actor, not a writer. If I'd had someone to write some subtle lines leading up to what I was thinking about I could have delivered them perfectly. Better than certain other actors do, I'm sure.

"No," she said, staring at me.

As I looked into her eyes I had the weirdest feeling she was trying to put ideas into my head. That wasn't possible. Was it? In case it was possible, I glared back at her and began to recite Othello's lines. Memorizing the lines to plays I hoped to be in someday was a hobby of mine.

After a while, Darci smiled at me and I felt I'd won a silent battle. I was still thinking about running away, but I was also thinking about something else.

"I've got six weeks," I began, and Darci said, "No!"

"I don't usually have free time but my girl-friend Alanna—"

"No, no, and double no."

"You've seen her movies. Right now she has one with Denzel Washington and—"

"So? My mother stars with Russell Crowe."

I nearly exploded. "What's he got that—" Her little smile made me stop. Obviously she'd seen something, felt something inside me, not that Crowe and I—or that I thought Crowe—

I decided to go a different route. "Okay, don't help me. Someone stole papers from my safe that tell about my son. Someone burned up my agent along with the photocopies. Somebody killed a woman, then said she was the woman who is the mother of my son, but she wasn't. And a bunch of church people and her coworkers paid for her tombstone and all of them said there were no surviving relatives."

I leaned across the coffee table toward her, feeling my anger rise. If she didn't help me find my son I didn't see anything else I could do. "I'll just go there—by myself— and ask people on the street if they've seen some sandy-haired little kid. Of course I don't know what he looks like, but then all white kids look alike to me so what does it matter?"

When she smiled I knew I was making headway. Even better, I had an audience. "So I'll just go there by myself and ask questions and probably get myself killed, since everyone else has. And that will be the end of Paul Travis."

She looked at me with twinkling eyes and said, "If he gets killed do you think we'll get to see his apartment?"

I laughed with her. She wasn't easily made to feel guilty, that's for sure. "Darci, the truth is that without you I can do nothing. Can you tell what will happen to my child if he isn't found?"

I didn't have to be psychic to read what was on her face. "He'll die, won't he?"

"No," she said. "The mother will but not the child. There's something about him . . . I don't know what it is."

"Maybe he's like you and someone wants to use him for nefarious purposes." When I saw Darci's too-pale face turn even whiter, I knew she was withholding information from me. "Spill it," I said. "Out with it."

She drained her glass, then held it out for

me to refill. "I can't do this," she said. "I don't have the time."

At that I pointedly looked around the empty house. No husband, no kids, no employees, no job. What the hell did she do all day?

"You don't understand," she said, running her fingertips around the edge of the wineglass. "I feel things all the time. Everywhere. But there's one of me and thousands, even millions, of them."

"Them," I said.

"Yes, them. Evil people. No, not evil, that's different. Greedy people, dishonest people. There are scams going on all over the world. I can't go to parties with strangers because I become aware that the man by the piano is thinking about killing his wife, or the woman in the kitchen is stealing from her employer, or I'll feel that the two children playing by the pool will be dead within a year.

"I can't change things. . . . I mean, I can change some things but not enough to make a dent in the horror that's in this world."

"So you isolate yourself in this house and do nothing."

"Not quite," she said, and I knew she was trying to make me think she worked on projects all day long. Probably did. Probably worked on getting her husband back and nothing else.

"You've been working on him for over a year. Think six more weeks will find him?" I was pleased to see her look shocked. Maybe I couldn't read minds but an actor learned to read expressions, and I'd read hers perfectly.

"Not possible," she said as she put her glass down.

"Not possible to do what?" I asked, putting on my innocent act.

She took a deep breath, then let it out slowly. "Okay, I'll make you a deal. You go to wherever this woman was killed, find out all you can, bring the information back to me, and I'll tell you everything I can."

"That makes sense," I said. "Two people are dead already but I'll be safe. I'll just ask about the kid and they'll give me information and snapshots."

She sipped her wine for a moment and seemed to think about what I was asking her to do. "Where did the woman last work?"

"A resort," I said quickly—too quickly—
and made myself slow down. "It's an old
. . . farm of sorts. Outbuildings. A couple of
old-maid sisters own the place and have
turned it into a sort of resort. Women go
there for massages and whatever."

When she started looking at me hard, I
couldn't meet her eyes.

"What aren't you telling me?" she asked.

"Read my mind," I said and when she
said, "Can't," I didn't believe her. I got up,
went to the foyer and fished inside my
jacket for the brochure, then went back into
the living room and handed it to her.

She looked at it for a few moments and I
could see her eyes widen in disbelief before
she looked back up at me. "It's a plantation
named 13 Elms, in Alabama, complete with
the slave cabins remodeled into guest
houses. It's owned by two women who are
the descendants of the original owners and
it's—" She opened her eyes so wide I
thought they were going to pop. "Among
other things available to their guests, they
conduct séances."

I gave her the grin Paul Travis uses when
he's trying to get information out of women.
It's meant to disarm them and to make

them think Travis is a nice guy. The look didn't work with Darci. I nodded at the brochure and said, "What else do you feel?"

"They're up to something. It's not evil but it's dishonest, completely illegal, and they're getting rich off of it. And, yes, a murder or two may have been committed."

"At least it's not evil," I said, and Darci smiled.

She quit smiling and said, *"You* do not want to go there."

"Great," I said and acted like I was about to leave. "You go, find my son, and let me know when you have him."

"Very funny," she said. "You know, I'm hungry. You want something to eat?"

"We just ate a huge meal."

"Yeah, but— Come on and I'll bake you some Jell-O."

She could see I didn't get what she meant—was it a joke?—but I followed her anyway, then sat and watched as she made herself an enormous sandwich. If she could bottle her ability to eat and not gain weight she'd be worshiped in Hollywood. I knew women who'd eat bear dung, or inject it into their veins, if they thought it would make them lose five pounds.

"We need to figure out how we're going to go about this," she said, her mouth full.

"Does this mean you're agreeing to do it?"

"I don't know. I'm thinking about it. Maybe—"

She stopped talking because the telephone rang and, instantly, she went running into another room to get it. I could hear her quick footsteps going deep into the house, probably into a bedroom where she'd have some privacy.

I was on the opposite side of the bar from the telephone but could see that the light on line four was on. Was that the super-private line? Slowly, I went around the bar and began to tidy up the countertop. Oops, I dropped one of those heavy kitchen knives on the telephone and when I picked it up, my hand accidentally hit a couple of buttons. When a man's voice came through on the speaker phone, I thought that someone ought to talk to Darci about phone systems that didn't allow other people to eavesdrop.

"Turkey," I heard a man say. "I'm in Turkey, but I've found nothing."

"You have," Darci said, "and stop testing me."

The man chuckled. "That's my baby. Yes, I found that big embroidered bag of Bo's."

"That's wonderful," Darci said. "Where? Tell me everything."

"You told me you felt something was in a shop in this area and it was. It was in an antiques shop. The thing was so worn and battered it looked like it was an antique."

"Where did he get it?"

"It cost me three hundred dollars to get answers and I'm still not sure he was telling the truth. He says some old man sold it to him with a load of things, old clothes, old household goods and—"

"Old mirrors," Darci said.

"Yeah. An old mirror. Cracked frame and so faded you couldn't see yourself in it. He didn't take the mirror. Said it was rubbish."

"Have you found the man who sold him the things?"

"Not yet. I thought you—"

"He's gone, Dad. I can feel that he's gone. He doesn't live in Turkey and the man has gone home. His old wife is ill. Egypt. Pyramids. I see pyramids."

"Okay, honey. I'll get on the first plane out of here. Are you all right?"

"Yeah," Darci said hesitantly.

"What's wrong? Other than what's wrong, that is?"

"There's a man here, Dad. He's an actor and my mother sent him to me. She wants me to help him find his missing son."

"An actor with a missing child would bring you a lot of publicity."

"No, it's not like that. It would take too long to explain but people don't know about the child and . . ." She trailed off.

"Look, honey, I need to go, but if you're asking me if it's okay for you to help somebody, yes it is."

"I'd have to go somewhere. I can't do it from here."

"Yes!" the man shouted into the phone. "Yes! Get out of that house. Take Adam's cell phone. I have the number. Help the man. And, Darci, call your mother. She loves you."

"Yeah. Sure," Darci said.

"I love you!" the man said. "Call you when I can."

Quietly, I pushed the button to cut off the speaker phone, then finished tidying up. When Darci returned, she sat on a barstool for a while and said nothing.

I put lunch meat and cheese away and

when I looked back at her she was staring at me. "Hear what you wanted to?"

I willed myself not to blush at being caught. "I heard that you can do what you need to do without being here in this house." I leaned on the countertop toward her. "Look, Darci, you must know whether or not we can do this."

"No, I can't see the future, but I can see—"

"See what?"

"Something in my life will change if I do this. I don't know how or what, but I see that something will change forever—and I'm not sure I want that."

"Does it have to do with your husband? Or that people find out about you? Or me? Maybe they say you and I—"

She waved her hand. "No, identity isn't the problem. We have to go in disguise. No one will recognize you. Me, maybe. But not reporters. Someone else, and I can't figure out who it is."

I had to work to keep from asking, "Why the hell won't they recognize me?" Instead, I said, "Good or bad? Are the changes you foresee good or bad?"

She looked as puzzled as I felt. "I don't

know. But I feel that if I don't do this, I'll never be able to find my husband. Somehow, going with you to this dreadful place, helps me . . . I hope it helps me find him."

"Okay," I said, "so now tell me why no one will recognize me."

"Oh," she said, as though it didn't matter. "They think you're gay and a look-alike, not the real Lincoln Aimes."

"Gay?" I said. "I am not gay. I am—"

"Speaking of which," she said, "you touch me and I'll cause you pain."

"I have no desire to touch you or any other white woman," I said. "Besides, you're—" I stopped because I knew Darci saw too much. The truth was, if I didn't get some relief soon I was going to do some things that were going to get me on the front page of the tabloids. "Okay," I said. "Hands off. A promise."

"On your mother's life?"

I sighed. She sure did snoop. "Yeah, on my mother's life."

DARCI ⊯

⊰ *Chapter Five*

There wasn't anything I could do but let him spend the night, but I made sure he was as far away from me as he could possibly be. Since he was such a snoop, I couldn't let him near my father's studio, so, in the end, I stuck him in the housekeeper's room. It had been the smoking room for some man whose wife wouldn't let him smoke in the house and, in retaliation, he'd added a couple of rooms on until it was his own apartment. After that, they'd been a fairly happy couple.

So, anyway, I put Linc downstairs, way at the back of the house, and thought about nailing a 2 x 4 across the door. The man needed a sex partner *soon.*

All night long I tossed in my bed. I

needed a sex partner, too, but not just anyone. I needed Adam Montgomery, the true
love of my life.

This actor, this Lincoln Aimes, thought my
power was wonderful, that I was a cross
between a witch and a superhero, but I
knew that my power was useless since it
couldn't find the one thing I wanted: my
husband.

Part of me knew I should be grateful for
the tiny bit of time I'd had with him. I guess
no one deserves a blazing light of joy such
as I'd had with Adam. Not forever, anyway.

Adam was such a complicated man, so
full of anger at what had been done to him
and his family, but he didn't allow that anger
to turn into evil. He could have used his
anger and his family's money to hurt a lot of
people, but he didn't. Instead, he helped
them.

To the people of Putnam, Kentucky,
where I was born and raised, Adam Montgomery was a hero second only to the Lord.
"Jesus saved my soul, but Adam Montgomery saved my ass," was what people in
Putnam said on a regular basis. I didn't like
the profanity or the easy use of our Savior's
name, but the saying was true.

That horrid book written about me said that I was obsessed with money, that I had been paid a fabulous salary, but wouldn't pay for anything on my own, and that I made Adam pay for everything. Basically, that was true and when Adam, who knew the extenuating circumstances, teased me about it, his family wanted to know why. He couldn't tell them about my abilities and he didn't want to tell them anything bad about the Putnams—who owned Putnam—so Adam had made up some story about my saving for my dowry.

Unfortunately, the whole family—except the few who knew the truth—picked up on it and began to tease me. I didn't mind. In fact, I liked it. It made me seem normal and one of them. In my own family I'd always been treated as though I was strange, someone to stay away from.

The truth about the money was that Putnam—the son, not the father—said that if I'd marry him he'd forgive all the debts of everyone in town, which was about seven million dollars. No one born in Putnam was ever refused credit; they just got more in debt.

I didn't want to marry Putnam. He was a

nice young man but he had the IQ of a
raisin and about as much depth. He only
wanted me because I was the only girl in
town who wouldn't go out with him, which,
translated, meant that I wouldn't go to bed
with him.

I came under a lot of pressure after Putnam told someone, which meant that
everyone in town knew within 33½ minutes,
that if I married him he'd forgive the town all
mortgages, car loans, store charges, whatever. After that, in the town's mind, it was a
done deal. I'd marry Putnam and they'd be
out of debt.

Putnam made everything worse by saying that he'd even write off the debts if I'd
marry him for just one day—meaning, of
course, just one night.

Adam once asked me what Putnam's
dad, also named Putnam, thought of this
but the town of Putnam had been given to
Putnam when he turned sixteen, so he
could do what he wanted with the place.
His dad was too busy trying to buy Dallas to
care about our town any longer.

I knew that I couldn't live with the burden
of not marrying Putnam and having the
town stay in debt, so I got Putnam to agree

to give me one year to pay off the debt. I'd done some concentrating and I could foresee enough to know that within a year I'd either be able to pay off the debt or I'd be dead. At the time, death seemed preferable to being married to Putnam.

The Montgomery family loved to laugh about how I'd searched for a nickel in change, how I'd refused to buy myself warm clothing even after Adam gave me the money to do so. Better they should laugh about such things than know the truth, I thought.

But Adam knew and after we were married, he went to Putnam and worked out a deal so that everyone's debts were paid. Suddenly, people owned their houses, owned their cars. It changed the town completely, and almost overnight, prosperity began to hit the little town. Because everyone had been so deeply in debt, no one had had the get-up-and-go to try new things. What money they earned went to pay the Putnams for Putnam-owned merchandise. But when the people owned their own buildings and all the money they earned was their own, they began to have some energy.

"Communism," Adam sad. "It's why when Russia was communist ninety percent of the food was grown on ten percent of the land that was privately owned. People are selfish creatures."

Anyway, it had all worked out. Putnam the town was beginning to thrive and Putnam the son had married and had two kids already. Putnam the father had moved to Louisville and was trying to buy it, as he'd been defeated by Dallas.

As for me, everything had backfired, and I couldn't defend myself. Right after that book came out, my dear sweet husband wanted to publish a book that told the truth, but we couldn't. We couldn't tell about the money I wanted to give to Putnam without telling of how positively feudal the place had been for about 150 years. The mountains of Kentucky got enough bad press without hearing something that was guaranteed to make a bunch of Yankees laugh their heads off. The people of Putnam were just regaining their pride, so how could I take that away from them?

It was Boadicea who'd made me stop feeling sorry for myself. "You have freedom; you have everything," she'd said in her childlike way. Having been raised by an evil witch had not given her an expansive vocabulary. It seems that witches didn't get their captured kids together for play dates. Ha ha.

All in all, everything had been okay for years because I had my family and love was everywhere. But that now seemed long gone. My daughter and niece seemed to be perfectly happy in Colorado. It was a child's dream place with animals, trees, and playmates. Best for my daughter and niece was that their cousins didn't think they were weird. When the girls made their dolls climb trees, the cousins thought it was hilarious. There'd been a problem when one of Mike Taggert's kids had started charging admission to shows, but Mike had sorted his son out soon enough.

I punched my fist into the pillow and tried to think about what to do. My father wanted me to get out of the house, but he was always telling me to do that. He said he didn't want me to become obsessed with Adam and Bo's disappearance. He said that for the children's sake I should try to create a life for myself.

He could give advice but he certainly

couldn't take it! He'd been on the road since soon after Adam and Bo had disappeared and he'd had no rest—or life—at all. When Linc had asked me if it was easier for me to find something if I was closer to it, I almost spilled my guts. Yes, definitely yes. My father was my legs, so to speak, in our continual search for Adam and Bo. He called me from points around the world and I told him what I felt and where to try next.

Of course I'd felt that he'd found something of great significance: Bo's bag. It was the bag Adam had used to take the mirror out of the witches' house in Connecticut, so there was a lot of energy attached to it. What I think happened was that it had been stolen. Earlier, I'd told my father I felt that Adam and Bo were being held prisoners somewhere and one of the guards had stolen Bo's bag—with that old mirror inside it.

If this was true, then my worst fears were alleviated. My fear had always been that Adam and Bo were being held for that blasted mirror. After all, why had they taken the thing with them when they left? Why had they left in such secrecy? Why hadn't Adam told me what had happened that so excited him? Why hadn't I made a point to *listen?*

I'd spent months beating myself up over my lack of attention to what Adam had been so excited about that day, but I couldn't change the past.

But perhaps I could change the future. I'd told Linc that there was too much evil and wrongdoing in the world for me to be able to help, but I wasn't about to tell him the truth.

I know that most people don't believe in psychics. And no wonder, with so many charlatans out there. Tell people they're one way in public and another in private and they'll say, "She really *knows* me!"

But you know what I found out after I married Adam? I found out that the FBI believes in psychics. It seems that the FBI will use anything there is to try to bring criminals to justice—or to stop them.

A psychic can walk into her local police station and be laughed out of the office, but if she goes to the FBI, they'll say, "Show us."

Adam had a friend in the FBI, a man who'd helped us bring down that evil woman in Connecticut, so we both felt we owed him. He showed up at our house one Friday afternoon with a hand truck and three big file boxes packed full. He didn't leave until the next Thursday. By that time we'd gone over every case file in the boxes and I'd told him all I could.

I really hated doing it. What was in those files was horrible beyond imagining. In spite of what I told Linc, I can block out some of the horror around me. It's not easy to figure out if a person is fantasizing about murder or is really about to do it. Also, people do things on the spur of the moment. Someone can be hugging his/her spouse one day, and kill them the next.

But, as much as I hated doing it, I went over every file and I talked about killers, and innocent people in jail, and missing people who were dead or living elsewhere.

As my father knew, because he'd studied my ancestresses, I was good at finding people and things. Give me a map and I could close my eyes and quite often find missing or kidnapped people. Too often, I found graves.

Since that first time, every week, the FBI had sent me papers to go through to see what I could.

What my husband, Bo or my father never told the FBI or anyone else about were the other things I could do. I could make people do things; I could put thoughts into their minds. I had an idea the FBI knew more than they let on because they were the ones who covered up how the four people in the underground tunnel had died. Their final report said that Adam and his cousin, Mike Taggert, had killed the people. Also, the autopsy report that said there were no marks on the people, just their burst brains, "disappeared" almost immediately.

I pounded the pillows again and saw that it was nearly four A.M. Last night I'd had a flash of a premonition, that I *needed* to go to this place in Alabama with this man. There was something there I needed to find and take. Okay, steal. But steal what? Heaven help me, I hoped it wasn't another stupid mirror. I hated that thing passionately. My father rarely left it and Bo talked with great sadness about how she could no longer see the future in it because she was no longer a virgin.

For me, I'd never seen anything in it and didn't want to. I got rid of my virginity approximately one hour after the wedding ceremony. Adam grabbed me and pulled me into—

No! I could not think about that. It was something I'd learned soon after Adam left. Thinking about, remembering, our joyous times in bed together was guaranteed to make me go insane.

I turned on the bedside light and picked up the photo Linc had given me. I knew the woman in the picture had given birth to Linc's child. So who was the woman in the car who'd been killed? The newspaper said it was this woman but it wasn't. When I touched the newspaper clipping I could see that the woman who'd been killed was taller, thinner and had darker hair than the mother of Linc's child.

For a moment I closed my eyes and tried to put together pieces I was seeing. Maybe if I had that dreadful mirror my father could look into it and see what was ahead. But we'd all learned that what he saw was what could be. The future could be changed—changed from what was in the mirror, that is.

"How do I do this?" I whispered, clutching the photo. "And how is this connected to my husband and Bo?"

When I had another thought I opened my eyes with a jolt. My mother. She had been given a movie audition because of the Montgomery name, but the talent that got her leading roles was hers. I was truly shocked when I heard she was going on TV. Why had she agreed to do that? Because she liked the show a lot? I'd read every interview she'd given—and there were many—but she'd never once explained why she'd agreed to do a TV show.

Suddenly, I sat upright in bed. Was all this too much of a coincidence? My mother steps down off her big-screen pedestal to do a TV show, and the next thing I know, she's sending me off to some real-life murder mystery weekend. In my heart I knew there was more to this than finding a missing child. There was a connection to my husband. A link, so to speak, I thought, then I smiled. A Linc, maybe? I lay back on the pillows and smiled some more. It would be just like my mother to use a gorgeous young man to run errands for her. Maybe I couldn't be in the same room with my mother for more than fifteen minutes without being made to feel inadequate, but she had rescued me. She'd risked her life to save mine.

So what was she doing now? I wondered. And even more importantly, where had she found out information that I couldn't?

I picked up the brochure Linc had given me, held it between my palms and concentrated. Whatever I was looking for I felt was there, so I wanted to make sure the place had empty rooms for us. And I wanted to make sure Linc would be allowed in because this was a females-only resort.

I smiled at what I saw. The pain I'd given his head was nothing to what he was going to soon feel. All those women—both dead and alive—and he wouldn't be able to touch one of them.

LINC ‡⟵

All I could think was, This kid better be worth it! He better be some adoring, worshipful little brat who idolized me or I was going to send him back where he came from.

I don't know what happened to Darci during the night but she woke up a different person. My first thought was that she was delighted to be going somewhere with me. I'd said I wasn't interested in white women, but that was a lie. Actually, if given a choice, I prefer . . .

Oh well, it didn't matter anyway. She told me I had to audition for her. She wanted to see if I could act gay. I didn't like it but I couldn't resist so I showed off a bit with a pretty good performance: tasteful, on the elegant side. I imagined myself as an art dealer, someone with a lot of knowledge, well-traveled.

Darci didn't like it. "Have you ever seen *The Birdcage?*"

I groaned. Gays hated that movie, saying it was too exaggerated. It made a caricature of gays everywhere.

She started looking at me hard. I got this tiny pain in the base of my neck. Loudly, I began reciting the Gettysburg Address. When Darci laughed, the pain stopped. I refused to think about what she was doing and what she could do. If I believed what I was thinking I'd be expecting little alien beings to pop out of my belly.

"Do you want to do this or not?" she asked. "I called the place, this 13 Elms, this morning and they're going to let you in only because I told them you're beautiful and you're gay. I don't know why the beauty makes any difference, but they said the women who came there have to sign a document saying they'll have no sex while they're there."

"Is that legal?"

"Probably not, but I guess they can do

what they want. They say that sex interferes with the spirits."

"What kind of place is this, anyway?" I asked.

"A rip-off. They tell these rich women they can't have sex because it's like telling them they can't have chocolate—it makes them crave it. The women get into some kind of frenzy of denial so they will believe what they're told to believe. I think one of the owners says her spirit guide is some dead Indian. I think he wears only a loin-cloth. Or did," she added.

"Maybe I could get his job," I said, and couldn't resist flexing a bicep.

"No sex," Darci said firmly.

"So how will they know?"

"The bedrooms are bugged. There are cameras hidden in the rooms. They use what they hear in the séances."

"If you can tell all that from a brochure, how come—?" I broke off. No need to get her angry at me. Just thinking about what she could do made me rub my nose.

"Why didn't I know who the witch was in Connecticut?" she finished for me, seeming not in the least upset. "She had power, lots of it. And back then I didn't know much. I'd just left my small town and the most I'd ever done was—" She waved her hand. "Forget that. Can you do *Birdcage* or not?"

I grimaced. Of course I could do *Birdcage* and I'm sure she knew it—but I hated it. I put a hand on my hip, shifted my weight and flexed my wrist.

"Perfect," she said, smiling.

"I'm going to be a rich divorcée from Texas and you're going to be my personal assistant. Can you type?"

"No," I said and gave her a hard look. This wasn't what I'd had in mind.

"Use a computer? Take dictation? Make coffee?"

"No, no, and no."

"What can you do?" She was smirking.

"Play any role ever written."

"Even a gladiator?"

"Honey," I said in a stereotype of a gay man, "I can out gladiate even a bipolar. If *I* had been in shock treatment . . ." I rolled my eyes to let her know that I would have done a better job than Russell Crowe ever thought of doing.

To my delight, Darci began to laugh and I don't know when I'd ever felt so pleased about performing. Maybe it was the thought of how much she must have seen and felt in her lifetime, yet she was laughing at my jokes.

"Okay," I said, "when do we go? And, by the way, why do you, a rich young woman, want to go there?"

"My husband, thirty-one years my senior, died without telling me where he'd hidden his first wife's jewelry. I want to contact his spirit and see if I can get him to tell me where the jewels are."

"Good one," I said. "So when do we leave?"

"In about three hours. My husband's cousin is sending a plane to take us. What?!" she asked me as she must have felt my sense of panic.

"I brought one bag of clothes. I need—" I cut off because I could see she was fighting with herself. Something had made her change her mind about wanting to go and now she seemed to be fighting something else. Overnight, she'd gone from refusing to go to wanting to go instantly. "Delay the flight and give me two hours in a high-end mall and—"

"There isn't time," she said. "We need to go now. I have to get something there or meet someone or . . . or . . ." When she looked up at me, I could see pain on her face. "My husband. He's taller than you and less beefy, but I think his clothes will fit you." Turning, she left the kitchen and headed into the bowels of that big house.

"Beefy?" I whispered. "I'm *beefy?*"

"Are you coming or not?" she called to me, and I hightailed it after her.

She led me to her inner sanctum, her bedroom, and from the way she ran past the neatly made-up bed, I wanted to tease her. I don't know where she was getting the idea that I was coming on to her because I wasn't. I guess sex was one area where her psychic abilities failed.

Truthfully I had no interest in her at all. She wasn't my type, no matter what color her skin was. As I followed her into a closet, I contemptuously looked her up and down. She had on a pair of black linen slacks and a rust-colored shirt that just reached to the top of her rear end. Her curvy little rear end. Too curvy for someone as scrawny as she was. And her legs—

"Cut it out!" she said over her shoulder.

"I have no idea what you mean."

She gave me a look that almost set my

eyelashes on fire. None of her voodoo magic, just a girl-look telling me to back off. The look kind of interested me. Since I'd been sixteen, I hadn't had many women say no to me. Actually, when I came to think about it, the only woman who'd ever said no to me was Darci's mother. Alanna's no's didn't count.

As she switched on the closet light, I said, "You're like your mother, you know that?"

"Is that good or bad?"

I busied myself looking at her husband's clothes. "You're the psychic so you figure it out." I really hoped I'd made her curious, but she didn't seem to be.

Yawning, she went back into the bedroom and sat down on a little chair where she could see me but was out of touching distance. Coward, I thought. But as I looked away I knew she was genuinely disinterested in what most women liked about me.

I looked at the clothes. Everything was of top quality, but was ultraconservative. This wasn't a man who wore red silk shirts out to dinner.

"So what can I borrow?" I asked.

"Anything, whatever." She looked half asleep.

"You don't mind that I wear his clothes?"

"Clothes are things. He's not in them."

"So where is he?"

She seemed to want to answer my question but didn't yet feel that she could confide in me. Yet, I thought. She might have no interest in me sexually, but women liked to talk to me.

I began to pull clothes out of the closet and put them on the bed behind Darci, then I started unbuttoning my shirt. When she looked at me, startled, I smiled. "I have to try them on, don't I?"

She got up, obviously planning to leave the room.

"Shouldn't we be talking about what we're heading into? Are you going to introduce me to these ladies as Lincoln Aimes? And maybe you should tell me what happened last night to make you so happy this morning. Your husband visit you in spirit form?"

She shot me a look and with it came a little pain to the back of my neck, but I just smiled. I watched as she walked to the other side of the room and sat down on a chair, her back to me. She'd said she was unaffected by me, so why didn't she want to see me in my underwear?

As I pulled on a pair of Montgomery's trousers, I told myself to knock it off. But I really wished I could spend a couple of hours with Alanna before Darci and I left.

In the end it took Darci and me a couple of hours to pack since I showed her each piece of clothing I tried on. She was right when she'd said he was taller than I was, but as Darci so indelicately put it, "Your behind sticks out much more than his so it shortens the pants."

So much for racial differences.

After we chose clothes for me—and I vowed to go shopping as soon as we got there—I asked Darci what she was going to wear. She looked at me blankly for a second, as though she hadn't thought about it, then led me to her closet. It was as large as his but only half full.

"Adam buys my clothes," she said. "He has such good taste and—" She looked away.

Since my usual way of cheering up women wasn't available to me, I decided to put my acting into practice. "Honey," I said, hand on hip, "with your coloring you can wear just about anything." I pulled down a cute little blue suit and held it up in front of her—and when I did, I said in my normal voice (which, personally, I thought was quite as deep and sexy as you know whose) that her hair color had to change.

Our first argument ensued. Or was it our twenty-fifth? I couldn't be sure. Darci stalked out of the closet. "Oh no," she said. "My husband likes this color. It's a strawberry blonde and he likes it."

If the guy liked redheads, maybe he wasn't as deadly dull as his wardrobe made him seem. "So do the tabloids," I said. "They love your red hair. Didn't they say something about your temper matching the color of your hair? And didn't your hairdresser give one tabloid an interview? Think no one at that place in Alabama will recognize you?"

When she stopped walking, I knew I had her. "There isn't enough time to change my hair color, even if there was some dye in this house, which there isn't."

I don't know how I knew it, but I knew she was lying. She may have all sorts of powers but, underneath, she was just human—and not a great actress. To me, who'd spent a lot of time around actors and liars, she was utterly transparent. "Tell me, Darci," I said, "do you lie often and if you do, does anyone believe you?"

I wasn't sure but I thought I saw a tiny smile at the corner of her lips. It was my guess that she lied often. If I had her abilities, I'd lie to everyone all the time. "So who has the hair dye?" I asked.

"The housekeeper may have some."

"In the room where you put me?" I asked. "The one at the far side of the house? The one so far away from your bedroom it has another zip code?"

She gave me a full smile. "That's the one." She looked at me for a second, then said, "Race you," and took off.

She won but only because she didn't get lost in that maze of a house. She was already in the housekeeper's closet and, way in the back, under four shoe boxes, was a stash of boxes of black hair dye. As I saw Darci pull them out I thought that I'd hate to work for her. I'd never be able to have a secret.

Twenty minutes later, I had Darci leaning over a sink and I was squirting the dye on her fine, silky hair. At that thought, she sent a little pain to the back of my neck and I shoved her head down until it clonked against the porcelain.

"I thought you couldn't read minds," I said, my gloved hands massaging her scalp.

"I can feel things and you are . . ." She twisted a bit to look at me.

"So horny I could screw the crack of dawn?"

"That's about it," she said, smiling.

"This kid better be worth it," I muttered. "By the way, this private plane that's picking us up, is it a jet? With a flight attendant or two?"

"Sorry to disappoint you but it's an old fishing plane. Smelly, dirty, slow and loud. We can't arrive in anything with the Montgomery name on it."

"Sure," I said. "I don't know why I didn't think of that. Okay, stand up. You have to leave it on for twenty minutes. Here, let me do your eyebrows."

"Yuck. I'll look horrible."

"Not to me," I said, then smacked her on the fanny. For a moment I held my breath.

Was she going to give me another nose-bleed?

She rubbed her rear end and said, "Save it for somebody who's interested, and touch me again and I'll show you what I did to those four witches in Connecticut."

With that, she left the bathroom to go to her closet to start pulling out clothes.

Damn! I thought, but she was a weird little character. And damn me, but I was more intrigued by the minute.

Darci ↢

↣ *Chapter Seven*

All the way to Alabama on that dreadful plane Mike Taggert had sent, I thought about my mother—and tried hard not to think about her.

Mike hadn't asked me too many questions except whether or not I might be in danger. "None whatever," I said, lying while using my mind to make him believe me. I think he did, but I wasn't sure. On the other hand, I'm sure he knew he didn't have much choice in the matter. Yes, he'd contacted someone he knew and got me a plane down to Alabama. He asked me some questions, but I didn't answer him, because the truth was I didn't know what was ahead.

As the day progressed, I kept feeling that

something was calling me to this place in Alabama. If I weren't such a lily-livered coward I would have called my mother and asked her what she knew. But I was like those women—and men—who ran corporations but turned into weaklings in front of their mothers. I'd walk into fire for those I loved, but just the thought of calling my mother made me want to sit down and take some long, deep breaths.

The plane ride was so noisy that there could be no conversation so I tried to concentrate on what I was feeling. "An object" was all that was in my mind. Some magic object was pulling me to it. Was it an object or was it a person? If it was a person, did it have a body? And if it was an object, what did it do? For a moment I closed my eyes and fantasized about finding Aladdin's lamp. If the Mirror of Nostradamus existed, why not the magic lamp? I certainly knew what I'd wish for!

The plane suddenly dropped in altitude and jarred me back to reality. I looked across at Linc and saw him cross himself. I could feel that he expected to die at any moment.

It wasn't long before we landed on a private landing strip where a long black limo was waiting for us. I'd told Mike that I needed to look rich when I arrived so he'd arranged it.

We drove for over an hour before we reached 13 Elms, the place where the mother of Linc's son was last known to work. Officially, she'd been a masseuse, but I felt that she'd done something else, something that involved the child.

Maybe I was being paranoid but I wouldn't talk to Linc inside the limo. I knew Mike had sent the limo, and the driver wasn't from the plantation, but, still, I had the feeling we were being watched. Watched and listened to—and scrutinized.

"What's wrong with you?" Linc asked. "You've turned whiter—if that's possible."

I smiled at him. Poor man. He was totally unable to suppress his sexual desires. Perhaps I should give him a talk about self-denial.

As soon as I figured out how to suppress my own longings I was going to talk to him.

"Holy Mother of—" Linc said under his breath.

"Please don't curse," I said, but there

was no conviction in my voice because I was seeing what he was seeing.

The brochure about the place, 13 Elms, had been crazy. They hadn't stated outright that they were a group of spiritualists, or that they held séances, or that anyone told futures. In the brochure they'd said they were "a place of rejuvenation." They said that your worries would be taken away at 13 Elms. I'd felt the truth of what went on there.

However, I'd not seen the actual, physical place as my visions aren't perfectly clear. Sometimes they are, but most often it's just glimpses of images. I'd seen bricks and trees, and I'd seen white columns. From this I'd drawn the conclusion that 13 Elms was an old plantation-type house, like something out of *Gone With the Wind.* The brochures had carefully shown only interiors and a cute herb garden with a sundial in the middle of it.

But what Linc and I were seeing wasn't cute, wasn't little, and didn't look very southern. It looked like a fortress more than a house, with two towers sticking up from it, one tall, one short. The whole thing was made out of bricks that I was sure were handmade. In front were the white columns I'd seen in my vision supporting a second story porch, but the porch area was narrow and looked as though it had been an after-thought.

Turrets, a cone-shaped roof, and small round-topped windows were all over the sprawling façade.

"Whoever built this was crazy," Linc said.

"I agree completely."

"Want to leave?" he said quietly so the driver wouldn't hear.

"Can't," I said and meant it. There was something in that house that was pulling me to it.

"Darci," Linc asked, making me look at him. "If you're going to do things that are scary, I think we should leave now."

"You mean like wander around outside at night even though we hear wolves howl-ing?"

Linc didn't smile. "There aren't were-wolves, are there? What about vampires?"

"Not that I know of," I said, trying to sound as though I really knew.

I didn't try to explain to Linc what I was feeling. All I knew was that the first second I had I was going to start searching that old place and see what I could find.

The driver of the limo stopped in front of the porch and Linc and I got out, both of us craning our necks to look around. I wasn't feeling evil from the place but it was definitely eerie. I wouldn't have been surprised to see bats flying out of a tower—bats with little people faces on them.

"This place gives me the creeps."

"Me, too," I whispered back to him. The driver was unloading our bags and, as my assistant, Linc should have been helping him, but I didn't think Linc would ever get the hang of being an employee. When the driver finished unloading, he jumped into the car and sped off, leaving us standing there. He was a local so maybe he knew things about the house.

"Now that is scary," Linc said, looking after the car. "That man didn't even wait for a tip."

"Maybe my husband's cousin took care of it," I said, still looking at the house.

As I reached for the doorbell, Linc said, "If that thing rings like a howling wolf, I'm outta here."

"Me, too."

"You're supposed to tell me you feel this place is safe."

"But I don't. I'm sure someone's watching us."

"Usually, when I feel that way I like it," he said. "But not now."

When I pressed the doorbell, we heard a pleasant chiming inside. A woman wearing a black dress and a white collar opened the door. She didn't smile or greet us in any way. We stepped inside, she closed the door behind us, then she quietly left the room.

Linc and I stood together, silently looking about the entrance hall. It was large, but not like the vast spaces Adam had shown me in the castles in England and Scotland. In fact, this room was rather nice. It was paneled in oak that had aged to a soft brown. A fireplace complete with cheerful, crackling fire was to our right and a wide staircase was on our left. It led up to a railing that went around the whole second floor. On the back wall were bookcases and in front of them was a big rolltop desk.

There were at least four doors leading out of this room and through one of them came two women who I was sure were the sisters who owned the house and grounds. I took one look at them and decided I didn't trust them. One was short, fat and sweet-looking; the other one was dark and thin. I could feel that both of them were up to no good. When they looked at me and all my jewelry—Linc had made me empty my jewelry box—they looked like cartoon characters, with dollar signs in their eyes.

"There you are," the plump one said, taking both my hands in hers, and when she touched me I felt a weak current of electricity go up my arm.

My goodness, I thought, the woman has some power and she's trying to read my mind. I sent her the thought I wanted her to feel, that I was greedy and angry, and that I wanted to get what I felt was mine. At least I hoped that's what I was sending. Ever since I'd walked inside I'd been feeling a little odd, not quite stable.

"I'm Narcissa Barrister and this is my sister Delphia, as in Philadelphia," she said. Narcissa had blue eyes and pink cheeks and she was smiling sweetly at me. "And you are Darci Nicodemus, is that right?"

Linc had made up the name. I didn't like it but considering that my life seemed to revolve around that horrid mirror, Nicodemus was close enough to Nostradamus to be almost the same.

"Miss Nicki," Linc said before I could speak. He swished over to Narcissa, took her plump shoulders in his big strong hands and kissed both her cheeks. I held my breath. No men were allowed here so what would she think?

I needn't have worried, for Narcissa giggled like a preteen. I watched in amazement as her body shimmied like Jell-O.

"Aren't you adorable?" Narcissa said.

Linc smiled at me, then approached Delphia, who was standing apart and silent. I'm sure his intention was to kiss Delphia and charm her, too—but one look from the woman halted him.

"No, dear," Narcissa said sharply. "No one must touch Delphia. She's a psychic and she feels things. We mustn't overburden her."

"Isn't that the most exciting thing you've ever heard, Miss Nicki?" Linc said to me, but I was looking at Delphia to see what I could feel from her. Not much. I was willing to bet that plump little Narcissa had more power than her sister did. If people hadn't been killed who I thought were connected to them, I would have sworn there was no harm in either of them—no real harm, just greed.

Narcissa was staring at Linc. "You look just like that boy on that TV show. What is his name?"

"Lincoln Aimes," Linc said quickly. "And don't I look just like him? But, honey, he's too butch for me. I couldn't possibly play a role as well as he does. By golly, if he were on the big screen, there's no telling what that man could accomplish. Honestly, I think he's one of the best—"

"What can you do?" He was cut off by the gravelly voice of Delphia. A voice that had been acquired from too many cigarettes—or an injury. I looked at her throat but it was covered by the high collar of a dress that was buttoned all the way up to her chin.

"I beg your pardon?" Linc asked, as startled as I was by the woman's voice.

"My sister wants to know if you can do

anything, like read palms, tarot cards, that sort of thing."

I had to look away so my smile wouldn't be seen. I think they were offering Linc a job to supplement whatever he was supposed to be doing for me. So far, all he'd done was bully me. "Masseur," I said. Maybe he could find out something from the other guests and maybe a job would keep him busy. "Linc can give massages. He's quite good at it."

Linc narrowed his eyes at me and I knew he was sending me the message that he was going to kill me.

"How wonderful," Narcissa said. "We had two people who gave massages but one of them . . . one of them . . . Oh dear. Perhaps, Mr. . . . What was your name again?"

"Forbes," Linc said. "Jason Forbes."

I hadn't liked the name Linc had made up for himself, but he said Forbes sounded rich and Jason sounded strong. I said the name sounded phony. Linc said, "You think Lincoln Aimes is real?"

At that moment a woman hurried into the room. She was about sixty, very overweight, wearing just a towel and a shower cap, and she was angry. "Narcissa! That

Maria has disappeared again. I was scheduled for a massage at four o'clock, it is now four oh seven and she is nowhere to be found. I demand a refund."

"Dear Mrs. Hemmings," Narcissa soothed. "We've just hired a new masseur and he'll take care of you right now."

"He?" Mrs. Hemmings asked angrily. "I was told that no men—" She broke off when she saw Linc. Six feet of muscle, all of it covered in café au lait–colored skin. I thought the woman was going to swoon—or worse, drop her towel.

"Oh," was all the woman could say. "Oh."

Linc, who I'd already learned would pretty much roll onto his back and purr for a compliment, gave the woman a look Paul Travis would use on murder suspects to get them to confess.

Both Narcissa and I grabbed Mrs. Hemmings's towel before it fell.

"He's not a real man," I heard Narcissa whisper to the woman. "If you know what I mean. Your virtue will be safe with him."

"Oh," Mrs. Hemmings said again. "Oh."

Narcissa looked at me. "Perhaps I should show Mrs. Hemmings and Jason where the massage rooms are. Delphi will take you,

Miss Nicki, to your rooms. Don't worry about your bags, they will be delivered to your room. And remember that dinner is at six tonight. We want our food to be well digested before Delphi's séance tonight. You will be there, won't you?"

"Only death would keep me from it," I said, then wished I hadn't because Narcissa looked at me oddly. I ignored Linc's expression of terror as he looked at Mrs. Hemmings's huge white body.

I turned back to Delphia, smiling, and thinking that I had two whole hours to explore before dinner. Even if I didn't explore, I didn't want to be around Linc after he got through with Mrs. Hemmings.

Delphia didn't say a word as she went up the stairs, then down the hall. From the way she moved I could tell that she was in fairly good shape physically. I wondered if there was a gym in the house.

"This is your room," she said, opening a heavy oak door at the end of the hall.

It was beautiful: high ceilings, tall windows, a bed big enough for half a dozen people, a couch, chairs, desk. One wall had an enormous fireplace with two carved marble sculptures of bare-breasted mermaids, their tails spilling down onto the hearth. The mantel was level with the top of my head and held enormous pewter jugs. A portrait of a man wearing a Confederate uniform was high up on the wall.

In front of the fireplace was a sitting area filled with fat furniture on a beautiful rug of green and rose tones. The bed was on the far side of the room and next to it was a door leading into a bathroom the size of the average master bedroom. Thick white towels were draped across heated bars.

"Is it all right?" Delphia asked in her gravelly voice. I could feel she had pain associated with her neck but I wasn't clear on what was wrong. There was something odd in this house. I felt like a compass placed on top of a magnet. My perceptions were going round and round like a compass needle gone crazy.

"May I see your palm?" she asked.

For some reason, I was hesitant. If I touched her, what would I see? Would my senses settle down or go more askew? "I thought we weren't to touch you," I said, smiling, my hands behind my back.

"I wish to know about you," she said, holding out her hand for me to put mine in her palm.

The instant I touched her I knew she was a charlatan. No psychic ability at all, but I was willing to bet she didn't let her sister know that. In fact, I got the idea that Delphia lorded it over her sister pretty strongly.

"You have a long lifeline," she said, "and you've had many experiences in your life. I see a man, very tall and dark."

"Good!" I said, "since my husband was blond. I'm missing something and I want to know where he put it—them."

She gave me what I'm sure was a much-rehearsed look, supposed to make me feel as though she "knew" things, and said, "All will be made known to you in due time."

It wasn't easy but I didn't laugh. If she were a real psychic, she would have seen that the only things I wanted to find were my husband and his sister. She dropped my hand and I stepped away from her. I didn't like being too close to her as greed beamed forth from her like a big green floodlight. Her aura was an ugly brownish red.

"I've never been to a séance before," I said honestly. "What's it like?"

She was looking at me as though I'd done something strange. Story of my life, I thought. I never seemed to act or react the way other people did. I sent a message to her mind that I wanted her to like me but I don't think she "heard" me.

"Do you conduct the séance?" I asked.

"Yes," she said slowly, looking at me. "I've seen you before."

I'd prepared for this and had my story ready. "Yes. I look like that woman, the Hillbilly Honey, the one who was in the news so much. Actually, she's a distant cousin of mine." I tried to put bitterness in my voice. "It's because of her that I'm here. My dead husband hid some things that I knew he owned, but if I went to normal sources to help me find them, I was afraid the media would pick up on it. I'd jump off a building rather than have the papers call me a hillbilly anything."

"So you came to us."

"Yes," I said, trying to look helpless and needy. "Do you think you can help me? Do you think your spirit guide can locate the jewelry that husband of mine hid?"

At just the mention of jewels I saw a tiny flame ignite in her eyes.

"We will do our best. Now I think you should rest from your journey. I'll see you in the dining room at six, then we will all meet in the library for the séance. If you'll excuse me, I have matters to attend to."

She left the room in a flash and I wondered what she was up to. I mention jewels and she leaves.

Ten minutes later the woman who'd opened the door for us brought my three suitcases into the room. When I tried to tip her, she shook her head and left. As soon as she was out of the room, the first thing I did was ascertain where the cameras and microphones were. People don't realize how much energy machines give off, but I'd found out long ago that I could find machines with my mind. It took just a few minutes of concentrating to find them.

Disabling them without alerting the watchers was another matter. I hung a hat over the little dried flower wreath that concealed a camera that looked toward the bed. In the bathroom (how rude! I thought) I sprayed my hair, then leaned over as though to get something and thoughtlessly sprayed the panel by the mirror, thus covering the camera lens.

The microphones were more difficult but I managed—after three tries—to smash the one under the bed with the suitcase. Since there was no camera to see me, I put on a little radio show as though I were using the poker as a fencing sword, then said "oops" just before I smashed the microphone with the poker.

I knew I was giving too much away by doing these things but, really—a camera in my bathroom!

Once I was alone, I started digging through my bags and soon found what I wanted: my black Lycra cat suit.

At the sight of the suit I refused to let myself cry. I hadn't worn it since Adam and I had gone into the tunnels in Connecticut. To cover his attraction to me, he'd complained about everything I did or said. Of course I'd known we were safe. And I'd known—

I made myself stop thinking about Adam, then went into the bathroom to change. When I emerged a few minutes later I halted. I could feel Linc near me. A second later, I saw his face at the window—the second floor window.

"What in the world are you doing?" I

asked as soon as I got the window open. He was hanging by his fingertips and I had to help haul him in.

"Episode twenty-three was about a cat burglar," he said as he fell onto the floor. "The director made me put on a leotard and crawl along the ledge of an eighteen-story building to see if it could be done."

I helped him stand up. "I thought all that was fake, that the actors were really only a couple of feet off the ground."

"I was, but I still couldn't slip or— Wow! You look great."

I stepped away from him. "So how's Mrs. Hemmings?"

Linc groaned. "You can't believe the offer she made me. She wanted to pay me to—" He waved his hand. "Anyway, I got no information out of her. She's never been here before. But I talked to another guest and she said that the masseuse who used to be here was named Lisa, but she said she had never seen a little boy around here. She said that Delphia didn't like men, children, or animals. You know, you really do look *good.*"

"Touch me and I'll make your head hurt,"

I said, but I was smiling. His desire for a woman was getting stronger every time I saw him. His aura was now about a foot around his body and it was bright red. "You should have taken Mrs. Hemmings up on her offer," I said, making sure there was lots of distance between us.

Linc plopped down on my bed and I could tell he was sulking. I wondered how many women had turned him down in his life.

"Did anyone see you climb up whatever you climbed up to get into my room?"

"I don't know. You're the psychic. You tell me. And why are you dressed like that anyway?"

I had no intention of telling him anything so I began sending him soothing thoughts that I hoped would put him to sleep, but since I was in a hurry I was a little too pushy.

"Ow!" he said, rubbing his neck, then he began reciting the Gettysburg Address again.

I didn't have time to deal with him. "I'm going somewhere and I want you to stay here and wait for me."

He didn't bother to answer. "What a fireplace!" he said, rolling off the bed, going toward the mermaids, his hands ready to grab
their breasts.

I put my body between him and the mermaids. A mistake. As his hands got near
me, I gave him a look that made him halt.
He stepped back, smiling. "Wherever you're
going, I'm going with you."

"To the library," I said. "I have to do some
things there. By myself."

"Such as disengage all machines that
make fake ghosts appear?"

"Now who's the mind reader?" I asked.

"We did a show that had a séance. A
woman went to one and never returned, so
I know something about the tricks. If you
go, you go with me," he said, and I knew he
meant it.

"All right." I sighed to let him know I
didn't like the idea, although, truthfully, I
didn't want to go sneaking around by myself. I couldn't cut wires or whatever while
using my mind to make sure I wasn't
caught. "Let me make sure the hall is clear."

When Linc started to open the door, I
shut it. "What do you think you're doing?"

"Checking the hallway. Excuse me. I forgot that you can do what no one on earth can do and that I probably know only fifty percent of what you can do."

"One percent," I said. "And hush." I closed my eyes and searched with my mind. I felt no one near us, felt that no one was about to come down the hall. I sent out thoughts that no one wanted to go into the entryway or—

Opening my eyes, I asked Linc, "Do you know where the library is?"

"What if I hadn't dumped Mrs. Hemmings and come here, ready to rescue you? How would you even have found the library without me?"

I opened the door slowly, peeking out just in case. Something was very strange in that house and I meant to find it. As far as I could feel, there were no cameras or microphones in the hall. It was my guess that there were certain people—namely Narcissa and Delphia—who didn't want their movements recorded. Since they used the hallway, there were no recording devices.

"I would have moved the library to me," I said over my shoulder to Linc as I left the room.

"You can't really move a room, can you?" he asked, following me.

Turning, I walked backward down the hall. Okay, so I was enjoying his lust. I planned to remain faithful to Adam forever, but it was nice to look at Linc's beautiful body and see the lust that encircled him grow and develop. If auras were tangible he would have had a wall of fire behind him.

"No, I can't move a room but I could, say, make a backhoe driver get lost and end up with his machine in the library."

"That wouldn't really move the room, that would destroy it. Not the same thing."

His voice was getting deeper and the flames of his aura bigger. "How about if I make someone think that she had to go to the library to get a book? I could follow her."

"She'd better be a locksmith because they keep the room locked."

His aura was now nothing but fire: red, orange, tiny bits of green at the tip. I could feel its warmth. As I went down the big stairs backward, I felt that my body had ice around it and he was the warmth I needed. Adam, Adam, Adam, I thought.

Linc broke the spell. "This is it," he said,

his arm on the door behind me, his head coming down close to mine.

The spell was broken when I saw a man's face behind Linc's left shoulder. I blinked and the face was gone. When Linc's face got to where mine had been, I ducked under his arm.

"Did you see that?" I asked, looking around but seeing no one.

"What?" Linc asked, his voice higher. His aura was cooling, like a fire going down, no longer flames, but a warm glow. It wouldn't take much to set it to blazing again.

"I think I saw a ghost. Isn't that marvelous? I've never seen one before. I mean, I've seen many of them inside my head, and talked to a lot of them, but I've never seen one in solid form. It takes a lot of strength to be able to appear in life form. One time I was in a new house but the people had used boards on the walls from some old cabin. I could feel bits of ghosts all over the walls. It was as though they'd cut pictures into strips and glued them back together. Can you pick the lock?" His aura was down to a reddish brown.

"You're a very strange person, you know that?"

"Because I want you to pick a lock?"

"No, because most people are afraid of ghosts."

"Most people are afraid of me," I said. "Did you know—"

He cut me off. "You mean, did I learn how to pick locks, hotwire cars, and was I in a gang when I grew up in Harlem? For your information, my parents taught college and I—"

Racism, I thought, and gave a sigh as I pulled the little fanny pack I wore around to the front. "I was just being polite. My cousin Virgil taught me how to pick a lock."

"Virgil?" he asked. "About so high? Mean-looking? Scar across the side of his face?"

"That's him." I was bending down and working with the little tool Virgil had made for me when I was a kid. I used to love to get sent to stay with Virgil because he never thought anything that happened around me was odd. He was the person I came closest to telling what I was able to do, but then I think Virgil, just by being quiet and listening, figured out more than others did.

I felt rather than saw Linc shiver. "I

wouldn't want to meet that guy on a dark night," he said. "Or in sunlight. In fact—"

He stopped talking when I pushed the library door open and we looked inside. If there had ever been any ghosts in that room, I didn't feel them.

I looked around the room while giving myself time to feel what was in there. Two walls were covered, floor to ceiling, with books in walnut shelves, the third wall had shelves and a fireplace, and the far wall had two big windows hidden under heavy burgundy-colored velvet curtains.

While I was looking, I scanned for cameras and microphones. I could feel that there was a lot of electronic equipment in the room but none of it felt "on." It was like when the electricity went off. You knew the refrigerator was there, but it wasn't humming, wasn't using electricity, wasn't "alive."

As I looked about the room, I couldn't help but notice the decor.

"Too dark," I said. "If this were my library, I'd do it all in greens and yellows. Don't you think yellow curtains would be nice?"

"I think two people have been killed and I think this is serious. And I also think that if we had any sense we'd get the hell out of this place."

"Watch your language, please." I really hated the use of vulgar words. They were for shock value, so what value was there in using a shocking word every time a person opened his mouth? Or her mouth?

When I looked at Linc he was pulling books out of the shelves, looking at them, then putting them back. "I don't think this is the time to choose reading matter. We should—"

"Bingo," he said, looking at me in triumph. He'd pulled out books that were glued together, their insides cut away so they formed a box. Behind the box was what looked like a projector. "Is it possible you know anything about electronic equipment?"

"Both my daughter and my niece have telekinetic powers, but I don't. If one of them were here now, she could—"

Linc looked at me in disgust. "You have a small Phillips screwdriver in that pack of yours?"

He'd meant "know" as in having read a manual. "Oh," I said. I gave him a tool that was Phillips on one end and flat on the other. The middle had a hole in it that fit a 3/8-inch hexagonal nut.

"Virgil?" Linc asked as he took the tool.

I nodded and watched him. From the look of the way he was adjusting screws, he could have built whatever the thing was.

"Cool," I said. "I'll find them, you disable them."

"Partners," he said, the top of his head hidden in the bookcase.

"Like Holmes and Watson."

"More like Lucy and Ricky," Linc said, and I laughed.

Concentrating, I tried to find the other machines in the room but with their not being on, it wasn't easy. I think someone had turned off the circuit breaker so that if there was a storm or an electrical malfunction, the machines in the room wouldn't blow up. They must be expensive, I thought.

We pulled more fake books out, found more machines, and Linc disabled all of them. He said they were high-tech recorders and a projector for storing holograms. "Simple movie stuff," he said. "No offense, but I see why they don't let men stay here. Any man would know what these things are."

"Sure," I said. "Men are so very clever. That's why you have a kid whose mother you've never even met. Tell me, Mr. Brilliant, when you were in that room with that little cup didn't you consider that what you were doing might result in a child?"

He didn't bother to answer me but I could tell that he was embarrassed. The next second, he said, "Oh ho!" sounding like someone in an English movie. He had found a tiny wire along one edge of the bookcase. As his hands followed the wire, it looked as though he was a mime because the wire couldn't be seen.

"It goes up there," he said, nodding toward the paneling above the fireplace. He looked back at me. "I don't know what this wire is but on our show about séances, the woman used one like this to make things in the room move and to make noises. She hooked it to her elbow and all she had to do was move her arm and voilà! things moved. Whatever we do, I don't think we should cut this wire. I've fixed the machines so it looks like normal machine malfunction."

I gave him a look.

"Yeah. Well, okay, so they'll know someone did it, but they'll also wonder if maybe the machines went out on their own. If we cut the wire I think it—"

"Would make them insane with rage and they'll murder us in our beds?"

"More or less," Linc said. "What else do you have in that pack of yours?"

I held it out to him; he rummaged in it and found a little pink knife I'd had since I was a kid. The blade had been sharpened so many times it hardly existed. "Perfect," he said, then bent the wire around the knife to make a kink in it. "All we need now is to hook this on the corner of the mantel and the wire won't move if anyone pulls it. I think I can climb up there."

The tiny decorative ledge on the book-case was too narrow for his big feet. "I'll climb if you'll give me a boost up."

"Oh yeah," he said, then held out his arms to me as though he meant to hug me. When I took a step away from him, he grimaced. "Now you think I'm a rapist?"

"Touchy-feely," I said, and he gave me such a lascivious look that I laughed. The next minute he cupped his hands, I stepped into them and he nearly tossed me up to the high mantel. "I almost hit the ceiling," I hissed down at him.

"Sorry. I have too much stored energy. You think this place has a gym in it?"

"I think there's a gym somewhere and that Delphia uses it. She's stronger than she looks."

"Speaking of looks . . ." he said, looking up at me as I stretched up to reach the top of the mantel and pull the wire into place.

I didn't respond because my senses came alert. "Someone's coming," I whispered.

"Wire fixed in place?" he asked and when I nodded, he grabbed my ankle and pulled me off the mantel.

If my senses hadn't been so full of the approach of someone I would have screamed as I went flying through the air to land in his arms. When I opened my mouth to protest, Linc set me on the floor and put a finger over his lips to be quiet. Softly, I ran to the door and leaned against it. I was puzzled. I had put a mental no-entry sign on the hallways, so who was out there?

Closing my eyes, I tried to visualize the person I felt but didn't hear. Images came to me but they made no sense. A man. A woman. A ghost. A . . . A dragon?

At that image, I started to open the door

but Linc put his arm above my head and held the door shut, which annoyed me. "I could make you—" I whispered, but stopped because I felt the person—or thing—move away.

"Gone!" I said, pushing Linc against his ribs. It was like trying to move a rock. When I looked up at him, he was smiling in a lewd way.

"We are finished in here," I said. *"You need to work out. Get rid of some of that energy."* His aura had erupted into flame again.

"I know a better way to get rid of energy," he said as he bent his head as though to kiss me.

I slipped under his arm and when he held the door shut, I stared at his hand. I used my mind to transfer the red-hot heat from his aura to his hand. It was a lazy trick since I didn't take the time to conjure energy, but I wanted to get out of there and see who or what had been able to get past the spell I'd put on the hallway.

With a yelp of pain, Linc moved his hand from the door. As he was blowing on his hand to cool it off, I ran toward my room. My mind was split as part of me tried to find the person who'd been in the hall and part of me sent Linc a message that he needed to find a gym and stay there until dinner.

Once in my room, I stripped out of my Lycra and put on jeans and a knit shirt. On my way out I took my sun hat from over the camera in the dried flower wreath and put it on my head. Let them look at the empty room for a while, I thought.

I wandered around the "castle" for about thirty minutes, not seeing much, but feeling all that I could. Six of the bedrooms were occupied and I felt that the women in them were sleeping. Drugged, I wondered? Drugs to keep the guests quiet would make the housekeeping easier.

A lot of doors were locked. In fact, nearly every door was locked. There was a pretty little sitting room where I think tea was served that was open, but I didn't go inside. There were at least four cameras hidden in the room and I felt that someone was watching me with great interest. I had to tamp down a desire to grin and wave.

I kept walking about the house, trying doors, but all were locked. I could feel there were many people in the house but it was difficult to pinpoint their locations. I could feel people under my feet and over my head so the basement and attic rooms were occupied—or at least used. I couldn't feel a child anywhere. Nor could I feel the ghost I'd so quickly glimpsed behind Linc.

As for Linc, I was attuned to him enough now that I knew he'd set off on a long walk around the grounds. His room wasn't in the main house. When I closed my eyes, I could lock into him and almost feel what he was feeling. This had always happened to me when I was around someone for a while. With a bit of concentration, I could almost blend into that person.

With love, the feeling was even stronger. Like spinning a dial, I could tell where my loved ones were and what they were doing. Right now my daughter and my niece were in the sunshine and they were flying. No, swinging. Some boy was pushing them. I could feel Michael Taggert nearby. It was his son who was pushing the girls on the swings. The girls missed me, they missed all their family, but they were all right. They were getting the two k's that I'd long ago seen were necessary for children: Kissin' and Kookin'. Love and food.

I "spun the dial" so to speak and tuned in

to my father. At the moment he was yelling
at someone who was yelling back at him. I
didn't feel any danger and didn't think he
needed my help. It was difficult for me to
control things from so far away, but my
connection to my father was so strong that I
could do it.

My mother seemed to be driving one—or
was it two?—men insane with lust. Since
she'd become a movie star I never felt her
having sex anymore. As a child, I'd had to
sing, dance, even stick my head underwater, in order to keep from feeling her in bed
with men. By the time I'd met Adam, even if
I was, technically, a virgin, I was far, far from
being virginal.

As I did every hour I was awake, I tried to
find Adam and his sister. I could feel them,
they were alive, but they were trapped
somewhere. As I did many times a day, I
sent a message to Adam telling him I loved
him and was trying to find him. Under normal circumstances, he could hear my mind-
words, but I didn't think he could now. Now
he was blocked from me.

I homed in on Linc and smiled. He was
running now and working hard to channel
his lust somewhere else.

Once I'd ascertained that everyone was all right, I kept wandering about the big house. I found a door that I knew concealed a staircase that went down to the basement but it was locked. I wonder if the fire marshal knows about this? I thought. Wonder if I should tell him?

I came to a door that had beveled glass panes in it and I could see sunlight. When I turned the knob and the door opened, I was joyous.

Looking through the trees I could see three long buildings, nearly hidden in the shadows of the trees. As I approached them I had to stop for a moment and calm myself. Slave quarters. The buildings had been slave quarters. Not much of the original buildings were left but there was enough that the ghosts of the slaves could hang on and remain. I knew that there was an old slave cemetery behind the buildings but Delphia had had many of the markers removed because she didn't want the guests being reminded of the bad times.

I walked toward the buildings where I knew Linc was staying but it wasn't easy. Spirits were all around me. They knew I could sense them so they were running toward me and begging for my help. None of them were very strong, not strong enough, angry enough or full of enough hate to form themselves into bodies that could be seen.

But I could feel them, feel their tears, feel their confusion, feel their anger—and hear their thoughts.

"I served her for years but she threw me out," one female spirit said. She'd been too pretty and the mistress had been worried that her new husband would like the slave better so she'd sent the girl to the fields. She'd died soon afterward and she was still angry and confused.

There were several women crying for children who had been taken away from them and sold. There were some ghosts of men who were crying in frustration because they were helpless to protect the people they loved.

I stopped walking and told them, "Ssssh, be still. It's over. You're at peace now." They calmed somewhat but I knew it was temporary. When I had time I would look into it to see what could be done to give these poor souls peace. Would that mean setting the slave cabins on fire? If the spirits didn't have an anchor, could they find the freedom of release?

When the spirits were calmer, they pulled back. They were still with me, still following me, but they were now content to wait. Wait for what? I wondered and couldn't help shuddering. Wait until I went to bed, then descend on me in full force so I couldn't sleep? When I sent them a message saying I'd not listen to any spirit who pestered me while I was in the house, they backed away farther.

Good, I thought, smiling. I'd always had a way with spirits. Just give them what they want so they could get the peace they craved. Only a few times had I run into bodiless bad spirits. For the most part evil spirits attached themselves to a person as soon as they'd demolished the body they had. Evil had an awful lot of power.

"What are you doing down here in the Quarters?" Linc asked as soon as he saw me. When I knew there were no cameras or microphones hidden anywhere, I started to speak, but instead looked at Linc. He was wearing big, clunky training shoes, socks, red boxing shorts and nothing else. With sweat running down his bronze body he

was a sight to behold! He didn't know it, but
there were four women, former slaves,
hanging around him, their lust for Linc as
strong as his for me had been. No wonder
the poor guy was going crazy!

"What are you grinnin' at?" he asked as
he rubbed a towel over his sweaty chest.

"Nothing. Where did you pick up the accent?"

There was a porch along the front of the
building and Linc sat on the rail. "I guess it's
bein' down here. It's almost like I can hear
the slaves who lived here."

When I started to say something, he interrupted me. "If you're about to say somethin' that verifies my creepy feelin's, don't."

"I was just about to say that I have a
question for anybody in this room." The four
women around Linc did not take their attention from him and give it to me. In fact, I felt
them moving closer to him, as though to
keep me away from him. He was theirs
alone. When Linc swatted at what he
thought was a bug on his shoulder, I
coughed to hide my smile.

Loudly, firmly, I said, "Has anyone seen a
man around here? He's tall, about six feet
three inches, and he has a little black beard

like this." I drew an imaginary line down my chin, then made a little beard at the tip.

Suddenly, the whole room went still and in the next second there wasn't a spirit in the room or outside of it. Every one of them had run back to wherever it was they hid.

"Did something just happen?" Linc asked, and when I looked at him his aura was a nice reddish blue. He was ready for sex but he could also wait. With four randy, bodiless spirits taken away from him, he could cope with life again.

I shrugged, not answering because I was putting out feelers as to where the spirits had retreated. The graveyard, I thought. Back to their unmarked graves.

"I haven't seen a man like that."

"What man?" I asked.

"The one you just asked me about. Six three. Remember? You know, don't you, that he's probably only about five eight. He just looks tall to you."

"Ha ha," I said. "I wasn't talking—" I stopped because I couldn't tell Linc who I'd been talking to. Long ago I'd found out that people got very upset about ghosts. "Are you ready for dinner?"

"A shower, shave and I'll be there. Looking forward to the séance?"

I shrugged as I headed for the door. Who
was the man I'd seen, the ghost-man, and
why had the slave-spirits been afraid of
him? "Linc," I said, "tonight at dinner, I want
you to eat just what I do. If I turn down
something, I want you to turn it down, too.
Understand?"

"You think they drug the food?"

"There sure are a lot of people sleeping
this afternoon and I think people who are
mildly drugged would be more likely to see
what they're supposed to see. I'll see you in
the dining room," I said, then went back to
the main house. All the way there I kept
looking for the spirit-man I'd seen earlier,
but I didn't see anyone, not even slave-spirits. They had run away and hidden.

I looked at my watch, my beautiful watch
that my dear husband had given me. I had a
mere ten minutes to get ready for dinner. I
had on a pink Chanel suit that ought to
keep people from thinking I looked like a
hillbilly.

At that thought I took a deep breath. I'd
rather sleep in the middle of the unmarked
graveyard and be pestered all night by un-

happy spirits than go to dinner with a bunch of rich women with too much time on their hands. I'd only met one of them, Mrs. Hemmings, but I was sure all of them were going to be just like her.

LINC ⟨⟨

⟨⟨ *Chapter Eight*

I was so nervous when I met Darci outside the dining room that I wished I'd called a taxi and had it take me to the nearest Dairy Queen. Maybe it was that I was in disguise, or maybe I felt this way because I'd been relegated to what had once been the slave quarters. In spite of a pep talk from Darci, I wanted to run away as soon as I saw that old battle-ax Delphia coming down the hall, half a dozen sleepy-eyed women behind her. The women were all dressed in terrifically expensive designer clothes and their jewelry would have filled a wheel barrow, but they looked only partially awake.

When Delphia saw me, her dried-up old face turned thunderous and it didn't take a psychic to know what her problem was.

She didn't want me at the dinner table. I don't know what was wrong with me but I felt like shufflin' away 'cause I was gettin' too uppity.

Darci ran forward and said something, or did something, because five minutes later Miss Pinch-faced Delphia walked into the dining room without a glance in my direction. I guess that meant it was all right for me to eat dinner with the white folks. I couldn't help it; I turned and started to go back to "where I belonged."

Darci caught my arm. "What's wrong with you?" she hissed. The women were filing into the dining room, too zonked-out to even look at us.

I ran my hand over my face. "I don't know, but like I want to live, I want to go back to the Quarters."

"Oh," Darci said flatly, then looked behind me. "Get out of here," she said under her breath, "or I'll sic . . ." She hesitated, then her face lit up. "Devlin. I'll sic Devlin on you."

The instant she said the name I felt better. Taking a deep breath, I scrunched up my eyes and made my hands into fists. "Okay, so tell me what that was all about. I. Am. Prepared."

"There are four drop-dead gorgeous women, all former slaves, who want you to go back to the cabins so they can . . . so they can, uh, play with you. I told them Devlin—that's the name of the ghost I saw earlier—would get them if they didn't leave you alone."

I thought for a moment, then opened one eye. "How gorgeous?"

"Halle Berry?"

"Yeah?"

"A dog compared to these four."

At that I spun on my heel and started for the door that led outside, but Darci caught my arm. "Come on. You have all night for them. Right now we have dinner and a séance."

As we stepped through the doorway of the dining room I nearly panicked. The two sisters, Narcissa and Delphia, sat at opposite ends of a long table. Between them on each side were three women and an empty chair. All six guests were of the type I greatly dislike: overdressed, overly made-up, stiff-postured and expressionless. I started to turn away, but Darci held on to my arm like a little shark. I knew that if I left I'd have to carry her with me.

"Come on," she whispered. "You're an actor, so act."

As I took my place across from her, I smiled at the women and they blinked back at me blankly. Even Mrs. Hemmings, now wearing a necklace that probably cost more than I made last year, was looking at me as though she'd never seen me before. And to think! Just a short while ago I'd had my hands all over her body, sinking them into soft white dough that—

I looked at Darci. "Halle Berry, huh?"

Quietly, Darci gave a little bark like a dog, then she looked around the table and said, "Excuse me, a cough."

Minutes later, three solemn women in black uniforms appeared and served us tiny plates of cold shrimp. Following Darci's orders, I waited for her to start eating before I did.

Ten minutes later I knew she was right about the women having been drugged because as soon as they started eating, they began to wake up. As the evening progressed, one by one, each woman declared she was very thirsty, then she downed a big glass of water. After about three glasses, a woman would excuse herself and when she returned she'd look much better.

Could Darci have done that? I wondered. Had she made the women feel thirsty and drink a lot so they'd flush the drug out of their systems?

By the time the fourth course of the dinner arrived, the women had begun to loosen up. One woman said, "Good heavens! What in the world am I wearing? I look like a traveling jewelry salesman. Who wears pearls at this hour?"

I tried to be cool as I saw several hundred grand in jewelry slip over well-cared-for heads and get tossed onto the table. I looked at Darci and saw that she was staring at Delphia, who was glowering. Narcissa, at the other end of the table, was smiling so broadly I wondered if she'd been given a few happy pills.

I had to admit, though, that I was pretty sure it was my presence that was causing the women to act up.

Okay, so I'm a ham. Can I help it? I'd grown up in a household of scholars. Years ago I heard someone say, "The only excitement in our house was when someone turned a page." My childhood exactly. No zip guns—whatever they were and did they still exist? No gangs. No anything but bloody learning.

My parents and I had dinner together and every night I was quizzed about every word my teachers had said. All my teachers came to hate my parents. If I told my father we were studying the solar system, he'd write a twenty-one-page lesson plan for my teacher and give it to her, along with a three-foot-tall stack of books he said she needed to study. And this was in the first grade.

Some kids rebel with drugs or antisocial behavior, but not me. One day my father said he knew nothing about acting. I looked at my mother. "What do you know about acting?" I asked. "Nothing," she said. In the fourteen years I'd lived with them I'd never heard anything that they weren't an authority on. Fishing? My father had written three articles about how to catch salmon. He'd never touched a fishing pole in his life but he knew, in theory, all there was to know. My mother had written about crafts and music but she'd never been to a craft show, never plucked a guitar string.

That was the day I decided to become an actor.

I must have inherited something from them because I poured as much single-minded effort into acting as my parents did into their work. However, my parents and I nearly parted forever when I invited them to watch me on TV and they said no. A flat, unbreakable no.

Seems that they knew nothing about acting because they didn't want to know about acting. Just because their only son had become an actor didn't change their minds.

As far as I knew, my parents had never seen me perform in anything. They didn't own a TV and if they'd ever seen a movie, I didn't know about it.

The end result of all this was that ever since I stopped trying to impress my parents, I'd done quite well in my chosen profession. I was getting pretty sick of the Linc-is-beautiful crap, but I was doing all right.

As the dinner progressed and the women relaxed even more, I came to enjoy being the center of attention. Of course they all talked endlessly about my resemblance to Lincoln Aimes. I had fun being Lincoln Aimes pretending to be Jason Forbes pretending to be Lincoln Aimes. It was when the women started saying that I was smaller and much less muscular than Lincoln Aimes and I was about to remove my shirt to settle the matter that Delphia announced that it was time for the séance.

I glanced at Darci and she was giving me a look that said I should cool it.

That was easy to do. Sure. I had four love-starved, bodiless women hanging around me, six women looking at me like I was the only man alive, I hadn't seen my girlfriend in two weeks, and I should "cool it." Right.

At the door to the dining room, Darci clamped on to my arm and I instantly began to feel calmer. By the time we took our places around the table in the library, I could have stretched out and gone to sleep.

My tranquillity didn't last long because the laughter I had to keep inside me over the next hour threatened to send me floating up to the ceiling.

Delphia, using that raspy voice of hers, conducted the séance. Each of the six women at the table wanted to contact someone from the spirit world. For Darci's sake—not mine—they went around the table and, one by one, told who they wanted to contact and why. According to them, their one and only reason for wanting to contact a dead person was love. Deep, deep love.

When it came Darci's turn she said, "I just want to know where he hid the jewels," and everyone burst out laughing—and the way they laughed made me even more sure the women had their own nefarious reasons for trying to contact someone who was dead.

One of the stone-faced maids entered with a tray of green liqueur in tiny glasses and we each took one, but when I reached for mine, I saw Darci look at me. No, she seemed to say. Drink nothing. When I put the glass back down, untouched, I saw Delphia frown at me.

Within minutes the six women had emptied their glasses and I could see that they'd relaxed. I was sure it was so their senses would be blurred during the coming show. The lights were dimmed; we held hands. The show began.

And show it was! The best nonshow I ever saw. Delphia called on her spirit guide but nothing happened. She glanced directly at the shelf of books where I knew the disabled projector was and frowned. Maybe I should talk to her about Botox, I thought.

We were there for forty minutes, with nothing whatever happening, and I was filled with laughter. I figured that when Delphia found out what had been done to her equipment she'd know who'd done it, but I wasn't going to ruin the evening by thinking about tomorrow.

"I hear nothing from the spirits tonight," Delphia finally said in desperation, seeming ready to dismiss the group.

Darci held on to my hand tightly. "Perhaps Narcissa could try," she said.

"Me?" Narcissa said, and I could swear she was suppressing laughter. She had to know about the projectors and the wires and know that they were failing Delphia. "I know nothing about the spirit world."

"But sometimes weak spirits . . . I mean, I've read that sometimes weak spirits just need a body to use. Sometimes spirits don't have the strength on their own to manifest themselves. Maybe if there were some spirits in this room they could use your body and talk through it."

Everyone at the table was looking at Darci as though she'd lost her mind.

Glassy-eyed, drugged-up, happy, the six women stared at Darci, not understanding her. Delphia was frowning in disapproval—but then she seemed to disapprove of everything. Plump little Narcissa looked like she wanted to run away at the very idea of spirits using her body.

"They could try," Darci said loudly, her eyes on the empty space just over Narcissa's left shoulder. Nobody had to tell me that Darci was talking to four pretty slave girls.

The next second, Narcissa changed. Years seemed to fall away from her as she leaned toward me and leered.

I couldn't help my involuntary reaction of repulsion. Darci tightened her grip on my hand and sent me a mental message to behave myself.

"I want him," Narcissa said in a sultry, sexy voice. "I been waitin' a long time."

If the room were dark and I couldn't see Narcissa, I would have been interested in a woman with a voice like that.

"What do you want?" Darci asked.

"Him." This was another voice, a little higher but just as sexy. "He's fine. I want him." I leaned a little bit toward Narcissa.

"No!" Darci said sharply. "Not you, but them. What do the people by the graveyard want?"

"They want to find their kin. That's been sold." I swear it was a third voice so I knew that all four beautiful slave women were inside Narcissa's old body. I couldn't help it but I looked at Miss Burns. She was the youngest of the six guests, about twenty-six. She was skinny, flat-chested, flat-assed, had stringy blonde hair and lips the width of a piece of string. I'd dismissed her when I'd first seen her but, maybe, if the four girls could be put into her body instead of Narcissa's . . .

Miss Burns saw me looking at her and gave a shy smirk. She had rich people teeth: perfect, white but not so white that they were vulgar. I smiled back, picked up my full glass of liqueur, and saluted her with it.

Thank heaven Darci jerked on my arm before I drank any of it.

"How do I do that?" Darci asked Narcissa. "Where do I find their relatives?"

"Are they like him now?" Narcissa purred, looking at me with hot eyes.

"No," Darci said. "They aren't all like him. When do I find—?"

I don't know what happened next. Narcissa was leering at me, Miss Burns was doing her best to flirt with her skinny eyes, Delphia looked like she wanted to take an ax to the lot of us, and the other women were watching it all with eyes that were so glazed I knew they were feeling no pain. Darci was quizzing the four slave women she'd invited to inhabit Narcissa's body. The next thing I knew Darci was standing up and staring into the darkness on the far side of the room. Her face drained of what little color she had. She whispered "Adam," then she fainted.

I caught her before she hit the floor, picked her up, and carried her out of the room. Once we were in the hall, I thought, Now what the hell do I do? If I'd had access to a car, I would have put her in it and driven away, but I had no car and I didn't think Delphia would lend me one.

When I heard voices from the library behind me, I turned and headed toward the door outside. I knew that if I took Darci to her room, soon all of them would be bang-ing on the door. But where could I take her so that she and I could be alone?

"If there really are any ghosts floating around me, I need help," I said aloud. "Show me where to take her where we'll be safe from them."

I didn't want to believe in any of them but it was like about a hundred soft hands started pulling me. Part of me wanted to drop Darci's limp body and run, but a part of me liked it. It felt so safe, like being in my mother's arms—not that I knew what that felt like.

I was so busy enjoying the sensation, and looking at Darci to see any signs of life, and hiding from people's voices as they searched for us, that I didn't realize where I was being led until I was inside. There was a closed door, I pushed it open, then I was inside. There was just enough moonlight for me to make out a rusty flashlight. Still holding Darci, I picked up the flashlight and saw a big white table and a bunch of candles and a box of matches. I put her down on the table, lit half a dozen candles, then looked around.

I was in a crypt. I'd seen it earlier but had had no desire to explore it. It was not too far from the slave cemetery and I'd assumed some of the Barrister sisters' ancestors were buried in it. Inside, there were four marble sarcophagi with the lids pushed aside, one lid broken. It looked as though someone had been looting graves, been interrupted, and the flashlight, candles and matches had been left behind.

A groan from Darci made me turn to her. She was a tiny thing and she looked even smaller lying on that hard, cold marble lid. I put my hand on her forehead and smoothed back her hair, then I removed my dinner jacket and put it over her. "How do you feel?"

"Awful," she said, looking up at me. When she started looking at the empty space around my head I said, "How many of them are in here?"

"All of them. Fifty or so, and they're almost all women. Interesting."

"I see," I said and swallowed. I wasn't going to let her see that I wanted to run away and hide. "Any of them tell you what they want?" I noted that, in death, there seemed to be equality as the slave-ghosts could enter their masters' mausoleum.

With her hand to her head, Darci started

to sit up. I helped her turn around so her legs were hanging down the front of the sarcophagus. There was a name and a date carved in the marble and I could have read it, but I didn't. Also, the lid was askew so I could have peeked inside, but I didn't.

Darci looked up at me. "They want me to be a travel director."

"Yeah?" I said as I took a seat beside her. Obviously, she wasn't yet ready to tell me what had upset her so much that she'd fainted. "What does that mean?"

"They're letting me know that there are records in the basement of the house that tell about their loved ones. They want me to get the papers and tell them where to go to find them."

"We're talking about slavery, right? One hundred fifty to two hundred years ago? Do they think their friends and relatives will be waiting there for them?"

"I think so. Maybe their graves will be there and the spirits will be attached to the graves."

I thought about all this for a moment. "I have two questions. One is, Why don't they all go to the Good Place and meet up with their loved ones there *like they're supposed to?*" I said this last loudly to make sure they heard me. "Second, if they want papers that are in the basement why don't they just—you know." I made a sliding gesture with my hands, palms slipping past each other. "Why don't they go through the walls and get the papers themselves?"

"They're afraid," Darci said quietly.

That sobered me. "What could ghosts be afraid of? That someone's going to kill them? Tear their arms off? No, wait a minute," I said, snapping my fingers. "They don't have arms and they're already dead."

"They're afraid of Devlin," Darci said as she jumped down from the sarcophagus.

"And who is he?"

When Darci put her hands over her face and burst into tears, it was natural for me to pull her into my arms. When we heard voices outside, I pulled her tighter and looked at the lit candles in panic. Suddenly, they were all extinguished and I said, "Thanks" without thinking.

As we heard people walking around outside, I held Darci even tighter. I was in a tomb with a skinny little white girl with supernatural powers and I was surrounded by about fifty ghosts. Maybe I should run outside and throw myself at the feet of Delphia and the others who were searching for us, I thought.

"Nobody in their right mind would go in there," I heard a male voice say just outside the door. "Come on, let's get back. This place gives me the creeps in the daytime. Old Delphie wants that guy in her bed she can get him herself."

"I heard he was gay."

The response to that was laughter of such derision that I decided I needed to work on my disguise a bit.

"Did you send them away?" I asked.

Silently, Darci nodded against my chest.

"You know, you're handy to have around sometimes." I could feel her relax in my arms. "Of course, we wouldn't be hiding in-side a tomb at midnight if it weren't for you."

"Me?" she said, pulling away. "You're the one who wanted to find his son so you came to me. I didn't—"

She broke off because I was grinning at her and my teeth, whitened at enormous expense, shone like white lights. "Thanks," she said, pulling the rest of the way away from me. "I'm pretty tired so I think I should go to bed now."

Fumbling along the top of the tomb I found the box of matches, lit one, then nearly screamed because I was looking down into the sarcophagus at a dead man's face. I jumped back and when the match went out so I couldn't see, I said "Thanks" again.

I struck a second match and lit a candle, all while staying far away from the open part of the big marble coffin. "Darci, you fainted in there and I think you should tell me why."

"It was nothing, just a trick, that's all."

"A trick that made *you* faint? Look, Darci, I don't know you very well but I've seen that you talk to ghosts like they're everyday people. You also walked into a mess where people have been killed, but you didn't give it a second thought. So, tell me, what could make *you* faint?"

She took a deep breath and seemed to relax but her hands were in fists. "That spirit, that man named Devlin, is very powerful, so powerful that I can't tell anything about him. I don't know if he thought it was a joke or what, but he—"

"He did what?"

Her voice lowered. "He made himself look like Adam. Like my husband. Like—"

She broke off, turned away, and I could see that she'd started crying again.

I picked her up under her arms like she was a kid and set her on the edge of the tomb. When she was too close to the dead face inside, I moved her down and put my jacket around her shoulders. Marble and ghosts tended to make a cold room.

"Okay, now tell me everything."

"About Adam?"

"No," I said nicely. I had a feeling that if she started that we'd be here for the next six days. "Tell me about this guy Devlin."

"I don't know anything about him except that he's very powerful. He can manifest himself."

"To you, or just to people like you, or could I see him, too?"

"People like me? What does that mean?"

"Stop stalling and answer my question."

"I'm not sure, but I think that if he wanted to he could make you see him."

"If you see him again, ask him not to make the effort. Is he here because you are or does he live here?"

"I don't know."

"What about them, do they know?" I waved my hand around the dark tomb.

"They're no longer here. Just the mention of Devlin and they skedaddle."

I sat down by her, on the opposite side of the dead face in the box. "If you want to leave this place, we can. I don't think my son is here. Maybe he was but he's gone now. I think this place is just a scam being run by those two women so they can get money from bored, rich women. I think we should leave here now. Tonight. We'll start walking until we find a motel, then we'll—"

Darci hopped off the tomb and headed for the door. "I'm staying here until I find out what's going on. I think this Devlin knows something about my husband. Maybe he came here to meet me so I'm going to introduce myself. Bring the flashlight."

With that, she left the big, cold, marble mausoleum and went out into the night air. I knew I wasn't a coward but I looked around at the vandalized coffins, grabbed my jacket and the flashlight, and followed Darci out. "You guys blow out the candle," I said over my shoulder, then crossed myself when the light went out.

I could barely see Darci in the darkness

but she was running quickly toward the house. When I reached her, she was kneeling down by a basement window. She didn't look up but she knew I was there.

"There's no alarm on this window," she whispered, "but it's locked. If you muffled the sound with your jacket do you think you could break that pane of glass, reach in, and unlock it?"

"What if I did? What good will it do? Holy sh—" I began, before I remembered Darci's moratorium on cursing. She was undressing.

"I can slip through that window but not in this suit. It's too bulky."

She had on a pink suit trimmed in black, very old-fashioned and very expensive. Underneath it she was wearing a one piece black teddy that was nothing but lace and a few panels of black satin.

"Are you trying to kill me or what?" I asked, looking at her in the moonlight. Her legs were covered with black hose. She was short and tiny but she was perfectly proportioned.

"Can you or not?" she asked impatiently.

"Anything," I said. "I can do anything." But I didn't move. I just sat there.

"Linc, so help me, if you don't get that window open I'll send all four girls into your bedroom."

I hesitated.

"How about if I put the four girls into Narcissa's body, *then* send them to you?"

That scared me into action. I wrapped my jacket around my fist, broke the little pane of glass, reached in, unlocked the window, and pushed the broken frame up—but I didn't take my eyes off Darci. When she lay down on her stomach in front of me I thought I might be the one to faint.

"Concentrate, Linc!" she said. "Take my hands and lower me down. I don't know how far down the floor is."

I did as she said, but I wanted to weep when she wiggled her curvy little fanny down through the window. When she was all the way inside I had to move to my stomach to put my arms through the window. When I was as far as I could go, she still hadn't touched the floor. "Drop me," she whispered, but I didn't. I stuck my head inside the utterly dark basement. I had an idea that she had no intention of letting me inside the basement with her. "If you don't open the door so I can get in I'll find Delphia and tell her you're down here."

"I'll—" she began, probably meaning to threaten me, but she seemed to change her mind. "Okay," she said.

"Watch out for the broken glass," I said, but I knew it had fallen to her right. I let go of her hands. She couldn't have had too far to drop but I heard a muffled "Oomph" as she hit.

"Wouldn't want to bruise that little rear end, now would we?" I muttered, chuckling to myself as I went in search of a door into the basement. The next moment I gave a little yelp as I felt a bite on my earlobe. Not a bug bite but more like teeth had clamped down on my ear.

I was standing there rubbing my ear when I heard a creak. I didn't dare turn on the flashlight so I waited and finally saw what looked to be something large rising out of the ground. I really did hope it was a door and not some strange-looking ghost.

"Linc?" I heard Darci whisper.

I was there in a flash and down the steps in seconds, closing the door over my head. "I think one of the girls bit me," I said.

"Jealous," Darci answered. "I think

they're getting more powerful. All of them are. Their shapes are becoming clearer by the minute."

She turned on the flashlight and looked around. We were in a narrow hallway that had several doors along it. I opened a door and we looked inside. Junk. Old newspapers, a rotting wicker baby carriage, a cardboard box that had been chewed on by rodents. Old lace spilled out of the hole in the box. "An antiques dealer's dream," Darci said.

"And a fire marshal's nightmare," I said. Darci started walking down the hall toward whatever lay at the end. I guess there was nothing of interest to her behind the other doors.

Holding the flashlight, I followed her.

DARCI 🕮

I didn't want Linc to know how afraid I really was. Years ago I'd walked into some tunnels with the man I loved and I'd been full of confidence. After all, all I'd ever known was Putnam, Kentucky, and the shenanigans people got up to there. I'd seen and talked to a few ghosts and only a few of them had been truly malevolent. Mostly, they'd been searching for something or someone and I'd done what I could to help them out.

In the tunnels with Adam, I hadn't felt anything bad so I'd been full of myself. It was only later that I realized the witch's power had been so great that she'd taken away anything that would cause me to be alarmed. She'd set a trap and I'd fallen into it.

Was this house and the fake séances a trap, too? I suspected, to the point of being sure, that all this had been done to get me into that house. Either my mother knew more than she let me know or she was being used by someone very powerful. She'd been the one to start this, the one to get me here.

Who was this strong spirit Devlin and did he have anything to do with Linc's child who was missing? I wondered.

I turned a corner and there, sitting at an old table, was a gray-haired man wearing a worn and dirty robe. He was using a big wooden-handled knife to cut cheese to put on a chunk of bread. Around his left ankle was an iron cuff attached to a chain that was bolted to a brick wall. He didn't look up when Linc and I walked into the room.

"Can you see him?" I whispered to Linc.

"No, no, and no," he said, looking around the big brick-walled room at anything but the man sitting at the table.

Of course Linc was lying. He could see the man very well. I knew the man before us was a spirit, but did the man know? I'd met a couple of ghosts who refused to believe they were dead.

I stepped forward, Linc close behind me, and stopped in front of the man. "Are you real?

"Of course I'm real," the man said. He had a Scottish accent, like Sean Connery's, and he had the black brows and gray hair of Sean Connery, too. "If you don't believe I'm real, go ahead and touch me. Feel for yourself that I'm flesh and blood."

I knew the man was challenging me, daring me, so I reached out to touch him. As I knew it would, my hand went through his arm.

"I'm outta here," Linc said and headed back down the hallway. But, immediately, an iron gate appeared across the hallway.

I kept my eyes on the man at the table because he was transforming himself into something else. His face grew leaner, his hair lengthened and darkened, and his clothing changed to that of a buccaneer.

Wow! I thought, and not only wondered who he was but what he was. I blurted out the question that was foremost in my mind, "How do I find my husband?"

The man propped a jackbooted foot on a wooden carton where the table had been and began to peel an apple. "Through him."

Turning, I looked at Linc. He was examining the iron gate to see if there was a way to open it.

"Me?" Linc asked in wonder, looking back at us. "I came here because I thought my son might be here. I didn't—"

He broke off as he looked at the spirit-man, as though fearing he might change himself into some monster next. I wasn't going to tell him that I knew the spirit had changed himself into a dragon earlier.

"What does Linc have to do with finding my husband?" I asked. "And the child? Where is the boy? And where do they keep him if they do have him? And why do they keep him?"

"So many questions," he said, smiling and standing up. "To find your husband you must find the child and to do that you must have a Touch of God. Ask the slaves. They know things, but they won't tell you until you give them what they want."

He moved his eyes off me and onto Linc. "As for you, you must remember."

With that, he was gone. There one second, gone the next. I knew there were no other spirits or humans on this floor. There wasn't even electricity near us. All was silent. Dead.

Linc turned on the flashlight and shone it where the iron gate had been. The hallway was unblocked now.

I had agreed to help Linc because my mother had asked me to, but now it seemed that someone—or something—had put all this into play, not for Linc, but for me. I was sure that if I found out what I was supposed to, it would help me find my husband. If this was about me, then Linc didn't need to be here exposed to danger. I hadn't been able to protect my husband and sister-in-law so I didn't trust my ability to protect Linc.

"Linc," I said slowly, "I think you should leave this house. You should go back to Hollywood and stay there."

"And what do you plan to do?"

"Go home, too, of course. The truth is, all this is pretty much over my head. I'm not used to meeting ghosts that change shape and make up riddles. It's over my little hillbilly brain, so I think I'll go home and see my daughter and niece. I really do miss them."

After that speech, I started down the hallway toward the door. We could leave by the
door, and I could get my clothes back on. I
was beginning to feel like a stripper standing there in my hose and a teddy.

I took only half a dozen steps before I realized Linc wasn't following me. He'd
turned the flashlight so it lit a path in front of
me, but he was still in the big room where
we'd seen the shape-changing spirit-man,
Devlin.

Turning, I looked at Linc in alarm. "What's
wrong?"

"I was thinking," he said. "I was trying to
remember what that guy said and it seems
like the first thing to do is give the slaves
what they want. Is that the way you heard
it?"

"Yes, but—"

He turned away, shining the flashlight on
the wall where the spirit-man had been
chained. "Aha!" he said. The wall was still
brick but now it contained an old wooden
door once painted green, with a big iron
lock on it.

Standing, I watched him search for
something among the piles of junk. He

picked up an old shovel, put it through the lock and pulled.

The metal lock didn't break but the shovel handle did and the rotten old door did. Linc put his hand on the hole in the door, opened it and peered inside, shining his light all around. "Nothing but old wooden cabinets in here," he said. "I think maybe they're filing cabinets, though. Probably full of old papers." He turned back to me and gave me that much-practiced Paul Travis smile, the one that melted hearts. "You go on, go back to your kids. I think I'll stay here for a while."

I knew what he was doing; I just couldn't figure out why he was doing it. He was goading me into staying at the house. But then I was sure he very well knew that I had no intention of leaving. So why did he want to stay? For a child he'd never met? And what was Linc supposed to remember? That he loved the child?

Slowly, I walked toward him. "I wasn't really going to leave, you know," I said.

"Yeah, I know." Inside the room, he went to a cabinet and pulled open a drawer. It contained file folders and old papers. Linc pulled out a folder. "Bingo," he said, holding up a paper for me to see. It was a bill of sale for a slave child, aged ten, son of Dinnah. The space for the father's name was a blank.

"If these papers are so easy to find, why haven't those spirits out there found them before now? They've had a few years," Linc said.

I was looking in a file cabinet and I paused to look at Linc. "If everyone who stayed in this house was as plagued as you are by the spirits of the slaves, no one would stay. This whole house would be nothing but ruins."

Linc didn't understand what I meant. I was asking why the ghosts had attached themselves to him. "If Delphia thought there was a buck to be made in it, I'm sure she'd put the ghosts back into chains."

"True," I said. It was difficult to see in the dark room, but as far as I could tell there were about a hundred years' of slave records in the drawers. "Is this normal?" I asked. "None of my ancestors were rich enough to own slaves but . . ." I couldn't help it but I looked at Linc. A couple hundred years ago it would have been possible to *buy* a man like Linc. A beautiful, gorgeous, delicious man like Linc.

He didn't even look up. "Honey, what you're thinkin' is makin' my ears burn."

I laughed. He was certainly perceptive!

"There are too many of these to go through, even if we knew what we were looking for," he said, shutting a drawer and opening another. "As far as I can tell, Narcissa and Delphia's ancestors only bought women. They sold all the male children and most of the females, keeping only—"

What Linc was saying hit me at the same time it did him. Narcissa and Delphia's ancestors had made their fortunes by breeding slaves. They bought women, bred them, then sold the children.

When I thought of my own daughter and my niece and how much I loved them, I was sickened. How could I have survived watching them sold?

"You okay?" Linc asked.

"Yeah. But this makes me sick. No wonder the spirits out there are still here, still wanting to find their loved ones. But, Linc, why can *you* feel them? I haven't felt any psychic power in you."

"None," he said, squatting down to look

at a bottom drawer. "On the other hand, maybe I'm related to some or all of them."

I smiled at that. "You don't exactly look like you just stepped off the boat. Your skin's the same color as my husband's when he has a tan. You must have had a white grandmother."

"Or white grandfather," he said, standing up and handing me an old photo. I had to shine the flashlight on it. In the background was the brick house where we were now. In front was a tall, older, gray-haired man flanked by four very black women. Scattered around them were about a dozen children, all of them with light-colored skin.

"I guess Delphia's like her ancestor," I said. "He didn't want to waste money on a . . ." I looked at Linc.

"A stud?"

"I guess that's what he'd be called."

"So he did the job himself," Linc said.

I glanced back at the file cabinets. "Do you think some of your relatives are in here? That would explain why the spirits of the slaves were flocking to you."

"I know nothing about my ancestry," Linc said. "The only people who ever visited my parents' apartment were colleagues of theirs. My mother once said she had a sister but I never met her. I never heard my father mention anyone he was related to."

I could feel the sadness in his words even though he didn't tell me this with self-pity in his voice. "I'm sorry," I said as I reached out to put my hand over his heart. I wanted to calm him and try to heal his pain.

"You know what the best way to make me forget is?"

Since I was touching him, his thoughts raced straight up my arm. Clearly, I could see the two of us in bed together, me on top, panty hose gone, crotch of my teddy unsnapped.

I pulled away as though burned. "You have a dirty mind," I said.

"Does that mean you lied about being able to read minds?"

For a moment all I did was blink at him, then I put my hand on his arm. "Think about something else. Not sex. Think about your first-grade classroom."

I closed my eyes and could see it. "Rich," I said. "You're in a uniform and it's a private school. You're a good student. Very smart.

And popular. All the children like you." I moved my hand off his chest, then took his hand. "Think about something else." I wondered if it was just touching his heart that made me able to read his thoughts.

"You think I should go home," I said. "You think I'll get hurt. You think you ought to call the police and have them search this house for your son."

Linc was looking at me without a smile as he held up one finger and I touched just the tip of it. "You're thinking—" I quit touching him. "I told you: no sex."

"Can't help it," he said. "Between the ladies around me and you wearing next to nothing . . ."

I moved farther away from him. I could read what was in his eyes in a general way, but if I touched him, I could read his thoughts clearly, down to names and colors.

"I'm getting cold," I said. "Let's go upstairs, go to bed, and tomorrow we can—"

"Come down here tomorrow and find out somebody's moved every one of these files? No thank you. Darci, baby, you and I are going to move these files out of here tonight."

I couldn't help my groan. It had been a very long day and I wanted to go to bed. I needed some time to think about what I'd learned and what I'd seen, and I needed an hour or so of meditation to check on the whereabouts of my family.

I didn't have to touch Linc to know what he was thinking. The spirits out there, the ones floating around the old slave quarters, could be the spirits of Linc's ancestors. His family.

And he was right that the files might disappear. Linc had broken the door so anyone who was in the basement would see that the room had been broken into and searched. If there wasn't a furnace down here there were certainly enough fireplaces upstairs that could be used for burning these old files. If the files were burned, would the slaves' spirits ever be able to rest?

"Okay," I said tiredly, "tell me what to do."

"Get your friends to find us a wagon, and can you make sure everyone in this house stays asleep?"

I assured him I could. Before I came here, I'd believed I could do a lot of things. Between what had happened in Connecticut and all the wonderful things my father told me I could do, I'd begun to believe in myself. True, I couldn't find my husband and his sister, but, always, I'd felt that it was just a matter of time.

It was five A.M. before I got into bed. Linc had left the basement to find a cart, but, unfortunately, the door had locked behind him, on the outside. To open it would take too much time. The only way for the files and me to get out was through the broken window. As a result, Linc made me run up and down that dark, dank, smelly old hallway carrying load after load of file folders.

I must say that he was handy mechanically. He found some rope in one of the storage rooms, and an old metal tray. After some adjusting, he made a sort of winch around the metal frame of the broken basement window. I would run down the hall, scoop up a load of papers, run back down the hall, put them on the tray, then Linc would haul them up to the window. He piled them into a big garden cart he'd found leaning against the house and when it was full he'd take them to the mausoleum.

By the time we finished, I was exhausted. I shoved four boxes in front of the broken door of the file room, then ran down the hall. I had to run to keep from freezing as the basement seemed to grow colder by the minute. Linc leaned in through the window, I jumped and he caught my hands. To be funny, as he pulled me up, he sent me an image of us together, him pulling my teddy off with his teeth.

"I'm going to tell my husband on you and he's gonna beat you up," I said when I was outside, and he laughed. I grabbed my pink suit, still on the ground beside the window, and put it on.

I knew that most of the windows and doors of the house were on an alarm system so I thought I'd have to wait until the kitchen help arrived to get back inside—I didn't have the energy to True Persuade anyone—but a small side door caught my attention. The door was closed but a large panel in the bottom of the door seemed to be askew. When I touched it, it shifted. Easily, Linc removed the panel and I slipped inside the house. It wasn't difficult to see that someone had fixed the door so people could use it without setting off the alarm. The question was if the door had been fixed for me, or for other people? If it had been fixed for me, had it been done by a human or a spirit?

Personally, of the two of them, I hoped it was a spirit. Around this house the spirit people were by far the nicer. As weird as the spirit in the basement had been, I'd rather deal with him than with Delphia. The greed I felt surrounding that woman made my skin crawl.

She was as greedy as . . . as a man who'd make babies with slave women, then sell his own children.

Just thinking of that made me shudder. If the man was capable of something like that no wonder so many slave-spirits were still here and were still in misery.

I reached my room and ran my mind around it to see if the cameras and mikes had been reinstalled. Yes. That meant someone had known I was out of my room. I was too tired to think of a clever explanation for why I'd been up all night. In front of the camera in the wreath I peeled off my pink suit down to my teddy and hose that now had a million runs in them. "That Devlin," I said. "What a man!"

With that I gave a yawn and fell onto the bed. I was much too tired to take a shower.

I hadn't been asleep but minutes when I began to dream. At least that's the way it seemed to me. But even as I was half unconscious, I knew it wasn't an ordinary dream, that it was more.

I saw Adam, my husband. I tried to run to him but I couldn't. He was there but he wasn't. It was as though he was frozen in a great block of ice. Beside him stood Boadicea, also in a block of some icy substance.

I looked down at my hands and I was carrying a box. It was big and black and bound by brass straps. The box seemed to be humming, vibrating, making a little noise that I could feel more than I could hear. Beside me were three people, two men and a woman, and hovering nearby was a spirit that changed form constantly, from animal to person, then back again.

I knew that I was dreaming but I also knew that through some magic I was being shown a future that could possibly be. Someone was showing me what I needed to do to free my husband and his sister.

I tried to look around me but I was hindered by my body as I saw it walking toward the frozen forms. That body was focused, concentrating, only looking straight ahead to the figures of Adam and Boadicea.

I couldn't see inside the box but I knew that inside it were three objects, objects of such great magic that when they were together they hummed. They were like old friends, so glad to see each other that when they were together again they started purring. Did that mean the objects were part of a whole? Should I look for pieces of something? What did the objects look like? What should I try to find? How would I know them if I saw them? Did they have any magic when they were by themselves? If the pieces had no magic how would I know them when I found them?

As I watched myself get closer to the frozen bodies, I tried to calm down. My instinct told me that when my body reached the frozen forms I would awaken, so I needed to see all I could.

Who were the people near me? Linc! When I saw him I smiled. Already, I had found part of what I needed to free my husband.

I looked at the other two people in the dream. One was a man, white, strong-looking, handsome on the outside, but I could feel that he was very angry. I knew I had never seen him before.

The woman had dark eyes that were as hard as iron. I knew without trying that I could not use my mind on hers. Something or someone had made her shut her mind, close if off so no one could probe into it.

My body had nearly reached the blocks so I looked at the spirit hovering above. I could feel that he was showing off by changing into shape after shape. Annoyed, I watched him change into my mother, my cousin Virgil, into Putnam . . . and then into a little boy. He was about seven and he had Linc's face, lighter colored skin, but it was Lincoln's face.

The child looked at me, his eyes wide and pleading. "Help me," he mouthed. "Help me." He reached out his hands to me and instantly I felt power. When I'd shaken Narcissa's hand a tiny current had run up my arm. I'd correctly guessed that I could use her to channel the slave women.

Narcissa's power was nothing compared to this boy's. This beautiful child had some specific power in his fingertips. He could . . . I could almost see it, but then it escaped me. When I looked back at my body I saw it was but a step away from Adam and Bo's frozen bodies.

Time, I cried in my mind. Give me more time to figure this out.

I looked back at the spirit, and he'd changed himself into a man from ancient times, Biblical times. He was walking among people who were crippled and diseased. The spirit was trying to tell me something but I couldn't understand what.

In the next instant, my body reached the frozen forms of Adam and Boadicea. I saw myself start to open the box, then, just as I was about to see inside it, the dream ended.

When I awoke, I had a headache and I was very tired. I wanted to lie in bed all day, eat candy and watch old movies on TV. I wanted my husband to be there and tease me about being lazy, and I wanted the girls to climb into bed with me and get chocolate on the sheets. I wanted to look out the window and see my father and my sister-in-law holding hands and gazing into each other's eyes, thinking they were alone in the world, unseen by anyone.

For a moment I put my hands over my

face, breathed deeply and tried to keep from crying. I tried to pretend indifference to Linc's beauty, to his beautiful skin, to the way the muscles on his body moved under his shirt, but I wasn't immune to him.

Last night at dinner, the women guests had done everything they could to get his attention. They'd preened and posed, teased and taunted, while Linc had flirted outrageously. His only concession to playing a gay man was to call a woman "honey" now and then. He was such a stereotype that if he'd been on camera he would have been picketed.

Turning over in bed, I saw that a piece of paper had been slipped under my door. Probably an eviction notice, I thought, then dragged myself out of bed. I felt awful. I was wearing a teddy that was grimy with dirt and had a tear on the side where I'd caught it on a nail. My hose were one giant run, and my body had a coating of dried sweat. My left arm had a bloody gash from where I'd scraped the metal frame of the window when Linc pulled me up and out of the basement.

As I walked across the room I could feel

eyes watching me, so I knew the cameraman was up and awake. The bedside clock
said it was 9:30.

The paper contained a schedule, my personal busy-every-minute list of where I was
to be when. I'd already missed breakfast
and an early-morning exercise session. As I
tried to flex the stiff, overused muscles of
my back, I knew I didn't need more exercise.

There was a meditation session in thirty
minutes; I wanted to make that one. Maybe
if I had time to meditate, I could figure out
what was going on here. As I stepped into
the shower, I wondered if Linc had been
given a schedule and if so, what was on it?
Carry in buckets of coal? Scrub the kitchen
floor?

I was still stiff when I pulled on a pink
sweatsuit I found hanging in my closet, but
I'd loosened up by the time I left my room
and went in search of the solarium where
the meditation was to be held. I wished I
could pop some caffeine pills to stay
awake. But I needed all my senses alert because I wanted to quiz each woman to see
what she knew about the goings-on in this
house. Surely the women knew the séances

were about as real as a Scooby-Doo movie. Didn't they?

Yawning, I took my place on a mat near the other women, crossed my legs and began to meditate.

LINC 长

长 *Chapter Ten*

I dreamed I was in bed with all four of the slave girls, their supple bodies all over mine, their hands running over my skin, their lips on my legs, on my neck. One took me in her mouth while another ran her breasts over my face.

When I awoke I was sweating, unfulfilled, and crazy with lust. Worse, I didn't know if I wanted to call an exorcist or take a couple of pills and go back to sleep.

I lay in bed awhile, dozing, remembering, half dreaming. I dreamed of the girls with their copper-colored skin and I dreamed of Darci in her black teddy wriggling backward along the ground, inching her way through the window.

Somewhere in there, in a state of half

consciousness, I began to try to remember things. Isn't that what that . . . that creature said I needed to do? I didn't want to think that I'd seen a ghost. People who saw ghosts ended up in the tabloids and were laughed at. There were some things that enlightened, educated American people knew for facts: There were no ghosts and there were no aliens. Not in real life. If a person who had a college degree met a person who said he'd seen a ghost, immediately the ol' college degree began to laugh in derision. And classify. People who saw ghosts were put into a lower class, "non-u" as the Mitford sisters called it. "Not upperclass." Ghosts belonged belowstairs, not in the parlor.

Okay, so where did that put me? Last night Darci had wondered if I was related to some slave who said, "He's fine. I want him," yet I'd grown up in a household that thought bad grammar was worse than homicide.

But I'd seen a ghost. I'd stood there and seen Darci's hand pass through the arm of some guy who had a Sean Connery fixation, a man who was chained to a wall. I'm ashamed to say that all I could think of was running away. When an iron fence had appeared in my path I'd wanted to sit down and start blubbering.

Later, it took all my strength and the courage I had no idea I had to stay in that basement and remove those files. But I knew Darci, little bitty female Darci, would do it if I left, so I couldn't go. After all, she'd started the whole thing for me, so I couldn't abandon her, could I?

As I began to wake up I tried to remember what the man-ghost had said. It was like that old rhyme about "dog won't beat stick." One thing had to happen before another could. The ultimate happening was for Darci to find her husband, but first . . .

I picked up a piece of paper and a short, stubby pencil off the bedside table—"13 Elms. Reflections" it read at the top. I wrote, one, give the slaves what they want. Two, the slaves will tell you things. Three, find something from God. Four, use the thing from God to find the kid. Five, find Adam Montgomery. And six, Linc must remember.

Gobbledy-gook. None of it meant anything to me, I thought, but suddenly I sat upright in bed. I hadn't exactly lied to Darci but I hadn't told her the whole truth either. I'd said I knew nothing about my ancestors, which was true. I'd never been told anything, but my parents couldn't very well keep me from knowing their names, could they? My father was born John Aloysius Frazier the Second. Second, as in my grandfather'd had the same name. Once, I'd asked my father who the first John Aloysius Frazier was and I was told, "He was my father." Just that, nothing else. Further questions I asked were met with glaring silence.

Because of my father's refusal to talk about his familial origins I'd formed the idea that they were people I wouldn't want to know. But then, actors were people my father thought were beneath his notice. Maybe my grandfather was something that my father wouldn't like, say, a descendant of slaves and proud of it. I'd always had the impression my father thought he sprang from Zeus's loins. Slaves in chains would have marred his image of himself.

I dressed quickly, then went outside to look for transportation into town. I remembered the way our cabdriver had nearly run from this hideous old brick house so I wanted to find out what the townspeople knew. I saw a woman driving a pickup and asked if I could bum a ride.

"Sure," she said, "hop on."

It took me a whole thirty seconds to realize she meant for me to climb into the back with the boxes of produce. Her big black dog was taking up the passenger's seat. Sighing, I got into the back with the cabbages and thought about how I'd tell my agent about this and make him laugh, but then I remembered that Barney was dead because of me.

When I returned from town hours later, I saw Darci straggling behind the other women as they did a slow, lazy walk through one of the gardens. She was deep into conversation with one of the guests, listening so intently that I wasn't sure she'd see me hiding in the bushes.

She did, and yet again, I wondered what other kinds of things she could do. I knew she could give a person a nosebleed and a headache, that she could sense where people and machines were, and that she could use her mind to make people do things.

She said she couldn't read minds but I didn't believe her.

"Excuse me," she said to the woman. "My shoe is untied."

I'd seen Darci step on the end of her shoelace with one foot and now she moved several steps off the path to tie it. I was but inches from her and I wasn't surprised to see the woman she was with turn her head away to look toward a small pond in the distance.

When I started to whisper my message, Darci shook her head no, then put her hand on my shoulder, letting me know I was to think my message to her. Since this left her one-handed, she held out her untied shoe toward me. Kneeling, I tied her shoe while sending her the message that I wanted to talk to her. I sent her the image of foot-long sandwiches and slices of cheesecake to let her know that she could miss dinner and come to my dingy little room in the slave quarters.

For no reason except that I could, I took an extraordinarily long time in tying her shoe so I could lengthen my message. In detail, I showed her my dream of the previous night, of me with the four beautiful women, all of them licking and biting on me at once.

I didn't have to look up to feel Darci's embarrassment. In my mind's eye I could feel her reddened face.

When her shoe was finally tied, she took her hand off my shoulder and stepped back on the path, saying, "Sorry I took so long. The lace was in a knot."

Chuckling, I thought that someone with Darci's powers wasn't used to someone like me, someone who wasn't afraid of her, who wasn't shocked at her strange abilities. I doubt if she—

I cut off my thoughts because I found that when I tried to get up, I couldn't. It was as though I were frozen in place. Paralyzed. I wasn't in pain and my mind worked perfectly well, but my body wouldn't move.

I knew Darci had done it. Part of me was in awe while another part was appalled. No one on earth could do what she'd just done. Yet she had.

I don't know how long I stayed that way, probably no more than two minutes, but it was long enough to make me vow to never again play a practical joke on Darci—or at least not a joke I knew I couldn't win.

After a while I heard Darci's laughter floating across the shrubbery toward me and I was released. I'd been straining my body so hard against the unseen force that was holding me in place that when it let go I went backward into a rosebush.

When Darci came to my room an hour later, I had three scratch marks on my cheek.

"Slave ladies do that?" she asked.

"You did." I tried to sound angry and hurt.

Darci smiled. "You wish. So what did you find out when you went into town today?"

"I have a grandfather," I said, not letting her see that I was amazed, as usual, that she seemed to know everything I was up to. "He's a faith healer."

"Holy saints!" Darci muttered, eyes wide.

In this day and age when even kids' movies have cursing, it didn't seem possible, but I was shocked at her language.

"No," she said, feeling my shock. "I'm not cursing. I meant, 'Like the saints did.' Healing. Curing illnesses."

"Wait a minute," I said. "The man's a faith

healer. If you believe, you'll be cured, that sort of thing. I doubt if he can really—"

Darci wasn't listening to me. She was looking about the room. It was as cheaply done as possible, the upper half of the walls covered in painted Sheetrock and the lower half with grooved batten board. There was an old iron bedstead with a cheap, hard mattress and cheap, rough sheets. A chest of drawers and a tiny table and chairs completed the furniture. The bathrooms were down the hall, "ladies" on one side, "gentlemen" on the other. Since I was the only person staying in the Quarters I had the bathroom to myself.

"I don't like this place," Darci said. "A lot of pain is inside these walls. I've been to other plantations and they aren't like this. This place was worse than the others. Do you know why Devlin had himself chained to the wall last night?"

"Imitation of what had been done in that room?"

"Yes." She put her hand against the wall for a moment. "Delphia's ancestors were not nice men."

I thought that was an understatement. I put the sandwiches on the table and as casually as I could, I asked her what she'd found out.

Smiling, eating as though she hadn't eaten in years, she told me what she'd found out from the other women guests— which was exactly nothing.

"They all know that Delphia is a fake, but they say they come for the food and the light exercise and the massages. By the way, you're booked solid for messages tomorrow."

I groaned. "I won't do it. And if the women don't have any information, why should I?"

"I think they know quite a bit, actually, but they're not telling. Each one of them was lying but I'm not sure about what. All I could really feel was that something is to happen here that will make the whole trip worthwhile. Maybe an actual psychic will show up."

"There isn't any such thing as—" I started to say, but then I remembered the way Darci had held me in place just an hour ago. "What else?" I asked.

"Nothing. They're all rich and hate someone intensely. I could feel the hatred around them."

I reached across the table and touched her wrist with one fingertip. "What about my son?" I asked. I sent images to her of my agent who'd burned to death and of the news photo of the car smashed against a tree.

"All I know for sure is that all of it's tied together. You, your son, a Touch of God— What?"

I got up to get my pad of paper to correct it. I'd written, "Three, find something from God," but that man had said "Touch of God" as though it were the name of something.

Darci wiped her lips and looked at the list.

"Anything I left out?" I asked.

"There's more to it to find my husband," she said, looking me hard in the eyes.

I knew she was asking me something but I didn't know what, so I just opened the cartons of cheesecake and waited.

Slowly, she began to tell me about her dream. It took me a while to understand that she believed it had been a dream of prophecy. It took me even longer to figure out that she was asking for my help. If she helped me find my son and his mother, would I help her find her husband?

Since I had no psychic abilities, no talent for anything except acting—and not good at that if the men outside the crypt were to be believed—I didn't see how I could help. Darci said she didn't know either but her dream seemed to indicate that I would be needed.

Maybe I was stupid but I agreed to help her.

When I said that, Darci breathed a sigh of relief and dove into the cheesecake. "So tell me everything you found out about your grandfather," she said.

When I'd finished, she said, "Tomorrow's Wednesday so we'll drive to— Where is he and how far away is it?"

"East Mesopotamia, Georgia," I said, still marveling over the name. "About two hundred miles from here."

"Tomorrow we'll drive to East Mesopotamia, Georgia, meet your grandfather, then we'll be back on Thursday. There's to be another séance, but this time I think it might be real."

"More real than last time?" I asked. "The séance where you fainted?"

Darci smiled. "That was before I knew

what Devlin could do. Now that I know he's a Shape-Changer I'm more prepared."

"Mmmm," I said, not convinced. When I picked up the empty cartons, I was careful not to touch Darci. I didn't want her feeling my excitement and nervousness at the idea of meeting my grandfather. I felt like a kid about to meet Santa Claus for the first time. At the same time I was full of foreboding. Would he be like my father, who believed that human warmth was a sin?

On the other hand, the Internet article I'd read said that John Aloysius Frazier was a faith healer. Did that mean loud praying accompanied by the sound of money hitting a silver plate? If the man had a gold tooth and wore a diamond pinky ring I'd call my father and thank him for never introducing me to my grandfather.

"Linc," Darci said, reaching out to take my hand.

I knew she meant to soothe me, to use her powers to calm me, but I didn't want it. I moved away so she couldn't touch me.

"Okay," I said, changing the subject, "what do we do with all those files in the tomb?"

"I have no idea," Darci said. "Let's look at them and see what we can figure out."

I didn't want to return to that cold crypt, so I suggested we haul them into one of the other bedrooms where it was warm and light. Darci agreed, saying she could put a shield around the files so no one in the house would find them, plus the many ghosts would protect them. I said that the sheer dreariness of the Quarters would keep the people from the Big House away.

As soon as I said the "Big House," I knew where it had come from. The four slaves were near me again and it was their thoughts I was reading.

Darci guessed—or heard—my thoughts and grinned. "Why do you think none of those women at the house come down here and beg you for massages? Those four beauties keep them away."

"They can be seen?" I asked, too much interest in my voice. I told myself to cool it.

"No, but they can make people feel so creepy they'll leave. Cold chills. Hairs on the back of the neck standing up, that sort of thing."

"No bites on the earlobe?"

When Darci smiled it made me feel good

to have caused that smile. There was a sadness in her eyes that never went away. I
didn't like to think about last night, when I'd
been in the same room with a ghost who
liked to chain himself to a wall, then change
into some sort of Central Casting pirate.

As I smiled back at Darci I wondered
what it must be like to live in a world of
ghosts and other things "normal" people
couldn't see. But then, maybe if you'd seen
ghosts all your life, they wouldn't be any
more strange to you than the next-door
neighbor's kid.

"Let's go get the files," I said, and Darci
and I headed toward the crypt. "How many
are here now?" I couldn't help asking as we
walked.

"All of them," she said. "Lots of them."

I didn't work her as hard as I had the
night before, but last night I'd felt sure that
if we left the files in the room, by morning
they'd be gone. In the crypt I felt they were
safe—except from rats, creeping mildew,
and dead people, that is.

I gave Darci a pile of folders to carry,
loaded the big garden cart, and took them
the short distance to the long building that
was the slave quarters. Cheap, I thought.

Instead of the expense of separate buildings, the original builder had made three
very long houses, put in interior walls and
lots of front doors. Row houses. At least
he'd gone to the added expense of putting
a deep porch along the fronts.

When we found that all the doors were
locked, Darci looked defeated. "I can't open
locks without any tools," she said, "and I
don't think you should break the door
open."

I took a guess, got the key to my front
door, and tried it. When I opened the door, I
said, "It's cheaper to make all the locks use
the same key."

Inside the little room were furnishings
more sparse than mine. "I didn't know they
gave me the presidential suite," I said, and
Darci laughed.

She dumped her folders on the old
stained mattress that had cotton ticking
protruding from it. "Think this is original to
the house?"

Darci again laughed, making me feel like
a comedian.

"My husband couldn't make jokes," she
said. "He tried, but they always fell flat. His
sister laughed at them but then Bo had had

a very unusual childhood." Her tone was so wistful that I was almost jealous. Alanna said she loved me more than life itself—but she didn't seem to love me more than she loved playing opposite Denzel Washington.

I looked down at Darci as she picked up an old folder. I wanted to ask her to tell me more about her husband's family. I knew her sister-in-law had been raised by a witch—one of the evil kind. Ever since we did a show about a cult of witches that had killed a couple of people as "sacrifices," I'd been careful to distinguish between good and bad witches. We'd received letters full of rage telling us we hadn't done our research, that there were witches who didn't do evil, only good. Ralph had said, "Witches want control. For good or bad, they want control and in my book, control is bad." The director had said, "Next time we'll call them tooth fairies. Somebody check the Internet and see if there are any tooth fairy cults." As for me, I thought those complainers should get a life: Those who do, do. Those who can't, complain about everybody else's work.

I sat down on the other side of the bed, the folders between us. "Now what do we do?" The folders looked much newer than the papers and I wondered when file folders had been invented, and who had sorted the bills of sale.

"Martha Jefferson," Darci read, then her voice lowered. "This is a bill of sale for her three children."

When she looked into empty space I knew what she was seeing. I didn't want to ask, but I couldn't keep the words out of my mouth. "What is it?"

"A light," Darci whispered. "The spirits are usually just vague outlines of people. I feel them more than see them, but now there's a light and—" She paused for a moment. "Are you Martha? Do you want to know where your children were sent?"

I guess I should have been afraid but, instead, the idea of helping my ancestors, or just "my people" as Moses called them, gave me a feeling of elation that I'd never had before. It was a high. Like a drug. I snatched the paper out of Darci's hand, scanned it and said loud and clear, "Fairway Plantation, Jackson, Mississippi, to a Mr. Neville MacBride."

I couldn't see "them," so I watched Darci's face. Her eyes widened for a moment, then she broke into a smile so bright that for a moment there was no sadness in her eyes. She looked at me in wonder. "She left. The woman heard the name and she left. Get another paper, read another name!" Darci said, grabbing the file on top, and when she did her fingers touched mine. "Me too," she said. "That's how I feel, too."

I knew what she meant. I'd never done anything that made me feel as good as doing this did.

For the next three hours we went through folders, scanning names and reading them as fast as we could. I knew Darci felt as I did, that we couldn't stop to think about what we were reading or we'd both start bawling. She would think about her daughter and niece being taken from her and I would think about being put on an auction block and sold.

Not long ago I'd seen a special on TV about some archaeologists who'd dug up a slave cemetery and analyzed what they'd found. Not surprising, but still horrible, they'd found that the slaves had, basically, been worked to death. Extreme manual labor had worn them out so that few of them lived to middle age.

What I'd seen on TV was in my head as I speeded up reading the old bills of sale. It didn't seem to matter that Darci and I were talking over the top of each other or that we were going so fast we could hardly understand ourselves. It seemed that the ghosts could hear us and understand us and that's what mattered.

"Uh oh," Darci said after I read one woman's name. The slave called "Vesuvius," I'd read. No last name. Vesuvius, the volcano in Italy. "She's one of your four. Sure you want to let her go?"

I hesitated, as though I were considering. "Is she sure she wants to let *me* go?"

"The light around her just got stronger. Boy! Is she pretty. I wonder what happened to her after her child was sold? Oh my."

"What?"

"She was—" Darci looked back at the pile of folders. "She was branded on her cheek with an R for runaway."

I quickly read the name of the place in Alabama her son had been sold to. "Gone?" I asked Darci moments later.

"Gone."

I sighed because I'd miss my midnight companions. "So I guess now you'll have to take her place." I said this as though it was something Darci *had* to do.

"With a houseful of women wanting you? I'd never have a chance. You know, with all these spirits gone, maybe the women in the Big House will be able to visit you at night."

"That does it, I'm outta here," I said, and we laughed. I grabbed another folder and read the names. Even to my unpsychic mind the room felt lighter, less as though it was packed full of centuries of tragedy.

By midnight we had finished them all. I wanted to burn the evil documents but Darci said no, that they might be needed for something later.

We went back to my bedroom and I showed her what I'd bought, a fat bottle of Grand Marnier, the wonderful orange liqueur, plus a big chocolate orange.

We turned out the lights in the room and went to the porch to sit and look at the moonlight. Never in my life had I felt better. It was the first time I'd ever done something so altruistic, something so much for others.

As we sipped our liqueur out of water glasses, the only kind I had, I turned to Darci. "Do you do this kind of thing often?"

"Not just like this, but I help . . . people find things."

I knew she wasn't telling me everything, but then I was starring in a TV series called *Missing.* Since I'd met her I'd thought how real life missing people could use her talents. Of course, someone like Darci—not that there was anyone else like her on earth—would have put us all out of work.

"Police?" I asked.

"Not hardly. People don't believe anyone can have any ability that they don't have. If a person can't see a spirit, then he knows for sure there are no spirits."

Why did I think her little speech was meant to distract me? The next minute I felt a tiny pain in the back of my neck so I figured she was trying to redirect my thoughts. "FBI," I said and the pain stopped.

"You help the FBI?" I asked. "No, don't look at me like you're going to make me fall asleep. I don't tell what I know."

"That's for sure. You want to tell me about your father and why you know nothing about your grandfather?"

"Not in the least," I said, smiling and holding out the box of chocolate orange to her. "What kinds of things have you seen?

Maybe I can get a show out of what you know."

When she smiled I knew I'd loosened her up. She reached for the chocolate and purposely touched my fingertips. I jerked back but it was too late.

Sucking on the slice of chocolate, she leaned back in the rocker and looked out at the moonlight. In the distance, to the right was the big old house, silent, dark, ominous.

"I don't know where the child is, Linc," she said, knowing it was the question I'd been leading up to. I wanted to shout, Why can't you find *my* kid, but I didn't. Not yet. Tonight we'd found the spirits of children of some long-dead people, but why hadn't *my* child been found?

"Do you remember when I said 'holy saints' when you told me your grandfather was a faith healer?"

"Yes."

"Last night in my dream, only it wasn't a dream, someone was trying to tell me something. The man we saw in the basement—"

"The Shape-Changer, Devlin."

"Yes. Him. He showed me your son and I felt great power in the child."

I looked at her sharply. Was the kid some kind of freak? If Darci "heard" me, she didn't let on.

"It seemed to be a specific power, rather like my daughter's and her cousin's. They are telekinetics."

I looked at her in question.

"They make things move. They're young now and it's only teddy bears and balls, but someday . . ."

I turned away so Darci wouldn't see me cross myself. Here again was something that did *not* exist.

"Anyway, I think your son has some specific power. Devlin changed from being your son to being . . . or showing me a 3D picture of a man in Biblical times. He was walking among crippled and sick people. I didn't understand it then but when you said your grandfather was a healer . . ."

She trailed off, wanting me to understand what she was saying.

"You think my son may have inherited the gift of healing?"

"Perhaps."

I looked out at the night for a while and

thought how a gift like that would tear the kid's life apart. If he kept his ability a secret he'd feel as though what he could do was something bad and dirty, something that needed to be hidden. If he let people know what he could do, the other children would shun him. No baseball for the kid because the other kids' parents wouldn't want someone weird like my son near them.

Then there'd be the skeptics and the hangers-on. There'd be people who'd want to test him, and people who'd want to use him to make money.

"You know what I think?" Darci said after a while. "I think the child doesn't want to be found. I think he knows people want him so they can exploit him, so I think he's with his mother and hiding somewhere. He's near here, I can feel it, but I don't know where exactly."

I finished the liqueur and thought about what she was saying. "Could he be as far away as two hundred miles? In East Meso-potamia?"

"No. He's much closer than that. My thought is that if your grandfather shares the same talent as your son, then maybe your grandfather could give us an idea where your son might hide."

"Could Delphia be holding my son here in this house? Do you think he could be that close? On Thursday they have someone special coming. Do you think it could be—?"

"A little boy who heals people? No, I don't think so. I feel that the child is in a sort of prison, but I don't know if he's in a prison he's made or someone else has. Let's go to bed."

"Yes!" I said enthusiastically, making Darci laugh.

It was late and when I stood up, I realized I was more tired than I thought. We spoke for a few minutes about arranging to rent a car for tomorrow and what she'd tell Delphia and Narcissa, then we said good night. I stood on the porch for a while and watched Darci walk back to the house. This time she'd taped a door latch and the alarm system so she could get back inside easily.

Smiling, I went back to my bedroom. I felt good, as though I'd made a second Emancipation Proclamation, but at the same time I felt bad about my son. As I climbed into bed, I again wondered what I'd find when I met my grandfather. As I closed my eyes and settled into sleep, I realized I missed my four slave ladies. They were all gone and the emptiness of the room seemed to echo around me. Tomorrow, I thought. Tomorrow I'd call Alanna.

DARCI ⟨⟨

⟩⟩ *Chapter Eleven*

The next morning, I lay in bed for a while and thought. I was beginning to like Linc a lot. He pretended to be cowardly and afraid of things, but as far as I could tell, he wasn't afraid of anything.

And he was a good sport, ready to try anything new. He made me laugh with his repeated flirtations with me. I was sure he'd be willing to go to bed with me and have a good time, but I knew there could never be a lasting relationship between us. He was too in awe of me. When I touched him I felt his wondering what I could do. Could I get him a role that would win him an Oscar? Could I put a spell on a movie that would make it sell magnificently?

No, I was too much of a freak to Linc for

there ever to be anything but friendship between us. My husband, Adam, was the only
person who knew what I could do yet never
so much as thought about using my abilities for personal gain. Adam loved me for
myself; what I could do with my mind was
of no more importance than if I could speak
another language. As a man might say, "My
wife speaks French," my husband could
say, "My wife can kill people with her mind."

In the precious time Adam and I were together, I used to tease him that I was like
Samantha on the old TV show. Her husband
did everything to get his wife to be "normal." "And it always backfired," Adam said
once, kissing me on the nose.

Adam never tried to exploit my abilities.
One of our few fights had been when one of
his investments had failed and I'd asked
him if he'd like for me to see if I could
change it. Adam had become angry and it
took me a while to understand why. The
witch who'd kidnapped him when he was a
child, the woman I'd killed, had used the
mirror to foresee about the stock market so
she could make money. Adam was angered
at the idea of using supernatural power to
make money.

He viewed what I did with the FBI as a proper way to use my abilities and stayed with me as I went through the files. He was always there to hold me when I saw a vision of something too horrible to bear. There were times when I saw things that had been done to a child that so upset me that Adam would carry me to bed and make me rest. If I was too upset, he'd make love to me until the images of horror were gone.

After breakfast, Linc and I got into the car we'd rented; it was raining outside, and I couldn't stop thinking about my husband. I closed my eyes to keep the tears from running down my cheeks.

"Like to talk to me?" Linc asked softly.

His concern and his perception made me smile. "How about if you tell me all about your childhood," I said, then began projecting that thought into his head.

"How about if I tell you all about your mother?" he shot back.

That thought so disconcerted me that I let up on my True Persuasion of him. "Okay," I said. "You win. Let's compromise. Tell me about your show. I've never been on a TV set before."

When Linc turned into an actor and

started entertaining me, I realized that both of us had escaped having to tell anything about our true selves.

This morning I'd told Narcissa that there was an emergency in my family so I had to be away for a day, and of course I'd have to take Linc with me.

Narcissa was in a tizzy, very nervous. "That's all right, dear," she said. "I don't know what we'll do today because some-one has broken into the house."

I must have looked as shocked as I felt because Narcissa patted my hand.

"It's all right. There's no danger, but we do need to be cautious. Delphi has men coming today to put bars on the basement windows."

It was at that point that I realized she meant what Linc and I had done. I wasn't an actor but I tried to keep my expression of worry. "Did someone steal something?"

"Oh yes," Narcissa said, looking as though she might cry. "Our family records. We had a locked room full of the history of our family, of our forefathers and their con-tributions to our great country."

It wasn't easy to not pull back in revulsion

at what she was saying. This place had been built with money earned by breeding and selling human beings. Ghosts were still crying over the horror of what had been done to them over a hundred years ago, but this woman was talking about the glory of her ancestors.

Narcissa was so upset that she didn't seem to notice the way I pulled back from her.

"Just be sure and be here tomorrow, dear. We have a little surprise for our guests."

I wanted to get away from her so I didn't ask who or what the surprise was. I wanted to get into the car with Linc and drive very far away from that dreadful house.

When Linc and I were alone, I found him to be good company. He was full of funny stories of things that had happened on the set of *Missing* and, okay, I was curious about my mother. All my life I'd been scared to death of the woman. When I was growing up, she used to dump me on one family in town after another, as though I were an orphan. By all rights, I guess I should hate her. But I don't. In my life she was always a remote goddess on an ice mountain who came and went as she pleased, did with me as she pleased.

I guess the real reason I didn't hate her is because where she put me had been so very interesting. She'd say, "You'll be staying with the Holdens," and five minutes later a car would show up. Always, without exception, the family she put me with would be in a mess. There were wife beatings, a case of incest, masses of adultery, and children who were abused or neglected. Putnam was small but it ran the gamut of human behavior and emotion.

When I wasn't in school, I worked on the family I was living with and did what I could to straighten them out. When a husband raised his hand to his wife I'd set his hand on fire—figuratively, that is. It was like Pavlov's dog and he soon learned not to strike anyone. I made people think their kids were great so they'd stop abusing them.

One by one, I changed the inner workings of several families in Putnam. However, I was always careful to make them think that someone or something else had changed them so no one would know it was me. Often, I made people think it was a pastor. Sometimes I'd leave a book lying about and it would get read. "That book changed my life," people would say.

After a few months someone would return me to my mother's house and I'd live with her for a while before she sent me to another family.

In all my years of living in Putnam only once did I try to use my True Persuasion on my mother. I still remember it vividly, even though I was only about five. She'd told me to come inside but I didn't want to. I went into the house but as she sat at the table looking at a magazine, I stared at her and tried to make her think she should let me go back out again. My mother looked up from her magazine, looked hard into my eyes, then she slapped me. She didn't say anything before or afterward. No explanation of the slap, just *wham!* It was the only time she ever hit me—and I never again gave her a reason to strike me. After that, I obeyed her without defiance. And I never again tried to manipulate my mother's mind.

After Linc had been driving for a couple of hours, I casually asked a question about my mother. He wasn't fooled. He gave me such a knowing look that I blushed to my hair roots. When I poked him in the ribs, he acted as though I'd used a weapon on him.

"Okay," I said, "so I'm curious. Tell me what she's like."

"You want me to tell you what your own mother is like?"

"Like you know everything about *your* mother. Ha! You'd love to find out what her colleagues at work think of her, what she thinks of you, and—"

"How did you form the opinion that you can't read minds?"

I shrugged. "I can't read exact thoughts but I can read feelings. You think a great deal about your parents. You seem to want to rebel against them but at the same time you want them to be proud of you."

"And what about you? You have a mother who's one of the most beautiful, sexiest women in the world. How's that make you feel?"

He was pretending to be a therapist and looked down his nose at me as though he was analyzing me. I wanted to reply in kind but what came out of my mouth surprised me. "Did you go to bed with her?"

"Nope," he said cheerfully. "Tried to, wanted to, but she wouldn't have me."

I looked out the window to hide my smile, ridiculously glad that he hadn't had sex with her.

"Darci," Linc said, all humor gone from his voice, "I read that book about you and none of it makes sense. In person you're as unlike that stupid girl as can be. And there was no mention of your . . . well, your talent anywhere in the book. According to the author, you got everyone into a mess and they all risked their lives to save you."

I didn't say anything because there was nothing to say. I was beginning to think Linc was my friend but I wasn't sure enough yet to confide in him. Besides, if I told him the truth I was sure he'd stop the car and push me out.

"There's the exit," I said, pointing. Linc sighed and I could feel his frustration, but I wasn't yet ready to talk about what had happened inside the witches' cave.

East Mesopotamia looked to have once been prosperous. The buildings in the center of the tiny town were well built and dripped embellishments that had been the height of fashion around 1910 or so. However, since then, all that had been done to them was to patch them up enough to keep them from falling down. Half of the buildings were empty and the half that had businesses were not upscale. As we slowly drove through town, we did not see a white face.

I looked at Linc to see what he was feeling. I didn't have to touch him to feel his misery. He earned a lot of money yet here were people like him, perhaps even relatives of his, living in deep poverty.

He was solemn as he rolled down the window and asked a couple of men sitting on a bench if they knew John Aloysius Frazier. The man said "Pappa Al" was at "the old school house," and pointed east.

We drove east and a few minutes later we saw a hand-lettered sign that said "Frazier School," and Linc turned down the long driveway.

As soon as I saw the place, I loved it. It was a big, square building with windows all the way around it. Overhanging it were oak trees that had to be a hundred years old. Surrounding the building was a driveway that was covered with crushed shells.

Linc stopped the car, we got out, our

shoes crunching the shells in a pleasant way, and we walked toward the front door. We were just a few feet from the car when a bell rang and out the back poured children, all running and screaming, all of them dark-skinned. Since they ran in the opposite direction, they didn't see Linc and me.

We walked to the back of the school and standing on the doorstep was a tall, older man, majestic-looking with his dark skin and gray hair. His clothes were good quality and beautifully kept, but I could see that they were frayed at the edges.

He didn't seem surprised when he saw Linc and it was easy to see he knew who Linc was. He didn't see Linc as a TV star, but as his grandson. The man's eyes threatened to eat Linc up and the hunger I felt coming from him nearly made me cry.

"And who are you?" he asked, at last turning to me.

"Darci," Linc said. "Friend of mine. Could we talk to you?"

"My life is yours," he said, holding the door open wide.

Pappa Al, as he was called, told a young woman to tell the kids to go home for the rest of the day, that he wanted to talk to his grandson. The young woman stood on tip-toe, whispered something to Pappa Al and the man laughed merrily. "Yes, he's the one on that TV show," he said, looking at Linc with such pride that Linc began to blush.

Ten minutes later the three of us were sitting inside a screened porch, drinking cold lemonade, eating molasses cookies, and looking out at the beautiful scenery. At least I was looking at the scenery. Linc and his grandfather couldn't take their eyes off each other.

I kept my seat slightly apart from them and tried to calm them down so they could talk about the subject at hand. I was afraid they'd start dragging out photo albums and lose sight of what we'd come to find out.

Pappa Al's voice was beautiful and I could well imagine that he could heal people with it. But he told Linc that it had been his wife, Linc's grandmother, Lily, who had been the healer. But she had been a shy woman, so she and her husband had been a team. He made people believe his hands healed, while his wife was just his assistant.

When Linc told the story of how he'd come to have a son, I feared that his grandfather would be judgmental, but he wasn't.

He was so pleased to have a great-grand-son that he didn't care how he got the child. Linc didn't say that we had reason to be-lieve the child had perhaps inherited some supernatural ability.

I leaned back in my chair and quietly lis-tened as Pappa Al told of his son, Linc's fa-ther. "He was always embarrassed by us, by the tents and the revival meetings," Pappa Al said. "He disassociated himself from all of it from the time he was a kid. But the money we made allowed your grand-mother and me to open this school."

My ears perked up at Pappa Al's tone and I wondered if Linc's did, too. I said nothing as Pappa Al gave us a tour of the school. It had once been the town school, all twelve grades in the six classrooms, but in 1972, the county had declared the school inadequate and started busing the children fifty miles away "to a school where nobody knows them."

Linc and Pappa Al walked ahead of me and I couldn't resist a smile. I knew a sales pitch when I heard one.

Pappa Al and his wife had traveled for years, dragging their angry son with them, as they put on one faith healing tent revival after another. In 1980, Linc's grandmother had a stroke, so they returned to their hometown of East Mesopotamia, Georgia, where she died. A year after his wife's death, Pappa Al bought the old school, abandoned, falling down, and rebuilt it. After two years of fighting with the state school board, he received accreditation for a school for "special" kids. "The smart ones," Pappa Al said. "The ones who have a chance to make it to college. The ones who have ambition and drive." Proudly, he told Linc that eighty-six percent of his students went on to college. He and his staff helped the students with loans and scholarships. "If they want to go to college, I help them do it."

By the time Pappa Al had finished his long speech it was late afternoon and when he asked if we were hungry, I practically yelled, "Yes!"

We got into the car, me in back, the two men in front, and drove to a nearby restaurant. It was an old, worn-out place but it smelled heavenly. "Bring everything you have for my grandson," Pappa Al said, then glanced down at me. "And for his lady friend."

Before I thought, I said, "His lady friends are dead."

Most people would have assumed that I meant someone had died, but I guess Pappa Al had been around faith healers and other such people for too long to be fooled.

"How long dead?" he asked as we sat down at a table covered with red-and-white-checked oilcloth. I was the only white person in the place.

"Before the Civil War," Linc said before I could stop him.

All my life, secrecy had been paramount. I'd learned to dissemble, to twist the truth, and to flat-out lie in order to hide what I'd found out that people didn't want to know. Since people liked to believe that ghosts didn't exist, they were happier not hearing that someone often talked with them.

Linc had no such background and it was easy to see that he was as gregarious as his grandfather. Within seconds, Linc was telling his grandfather much too much. When I sent a message to him to stop talking, he just rubbed his neck and kept on going.

I was distracted by huge bowls of food that were put on the table. There was fried chicken, chicken and dumplings, beef cooked until it was falling off the bone, half a dozen vegetables, and what looked to be six pounds of mashed potatoes and a quart of gravy. I forgot about trying to rein Linc in and dove into the food.

"That's an evil place," Pappa Al said, his plate loaded with half the food I had on mine. "Did you know that there was a slave uprising there? It was led by your ancestor, a slave named Martin."

"My—" Linc said, so stunned he paused with his fork halfway to his mouth.

"It's my guess that's why your son stayed there. My wife, God rest her soul, could heal people sometimes, but *all* the time she felt things." Pappa Al looked at me. "You know what I mean? She felt things others couldn't feel. Honey, can you eat all that?"

"Don't worry. She'll clear the table," Linc said. "What do you mean that my son stayed there?"

"If the child is anything like his great-grandmother, he can feel things other than people's pain. My guess is that someone was using him to make money. You can't imagine the offers your grandmother and I got to make money off people's illnesses. A couple of times we had men tell us they'd give us a big house to live in and they'd bring sick people to us. They made it sound really good, but what we figured out was that they meant they'd bring rich people to us, people who'd paid hundreds of thousands, even millions, to be cured. The poor people who couldn't pay could die in the street for all they cared."

I looked at Linc and we both knew that what Pappa Al was saying had something to do with the missing child. I reached across the table to touch Linc's arm. I saw visions of the rich women at 13 Elms and, like me, Linc was trying to figure out why they went there. Obviously, those women didn't go to the 13 Elms for a fake séance. So why did they go? To be cured of some illness? But I hadn't felt that any of them were ill.

"Yes," I said to Linc, then pulled my hand away. He had the same thoughts as I did.

"What was that all about?" Pappa Al asked, nodding toward our arms.

"She can—" Linc began, then shrugged. "Tell me everything you know about 13 Elms."

I continued eating while Pappa Al talked.

The place was more evil than even I had imagined. Yes, it had been a breeding farm before the Civil War. Narcissa and Delphia's ancestors had been too lazy to farm. The story was that around 1810 the wife of the owner got sick of her husband doing nothing but spending his days and nights in the slave quarters. The house's roof was falling down, the crops were rotting in the fields, but all the man did was fornicate with the slave women.

One day the woman's husband announced he was going to New Orleans for a couple of weeks. The minute he left, she called a slave broker.

"She sold every one of the little light-skinned children running around the place," Pappa Al said. "I was told that she expected her husband to kill her when he returned, but when—"

"When he saw how much money she'd made he was pleased," I said.

"Yes," Pappa Al said. "There's a legend that every bill of sale for every slave is somewhere in that house."

"Not anymore," Linc mumbled. "They've been liberated."

I knew his grandfather thought Linc

meant the bills of sale, but I knew he meant the people.

"Slave breeding grew into a business after that, passed from father to son."

I pushed my empty plate away, sickened by the images in my head. No wonder I'd felt so much tragedy in that place.

"What about the uprising and my ancestor?" Linc asked.

"Your grandmother felt it. We were asked by . . . What's that woman's name? It was some city."

"Delphia," Linc and I said in unison.

"She sent a servant to us to ask us to come to her house. We thought it was an invitation for dinner, but it was an invitation to put on a show for their rich clients. My wife said Delphia was charging the guests plenty but planned to pay us only with a meal."

"Slavery is alive and well at 13 Elms," Linc said.

"It was at dinner that one of the women, the fat one—"

"Narcissa."

"Yes. Her. She was talking about the glorious history of 13 Elms when my wife asked her about something that had hap-

pened there before the war. I knew Lily
sensed something but I didn't know what.
Lily had to ask several questions before
Narcissa reluctantly said that she'd heard of
a slave uprising at 13 Elms, but it had been
taken care of.

" 'How?' Lily asked.

"The skinny one said, 'They hanged him.'
That was the end of that. The subject was
changed.

"After dinner Lily told me she was going
to do the healing alone, something she
never did. She said she wanted me to
sneak into the library and see if I could find
any books on the family's history. She
wanted to know who it was that had been
hanged and why they'd done it."

"Did you find anything?" I asked.

"Oh yes. Lily told them I had a stom-
achache so I was allowed to lie down in a
bedroom. As soon as I heard them lock the
door I was out of there."

"They locked you in? A dinner guest?" I
asked.

"How did you get out?" Linc asked.

Pappa Al smiled. "Let's just say that before I married your grandmother I learned a
few things that caused me some problems

with the law. Picking locks was one of the things I learned. I let myself out of the room and went snooping. There was a locked case in the library and I found a book in there, an old diary, and the dates were right. I flipped through the book and toward the back it said, 'They hanged Martin today. How will I live without him?' "

"Where is the book?" I asked.

"Back at the school."

Immediately, I stood up, ready to go get the diary, but then the waitress put a banana pudding, a coconut cream pie, and a chocolate layer cake on the table. I sat back down.

"A little thing like you can't possibly—" Pappa Al began, but Linc silenced him. I didn't bother to answer. The whole United States, the whole world, had laughed at my eating habits. Some people had said it was a physical impossibility for me to eat a lot and not gain weight. I never answered anyone's questions about the subject.

"Haven't I seen you before?" Pappa Al asked, squinting at me.

I ducked my head lower over a huge piece of pie. Perfectly toasted coconut was across the top of the meringue.

"She looks like a lot of people," Linc said quickly. "Could we see the diary? Maybe there's something in it we can use. And, by the way, why didn't they prosecute you for thievery?"

"From the dust on those books, it's my guess nobody'd read them for years, so who knows when, or even if, they found out the book was gone. Besides, it couldn't have been me. I was locked in a bedroom."

At that Linc and his grandfather shared identical laughs. Whatever else happened, I thought, Linc had gained a grandfather.

Before we left, Pappa Al suggested that if we thought the boy was being hidden somewhere, we should check the old church. The instant he said it, I knew there was something or someone there. It was the church that had supposedly taken up a collection for a gravestone for a woman who wasn't who they said she was.

As the sun began to set, we knew we needed to leave, but it was a sad parting. I could feel Linc's sadness at leaving, but also feel his elation at having found his grandfather. Like me, he'd always felt he was different. His parents had been as strange to him as the rest of the world was strange to me. When he hugged his grandfather good-bye, there were tears in both their eyes.

"If I find my son, can I send him to you?" Linc asked his grandfather. "My life in California isn't for a kid. I'll—"

"Don't worry about a thing. I'll take care of him."

I hugged Pappa Al, too. He picked me up, swung me around and told me he thought I'd make a fine daughter. I told him I already had a husband.

Knowledge came to his eyes. "That's who you are," he said. "You're the—"

I didn't have to use any True Persuasion to cut him off. I just gave him a human look and he didn't finish that hideous phrase.

He set me down, put his hand on the top of my head, and said he'd pray for me. I thanked him, then ran to the car where Linc was waiting. As we drove away, I waved until he was out of sight.

"How much?" I asked as soon as we were back on the road into the little town.

"You mean how much money did he con me out of?" Linc asked, grinning. "Fifty grand."

"What's that? One week's pay?"

"Less than half," he said, glancing at me. "I thought I'd start off small before he got the studio to send my paychecks directly to him."

We laughed together and were silent for a while. Whatever Linc gave we knew was for a good cause. For a moment I enjoyed feeling Linc's pleasure at having found something to do with his life—for that's what I felt that he was going to do. I wasn't really able to foresee the future, but I could easily imagine Linc heavily involved in the school in East Mesopotamia. A school for "special" kids, the ones who caused no one any problems and so were often neglected. I could imagine Linc using his fame—and his beauty—to give benefits to raise money for the school. Or schools.

I quit thinking of Linc's possible future when he pulled into the parking lot of a strip mall. "Wait for me while I go get something," he said. "Need anything?"

I said no; I was content to sit alone and think. Moments later, he returned with a bag. Inside were bottles of lemonade, bags of pretzels, and a little light, the kind that clips on to a book.

"You read, I'll drive," he said as he handed

me the plastic bag his grandfather had given him. In it was the diary written by Amelia Barrister, 1840 to 1843.

It took the whole trip back to 13 Elms to read the diary. I didn't tell Linc but the sadness I felt from the diary made it difficult for me to hold it.

In 1840, Amelia had started the diary as a young bride full of hope. She'd grown up in Ohio, met her husband at a church social, and married him three months later. She wrote of her excitement about going to live on her husband's "farm." A few pages later, she wrote that tomorrow she'd see it, that she'd heard so much about the place she dreamed of it.

There wasn't another entry for eight months, and when she did write, the tone was of a severely depressed woman.

Linc and I couldn't imagine how she must have felt to find out that the "farm" was for breeding and selling human beings. "And her husband was the breeder," I said.

In 1842, Amelia's tone began to lighten; something had changed. When she mentioned Martin, the name nearly leaped off the page. "She's in love with him," I told

Linc, looking at him. If he was Linc's ancestor, had Martin looked like Linc?

In 1843, Amelia wrote that she was ill and
stayed in her room most of the time. I ran
my hand over the page. "She's expecting a
baby and she doesn't know if it's her husband's child or Martin's." Amelia hadn't
written that but I felt it. "She wants her husband to sell Martin, to get him off the plantation before the child is born. If the child is
dark she knows her husband will kill Martin."

"What about her and the baby?"

"She knows that if the child is dark that
she and the baby will be killed, but she
hopes that maybe she can save Martin. But
her husband won't sell him. Martin's too
smart; he runs everything." That made Linc
smile in pride. "So what happened?"

I continued reading, but there wasn't
much more. Amelia never wrote of her
dilemma, but I could feel it. At last I came to
the passage, "Martin was hanged today."
Dutifully, Amelia had written that Martin had
tried to lead the slaves against them, so her
husband had had to hang him.

"Martin supposedly led a revolt with a

plantation full of women and children?" Linc asked angrily. "Go on."

Amelia wrote that she'd given birth to a child in the early morning so she'd not seen the hanging. The birth had not gone well and she was invalided; the doctor said she'd have to spend the rest of her life in her room. Her child was to be given to the "servants" to raise.

That was the end of the diary. I closed the book and held it. "Her husband locked her away. She was never allowed to leave the room where the baby was born. Never to go outside again, never to speak to anyone. She was condemned to solitary confinement for the rest of her life."

"And the baby?"

I took a breath. There were times—like this one—when I wished I had no power to see or feel things. "He was moved to the slave quarters and her husband made sure his incarcerated wife saw the child grow up. The child played beneath her window. Her husband also made sure . . ." I took a breath. "He made sure his wife saw the boy in chains when he was taken away to be sold."

I put my hand on Linc's arm to calm him.

"Think one of those bills of sale was for my ancestor?"

"I think so. Martin's name would probably be on the certificate as the father and my guess is that the child was sold to someone in East Mesopotamia, Georgia." Suddenly, I thought of something. "You know, don't you, that this makes you and Delphia and Narcissa blood relatives?"

Linc gave such a heartfelt groan that I laughed, and our laughter helped dispel the horror of the story in the diary. If her husband had killed Amelia, it would have been kinder. But she had been locked up, isolated. She'd been allowed to see her child grow up, but she hadn't been allowed to hold him, kiss him. And she'd had to watch as he was put in chains, to be taken away to be sold.

"What happened to her?" Linc asked. "What happened to my great-great-whatever grandmother Amelia?"

"I don't know. I only know what I feel from this book. Maybe there's something else about her in the library."

"In that glass cabinet next to the fireplace? Maybe tonight—"

"No, tonight there's 'something special,' remember?"

"Yeah, I remember," Linc said.

"We need to make a plan for tomorrow," I said. "While you're giving massages—"

"What?!" Linc yelled and an argument ensued. He said he was absolutely not, under any circumstances on earth, going to massage a bunch of lazy, rich women.

"You can ask them things," I said. "It's all well and good to find out about the past but as far as I can tell, that only tells us why your child felt at home here. His mother and he moved from one place to another, but they have remained here—at 13 Elms, I mean. Why? Is something here?"

"What was it that that Changer called it?"

"A Touch of God," I said, trying not to betray myself. I didn't want Linc to know how badly I wanted to know what that was. I wanted to find Linc's son and I was beginning to feel that we would, but what I really wanted in the long run was to find my husband and Bo. A Touch of God, I thought, and wondered yet again what it could be.

"No massaging," Linc said as we pulled into the driveway of 13 Elms. "Tomorrow I'm going to the church and talk to people."

I said nothing. The last thing we needed was for him to go to the church and ask questions. Why had the church said that the woman killed in a car crash was Lisa Henderson when it wasn't? he'd ask. How did Linc know another woman had been killed? they'd wonder. If it wasn't in the newspapers that she'd had a child, why was Linc asking questions about a child?

No, I could see that it was better that Linc let me use what small ability I had to find out what I could my way and not make people more suspicious than they already were. So far, no one suspected me, with my ugly black hair, as being the woman they'd read about. Besides, that was yesterday's news. But I could tell a couple of women had suspected that Linc wasn't a look-alike, but was actually the man they saw on TV.

This time I didn't sneak in the back way of the house, but rang the doorbell. I rubbed my eyes to make them look red, as though I'd been crying from my "family emergency," thanked the woman who answered the bell and went directly upstairs to my bed.

I wished I could take a shower and go to bed, but I needed to sit down and meditate and see what I could do to strengthen Linc's cover. I put a hat over the camera in the wreath, but left the microphones on. They'd hear nothing from me.

LINC ✥

✥ Chapter Twelve

I was sure Darci had done it to me. I'd been adamant about not doing massages but the next day, as though I couldn't help myself, I gave massages. As though I knew what I was doing. Ha! I'd had lots of massages but never given any. Except to Alanna and that had been for sex—if I remembered correctly. Sex was beginning to be something I only vaguely recalled.

Even though the women whose naked bodies I was slathering with oil were out of shape and unappealing, they were women and I'd been celibate for what seemed like years. But I wasn't the least bit turned on by them.

All in all, the whole thing was so odd that I knew it was witchcraft and therefore Darci.

"Conniving, manipulative, control freak," I muttered.

"Did you say something?" the woman on the table asked.

"I was just saying that this lavender lotion smells divine."

That was another thing Darci had done to me: I was so nonmale today that she may as well have cut it off. As I smeared lavender-scented oil on my hands and prepared to stroke the Great White splayed before me, I thought I was going to kill Darci. Garotte her with a pink satin ribbon.

At dinner I was so angry that I couldn't bear to look at her. I swished and pranced my way through the meal until one woman said, "What a pity," and another said, "Isn't it?"

As we left the dining room I got behind Darci and touched her shoulder so I could send her vivid images of all the most horrendous deaths I could contemplate.

"Twenty-four-hour spell," she whispered, then headed off to the library with the others.

It seemed that the "something special" was just another séance. I yawned and thought about excusing myself. Maybe I'd go to a bar and find myself a construction worker. Kill her, I thought.

As I turned toward the door a couple of the women grabbed my arms and pulled me into the library. As I passed Darci I narrowed my eyes in threat. She smiled and blew me a kiss.

Minutes later we were seated around the big library table awaiting what came next. I was suffering—for the first time in my life—from ennui.

In walked a tall, thin woman with honey-blonde hair down to her waist. She was wearing tight black trousers and a tiny black shirt that was like paint on her perfect body. If I'd been myself I would have jumped up and pulled a chair out for her. As it was, I looked at my nails and said, "Clairol or L'Oréal?"

Death was too good for Darci.

The blonde looked me up and down, then dismissed me as of no importance.

Oh yes. I was going to murder Darci.

However, even in my altered state I could feel Darci's excitement. Feel. Was that sentiment from Darci's emasculation of me, or had I become so attuned to her that what I felt, she did?

Whatever, I looked across the table and saw that Darci's eyes were wide open and staring. The other women's eyes were like that, too, but I'd never seen Darci with that look on her face. Even when she was watching Devlin the Shape-Changer, she'd been calm. I'd been scared out of my mind, but Darci had acted as though she saw and talked to ghosts every day—which she probably did.

I tried to reach deep inside myself and bring the real me to the surface and override whatever voodoo hex Darci had put on me. Hmmm, I thought. Wonder if she could use her power to put me into the role of someone? So I really felt as though I were the character? For a few minutes my mind wandered to critics' ravings about my "brilliant performance" and "Lincoln Aimes *was* Othello."

I pulled myself out of my fantasy and realized that Darci wasn't staring at the woman but at the big, round, glass ball she was carrying. How hokey, I thought. Not even Hollywood used crystal balls anymore. But here was one. It was the size of a bowling ball, clear glass around the edges, but cloudy inside. No doubt the clouds cleared when the woman's beautiful hand was crossed with gold. Was that a French manicure?

Darci sat there staring at that crystal ball, not even blinking. Please, I thought, someone tell me that thing isn't real. Darci could already do things no human should be allowed to do, but if she had some magic object that increased her power . . .

I decided not to allow myself to think about any of this, as I wasn't myself. If I remembered correctly, the idea of adventure usually exhilarated me.

The blonde introduced herself as Ingrid; she sat down at the head of the table, put her cloudy crystal ball onto a rosewood base, then waved her hands over it. I had to work to keep from groaning out loud. This was from a bad Theda Bara movie, before the talkies were invented.

I tried to get Darci's attention, but I couldn't. She was staring at that crystal ball so hard I expected it to explode.

DARCI 🙵

🙶 *Chapter Thirteen*

The woman who walked into the library was the one who'd broken into Linc's house and stolen the papers from his bedroom. I knew that the second I saw her. She'd also killed Linc's agent. She hadn't meant to. All she wanted was to destroy his records of Linc's son. She'd gone to the agent and told him she'd wanted to become an actress. She'd flirted with him, then knocked a cup of coffee over on him. While the agent was in the bathroom, she'd put some kind of detonating device under his desk. In the wee hours of the next morning she'd set it off, meaning only to burn out the agent's office. Unfortunately, the agent had fallen asleep on the couch that night and died of smoke inhalation. In my mind's eye I saw that the

agent had had a few drinks and was snor-
ing loudly. He hadn't even woken up but
died from the smoke before the flames
reached him.

I could tell the woman knew who Linc actually was. That he was gay didn't seem to
surprise her—and from the way Linc was
acting, I knew I'd overdone my True Persuasion.

What bothered me was that she wasn't
worried that Linc was here and had found
her. Had she expected it? Or did she have
something—or someone—who could coun-
teract anything Linc could do? Why was
she so sure that Linc's presence didn't matter?

I tried to look into her mind as best I
could, and I tried hard to find out where the
child was, but I could see nothing. I don't
think she knows, I thought.

For a chilling moment I wondered if she
had been the one to send the note to Linc.
"Your kid's missing." Had this woman
drawn Linc to her? If so, why?

All of this information, all these questions,
came to me in an instant, as soon as I
looked into her eyes. There were visions

around her that I could see as clearly as a movie.

In the next second, all my attention went to what she had in her hands. It was a big crystal ball. It looked like something out of a cheap magic store, but I knew that there was something inside that ball that had power—great power. A Touch of God? I wondered. All I knew for absolutely sure was that I *had* to get that hokey crystal ball. If I ever wanted to see my husband and Bo again, I *had* to have it.

I had to sit through nearly two hours of fake fortune-telling. I had to listen to the women being told that they gave too much and that they should think of themselves more.

Each woman agreed with that and if I hadn't been so preoccupied with staring at the ball, I would have gagged.

However, whatever was inside that ball was giving the woman some insight because she told a few things about the women's futures. I felt she saw more but wasn't telling. One woman would be dead within a year. Since I didn't feel that she had illness inside her, I figured it would be an accident. Ingrid told the woman she should party more, go on a long vacation, do three things she'd always dreamed of doing but never had.

I was curious what she'd tell Linc. Ingrid said he should give a hundred percent attention to his career. If he did, there were great things in store for him. In case Linc didn't get it the first time around, she told him to put everything and every person out of his mind. Let nothing distract him. One phone call could change his life.

I glanced at Linc to see if he'd be running back to his room to call the airport, but he looked at the woman with an arched brow. "And leave all this beauty?" he said. "I couldn't possibly."

I looked away to hide my smile, but Ingrid didn't hide her frown.

"What about me?" I said at last, staring at her hard. I wanted her to think what I wanted her to think.

She waved her hands over the ball and the "clouds" inside seemed to move around. She told me what I wanted to hear: that I'd find what I was looking for. The way she said it made me look at her. Did she mean the jewels I was supposedly looking for, or did she mean I'd find Linc's son? Or did she mean I'd find my husband?

As the evening wore on I could see that my True Persuasion of Linc was wearing off. He was looking at Ingrid with interest and he was looking at me in question. Eventually, the little glasses of green liqueur were served and the women grabbed them eagerly.

"These things are lethal!" they said, giggling, and yet again I wondered why they were there. The place wasn't great as a spa and the two séances hadn't been worth the expense of the stay. What did they know that I didn't? When I'd called to make a reservation I'd had to use lots of True Persuasion to get them to allow both Linc and me into the place.

Reaching across the table, Linc touched my hand for a second, pretending to remove a piece of lint. The touch showed me his idea of switching liqueurs with Ingrid. I gave a little nod and in the next second I laughed and sent my glass of liqueur flying across the room. It caused so much commotion and noise that everyone looked— and Linc switched his glass with Ingrid's.

Apologizing profusely, I knelt to clear up

the broken glass. Angry at my clumsiness, Delphia pushed a buzzer on the wall and called the maid. When I stood up, Linc nodded to me. Ingrid had drunk her drugged liqueur.

Ten minutes later everyone was sleepy, so we were hurried off to bed. Delphia said she'd send some warm milk up to me and hoped it would help me sleep. For how long? I was tempted to ask.

Once in my room I covered the two cameras yet again but didn't dare disable the microphones for fear I'd raise an alarm, then I dressed. It was eleven when Linc hove himself over my little balcony and entered my room. I put my finger to my lips for silence and we left the room together. As we walked, Linc put his hand on my shoulder so I could feel his thoughts about how much he liked me in my black cat suit. He made me laugh because he was so happy to no longer feel, well, other than himself.

Once we were in the hall I knew we were safer—not safe, but safer. Since the break-in in the basement had been found, I knew that the vigilance of the house had increased.

"Let me guess," Linc whispered.

"There's something in that ball that Ingrid has and I mean to have it."

"Find her room and I'll subdue her. All night if I have to."

He made me laugh as I began to tiptoe down the corridor in search of Ingrid's room. I knew she hadn't left the house; I'd made sure of that. Linc and I crept about as I touched one door after another.

At one door I jumped back.

"What?" Linc whispered.

"It's Amelia's room and she's still in there."

"Still? What does that mean?" He halted. "Not *that* Amelia."

"Yes, that one."

"She's dead, but she's still in there. Why didn't I know that?"

It wasn't until we reached the attic floor that I felt Ingrid and whatever was inside that ball.

I knew she was asleep and the ball was inside her room. It was pulling me as though it were a magnet and I a piece of steel. The door was locked. "Too bad Pappa Al isn't here," I said, leaning against the door, frustrated.

"Follow me," Linc said as he tiptoed

down the hall. When he reached a window seat, I knew what he was going to do.

"It's too dangerous," I said. "You can't—"

There weren't any alarms on the windows on the top floor so Linc opened it to climb out onto the roof. Pausing, one leg out, he said, "How about a good-bye kiss?"

"I'll kiss you if you die in my arms."

"That's encouraging," he said as he disappeared onto the roof.

I climbed onto the seat, stuck my head out and used all my power to guide him and his feet as he inched along the very steep roof. There was a place where the gutter was loose and he nearly fell, but I concentrated hard.

"You wanta back off on that?" Linc said across the roof between us. "You're making my head hurt."

"Sorry," I said and tried to calm myself. My father and I had worked on ways I could calm myself so I wouldn't inadvertently hurt people. Making Linc's nose bleed had been the first violent thing I'd done since the witches in the tunnel.

When Linc held on to the frame of the dormer window and pointed inside, I knew he'd found her. He pantomimed sleeping.

For a second I panicked. What if her window was locked? But it wasn't and Linc easily opened it and slipped inside.

I pulled my head back inside and tried to guide him through the room. I knew there were no cameras in the room.

Suddenly, my eyes flew open. She was awake! Worse, she'd seen Linc. My mind whirled with the problems this would cause. Would we ever find Linc's son now? Would I—?

I needn't have worried because, soundlessly, without a word, I knew that Linc had slipped into bed with her and he'd already started making love to her.

There were times when I really and truly hated my ability. I could see the two of them as clearly as though I were in the room with them. They were languid lovers, slow, sensuous. Linc loved women and he gave them what they wanted. If they wanted fast and hard, he delivered.

Ingrid wanted slow, sensual. Maybe it was because I'd spent so much time with Linc or because we were connected in some way, but I could feel what he felt. Heavens! I could feel what she felt, too.

I closed my eyes for a moment and

leaned back against the wall. I'd hardened myself against sex over the last year. I'd refused to allow myself to remember Adam's hands on my body, his mouth on my skin. I wouldn't even let myself remember the warmth of him, his skin nearly as dark as Linc's.

But now, connected to the couple making love on the other side of the wall, I could feel Adam, feel his mouth on my breast, his hand kneading. I could feel his lips on my stomach, his hands on my thighs, moving upward, stroking, caressing, driving me mad with desire. When he entered me, my legs grew weak and I slid down the wall, feeling him, smelling him.

"Adam," I whispered, "my Adam."

For a moment I sat there, my legs spread in front of me, feeling my husband's caresses as though he were with me. I could feel every move that Linc and the blonde woman were making, her hand on his skin, curving over the muscles of his chest, down his washboard stomach. Since I'd met him I'd refused to look at the beauty of Linc, refused to acknowledge his rampant sexuality, but now . . . Now it was as though it was me in that bed with him. I was the one stroking his thighs, running my hands over his buttocks. I was the one with my arms open to him, longing for him to enter me.

"Could this be classed as adultery?"

My eyes flew open and I was embarrassed. I closed my legs, closed my mouth that had been open to kisses, and tried to stand up, but my knees were so weak I stumbled. "Who are you?" I asked, my voice hoarse.

"Oh. You," I said. It was Devlin—or at least that was the name that had been put into my head. This time he was dressed in full Highland regalia, from brogues to a ribbon pulling his long gray hair back. "What do you want?" I sat down on the window seat. I was embarrassed to have been seen in a lustful fantasy, but also angry to have had it interrupted.

"This is a philosophical matter," he said, his hands behind his back and pacing. "Is it adultery to be in bed with a man who isn't your husband if you only do it with your mind?"

"Of course not." I tried to smooth my hair and wished I had on more clothes than a silly little cat suit. I crossed my arms over my chest as my nipples were still hard. I could still feel what Linc and Ingrid were doing just on the other side of the wall from me, but it was fading from my consciousness. I could tell they were going to be at it for hours and I wanted . . . I wanted to weep with envy.

"Who are you and what do you want?" I snapped at Devlin. "And why were the slaves so afraid of you?"

"They know their master," he said.

"Your ego is without limits."

"Why isn't something as tiny as you afraid of me?"

"Little body; big mind," I said. I could feel the rhythm of Linc and the woman.

"Now who has the ego?" Devlin said, but I could see he was pleased with me. He sat down on the seat beside me, which was disconcerting because his body overlapped mine by half a foot. I moved over.

"How galling life must be for you," he said in a chummy way. "To have the power of your mind yet have to hold back. Tell me, how much of it do you use? Fifty percent?"

I couldn't help it but I began to relax. This man was dead; he was a ghost. And even at that he was a weird ghost, changing his see-through body whenever he wanted. In other words, here was a man/thing who was stranger than I was. "About ten percent," I said. "Shall I experiment on you?" A couple of times I'd dealt with angry ghosts who didn't want to leave a place. I'd always won.

"Shall I show you what *I* can do?" he asked companionably.

I didn't want to see what he could do, but I also felt that he didn't want to see what I could do. My father said that if I were ever to tap into my power . . .

"Where is Linc's son?" I asked.

Devlin got up and went to lean his back against the wall. The bed where Linc and Ingrid were making love was against that wall. He closed his eyes for a moment. "Ah, I do remember those days. I remember a girl in 1206. She was—"

As he spoke, the wall began to disappear. It was a small circle at first but it began to enlarge until I could see Linc and Ingrid on the bed. They were beautiful together, him with skin like pale chocolate, hers like cream.

It was one thing to feel someone else's lovemaking but it was another to make a wall disappear and actually see what was going on. I concentrated on the wall and made it start reappearing.

Devlin, still leaning where the wall had been, opened his eyes and looked at the reappearing wall in surprise. "I was just try-ing to share," he said.

I didn't answer, just kept filling in the wall.

"Oh, so it's a war you want, is it?"

Had anyone seen us, I'm sure we would have looked like cartoon figures as we both glared at that wall. I would begin to fill up the hole, then the hole would widen, then fill, then widen.

It was Linc who stopped us. I hadn't thought about it but I would have assumed that what Devlin and I were doing with the wall couldn't be seen by . . . By what? Mor-tals? Normal people? Others?

But Linc saw the wall telescoping in and out. Worse, he saw me, and maybe Devlin, standing there and spying on him.

Devlin laughed and the wall was solid again. "Know you could do that?" he asked.

I tried to get over my embarrassment while seeking Linc's mind to make him for-get what he'd seen. "I had no idea, but I don't think I can do it unless someone starts it." I tried. I put my mind on the wall but it didn't move. Unlike my daughter and my niece, I couldn't move tangible objects. "I don't have the power."

"Ah," he said in a way that irritated me.

"What's that supposed to mean?" I looked at him hard. "You haven't answered any of my questions."

"I did!" He sounded offended. "I told you how to find the child."

"Oh yes, your riddle. Is the Touch of God in that crystal ball?"

"That one?" He opened the wall a bit so I could see a leather bowling-ball bag, then could see inside the bag. The ball was in it. He closed the wall. "She has no idea it has any power. She found the thing in the basement and took it to play her game."

"She broke into Linc's house and stole papers. She killed his agent."

Devlin reached toward the window seat, picked up a box of Godiva chocolates, and opened it. "Want one?"

I hesitated.

"Worried about calories?"

"No, poison."

"Darci, dear misunderstood Darci. Don't you yet realize that I've been sent here to help you?"

"Sent by whom?"

"The Good Guy." He held out the box again and I took a chocolate. I wasn't sure if they were real or an illusion, but they tasted good.

"Why would you help me find my husband?"

"You do know why you were given your powers, don't you?"

"World peace?"

Devlin chuckled. "More or less. You fight evil with evil. You—"

"I am *not* evil."

"No, but you have powers that in the wrong hands could cause great evil. Do you not know why your husband was kidnapped?"

I wanted to scream. I wanted to grab his collar and shout in his face, "Why?" but I didn't. I choked out a quiet, sedate, "Why?"

"Good control," he said, taking his hands off the box of chocolate, which hung in the air.

A floating box annoyed me so I snatched the box to put it on the window seat, but it disappeared in a poof. "You should meet my daughter and niece," I muttered.

"Who do you think taught them how to make their teddy bears belly dance?"

I took a step toward him. "If you ever harm them in any way, I'll—"

Suddenly, I was inside an iron cage, something old and dirty, like from a medieval dungeon. I could feel people behind me, smell their unwashed bodies, feel their fear. I refused to believe any of it. I concentrated and the people vanished. I think I could have made the cage disappear but, laughing, Devlin removed it.

"You have little power now, but you could have more."

"Why?" I said. "Why were Adam and Bo taken?"

"For you, of course. To get you, to pull you to them so you could be destroyed." His body was growing dimmer, fading. "Your power can be taken. The witch knew that. Darci, you must know that your power can be increased. If you are to win, it must be strengthened."

He was now just a faint outline. I concentrated but he didn't get more solid. When I doubled my concentration, he laughed. "Not yet, Darci, dear. Not yet. When you can keep me from leaving a room you'll be ready.

"You're to be tested. Are you worthy of so much power?"

With that he was gone.

I sat down on the window seat. After I'd killed the people in the tunnel in Connecticut I'd been so exhausted I'd had to be hospitalized. I wasn't near that now but I did curl up on the pillows and close my eyes.

All I wanted was a normal life, I thought. I wanted a husband and a couple of kids. I didn't want to talk to people who faded in and out and talked in riddles. I didn't want to have cages dropped around me. I didn't want evil people murdering others to try to get a power I never wanted in the first place.

Most of all, I didn't want to be "tested." Was what had been done to me by the media a test? Could I bear being so misjudged, so hated, when I was innocent? I couldn't defend myself, nor could those who loved me defend me. People around the world laughed at what they saw as my extreme parsimony. One night on the news was a segment someone thought was funny. The newscaster said, "Move aside Scots, we now have Darci." He went on to say that a new word had entered the English language. Whereas in the past the Scots had been the epitome of penny-pinching (How do you make copper wire? Give two Scots a penny.), now it was Darci, as in "Don't be such a Darci. You can afford it."

Adam had wanted to tell people that I'd collected nickels and taken any money he gave me because I'd wanted to get the people of Putnam out of debt, but I wouldn't let him. I couldn't embarrass my hometown like that. Adam said that what had been asked of me was blackmail. "It's primitive," he'd shouted. "The boy was offering you seven million dollars for your virginity."

I refrained from pointing out that Adam had made me risk my life for that same virginity.

Anyway, the last thing I needed was more "testing." Testing to find out what? That I was a good person? May God forgive me, but if I could get my family back I just might be persuaded to do something for the other side.

Even as I thought it, I knew it wasn't true.

I sat up on the window seat and tried to stop feeling sorry for myself. I could feel that Linc and Ingrid were still at it in the room. Poor Linc had so much pent-up desire that he might never quit.

Part of me screamed, "What about *me?!* What about *my* pent-up desire?"

Slowly, I got off the window seat and walked to the door of the room. Maybe I could make just a tiny hole in the wall, one that I could slip through so I could get the ball. Or maybe I could hex the door so that it unlocked. I hadn't tried that.

As I thought, I put my hand on the knob. "Oh," I said when it turned. It looked as though before Linc had succumbed to Ingrid's lust, he'd remembered to open the door for me, his partner.

I opened the door the narrowest crack I could, then crawled in on my hands and knees. Even so, Linc saw me. I felt his eyes on me more than saw them. I couldn't bear to again see him in bed with the woman. I tried to block out the noises of pleasure the woman was making, tried to not feel Linc's eyes on me. I grabbed the bag off the floor and started to take it. On second thought, I saw an old iron bunny rabbit on the hearth. I opened the bag, removed the glass ball and inserted the bunny. If I used my True Persuasion I could keep the woman from looking inside the bag and seeing that the ball was missing. In fact, if I worked hard enough I could make her lose the bag. Perhaps she'd leave the back door of her car unlatched, turn a sharp curve and all her luggage would roll out, down a hill and into a lake.

As soon as I had the ball, I clutched it to me and ran down the stairs and back to my bedroom. I wanted to get as far away from Linc and what was happening in that room as soon as possible.

When I was back in my room, part of me wanted to stay up all night and see what I could find out about the ball, but another part of me wanted the oblivion of sleep. Sleep won. I put the ball into the middle of the bed, under the covers to keep it safe and warm, then I took a long and somewhat cold shower. I needed to cool my body off from what I'd been feeling from Linc.

I got out, dried, and put on a long cotton nightgown. I was so cold I was shivering as I got into bed and pulled the ball to me. I put it against my stomach, wrapped my arms around it, pulled my legs up to it. I hadn't felt so comforted since the last night I'd spent with my husband. Whatever was inside that ball, I wanted it. No, I needed it. Even more, I felt it needed me.

"I can't do it," Linc said. It was afternoon, two hours after lunch, and we were at the slave quarters. What Linc couldn't do was break the glass ball. He'd used a hammer, a tire iron, and he'd repeatedly thrown it against rocks. The "glass" had not so much as chipped.

I was sitting on the ground surrounded by the old files and was going through them one by one.

This morning at breakfast Linc had been yawning, but he'd been so happy that I'd wanted to hex him out of sheer jealousy. The spell of nonmasculinity had worn off so he was himself again and flirting madly with all the women. He was kissing hands and cheeks and saying he was dying to get their naked bodies back under his hands. I didn't interfere as I had other things on my mind. I wanted to get back to my room to see what I could find out about the crystal ball.

Delphia stopped me after breakfast and pointedly asked me when I was leaving. Not Linc but me. I sensed that she was planning to ask Linc to stay on. When I touched her hand I could see that she was imagining a photo of him in their brochure; beautiful Linc was guaranteed to bring in more guests and more money. And if they tired of him would they sell him? I thought.

I used my True Persuasion on her to make her leave me alone so I could go to my room and study the ball. I spent four hours with it but achieved nothing. I could not connect with the power I felt inside it. I tried everything I could think of. I managed to make it roll across the floor, and, to my amazement, even lifted it a couple of inches. When I couldn't hold it off the floor, it dropped with a bang. Anxiously, I ran to it and inspected it for damage. One second I was feeling like I'd dropped my baby, then the next second I flung it as hard as I could against the stone fireplace. I chipped the rock but not the surface of the ball.

I was so absorbed in what I was doing that I forgot to protect myself. There was a knock on the door. I hid the ball inside the storage compartment under the window seat and opened the door. It was Narcissa.

"Are you all right, dear? We heard a noise and—" She broke off, looked around the room and saw my sunhat hanging on the wreath. "What a very pretty hat," she said, taking it down and pretending to look at it. "We wouldn't want it ruined, now would we? That nail that holds the wreath up could damage it. Perhaps you'd better put your hat here on the mantel."

She was, uninvited, now standing in the center of my room, and she was looking around, trying to figure out what I was doing in there all alone. "Won't you please join us? We have a florist coming today to show us how to arrange spring flowers. And later a woman is coming to teach us some yoga. We'd really like for you to join us."

Involuntarily, I shuddered. This woman looked and sounded as sweet as something off the Angel channel, but I knew she and her sister were doing something really bad. I wanted to scream at her, "Where is Linc's son?"

Instead, I burst into fake tears, covering my dry eyes with my hand. "I'm so sorry,

Narcissa," I said. "I've just had some terrible things happen to me lately."

As I hoped she would, she sat down beside me on the window seat and patted my hand. Again I felt the faint electric current run from her hand up my arm. Didn't she feel the ball under us? To me, it was as though we were sitting on a star. I could feel its extreme heat and light.

"What's wrong, dear? You can tell me anything."

I could feel her trying to will me to tell her everything about myself, tell her my deepest, darkest secret. I knew she couldn't help me with *my* secret but maybe I could get her to tell me *her* deepest secret.

"I need help," I said, stalling for time. I was trying to talk and work on her at the same time. That wasn't easy. I work best when I put myself into a state of meditation and concentrate hard.

"Help with what?" she asked. "You can tell me. I . . . know . . . lots of secrets."

"Not like mine," I said, "and I can't tell anyone what I want. It's too—"

"Too evil?" Narcissa asked, still patting my arm. "I doubt that it is. You should tell me. I've heard a lot in my life."

"I couldn't possibly tell."

"Then let me guess."

I made no answer, just covered my face with my hands and concentrated.

"You say your husband died and now you want the jewels, but it's my guess that you don't want the jewels for yourself. You try to appear sophisticated, but I can tell that you're not."

I looked at her sharply.

"It doesn't matter what I've seen but I know things. Delphi says I have half the women's intuition in the world."

It looked like jealous Delphia had reduced her sister's psychic abilities to that derogatory term of "women's intuition."

Narcissa picked up my hand and began to caress it. Instantly, I knew that *she* wasn't interested in Linc or any other man. I didn't snatch my hand away.

"My guess is that you grew up in deep poverty, then married a despicable older man for his money, but the old goat died and left you nothing. What did he do? Convert all his assets to tangible goods, then hide them?"

I was looking at her. What made her think I'd grown up in poverty? The clothes I was wearing and the three strands of gold around my neck were quite expensive. Did I—? I had to calm myself as her words were making me lose concentration.

"Are you in love with someone?"

"Oh yes!" I said.

"I see." She took my hand in both hers and kept caressing. "You want the jewels so you can give the money to someone else because he . . . she . . . ?"

"He," I said, and she lightened her grip on my hand.

"He is now demanding that you pay him or he'll go to the police."

"Police," I said, not understanding what she was saying, then it hit me. Good heavens, the woman believed I'd killed my husband and now someone was blackmailing me. I was to pay him or he'd tell the police. I needed to find some jewelry so I could pay the blackmailer. I put my hand over my face again. Murder and blackmail. Were the other women here for similiar reasons?

"I know," Narcissa said. "No one comes to us unless they've been given information about us. We advertise, but the truth is, we can't compete with other spas." She ran her hands over her ample belly. "Light cuisine and exercise are not what we're known for."

"Then you do . . . do what . . . what I was told?"

"We can, yes," she said softly.

I looked into her eyes so hard that mine began to ache. "When?" I asked.

"Soon. Others were here before you, and, as you know, we can do only one a day—or even less."

I put my hand on her shoulder and did what I could to read the images in her mind. Unfortunately, all I could see was a vision of the cherry pies that were being served at dinner.

"Won't you come downstairs and join us?"

"I'm rather tired. I'd like to stay in my room and—" I smiled at her. "I'd really like to read. Do you have any books that could take my mind off my worries?"

"You're free to use the library. There are some excellent local histories in there."

"Histories of this beautiful house?" I was afraid she'd refuse to let me see them as I was sure she'd not want anyone to know the truth of her ancestors. Instead, she turned pink with pleasure.

"How kind of you to say that. Most people say the most dreadful things about this house. Did you know that this house was once called A Hundred Elms? There were one hundred huge elms on the property, but after the war and the plantation workers were let go, the lumber had to be sold. One of my ancestors said he wanted thirteen elms left because thirteen was an evil number and that what the Yankees had done to us was evil."

I couldn't reply to that, because I didn't think the evil had come from a Yankee.

"Please," Narcissa said, "read all you want. Neither my sister nor I are readers so perhaps you can tell us about our family's history." With that, she left the room.

I stood there for a moment trying to recover. "Blood will tell," went through my head. If they didn't like to read, maybe both Narcissa and Delphia really did think that the locked room in the basement had contained the history of their illustrious family. Maybe their recent ancestors hadn't bothered to tell them the truth. Whether they knew the truth or not, I knew that whatever they were doing now was as horrible as what Amelia's husband had done to her.

After Narcissa left, I put on a show for the cameras. I pulled clothes out of my closet and looked at them as though I was trying to decide what to wear. I had on jeans and a cashmere sweater so I looked at the two suits and three dresses I'd brought with me. I hung one on the bedpost, another on the corner of the mantel and the last one on the flower wreath and covered the camera lens. As for the lens in the bathroom, I kept the door closed or I tossed a hand towel over it. Once I had privacy I withdrew the ball from the window seat and began to work on it again.

By lunch I'd still had no success, so when I went downstairs and saw Linc I told him we needed to get together. All through the meal he was the center of attention as he teased the women—and canceled all his afternoon appointments.

I met him at the slave quarters, the ball held against my stomach, hidden as best it could be by my big brimmed hat and a scarf. "I want you to break this open," I said, handing it to him.

He rummaged around in an old tool shed at the edge of the slave cemetery and found some rusty items that he used to try to break the ball, but nothing scratched it. Meanwhile, I started, yet again, going through the old slave documents. I was willing to sit outside the mausoleum and work, but Linc refused to stay near any cemetery, so we went back near the Quarters, out of sight of the house.

"I don't know what you're afraid of," I said, trying to keep pace with him. "All the restless spirits have gone in search of their loved ones, so the place is clean."

"Darci," Linc said in exaggerated patience, "most people in the world don't like cemeteries. They don't know for sure that there are ghosts but they're not taking chances."

"I'm telling you that there are ghosts but there are not any here."

"Great," he said, "I'm glad we cleared that up. Now let's get out of this place."

"I would have thought that after last night you'd be in a better mood today," I said under my breath, but Linc didn't comment.

I sat on a bench and watched as he put the ball on the ground under a shade tree— one of the thirteen remaining elms—knelt, and raised an old hammer above it. "Would you mind telling me what you and that . . .

that creature were doing with the wall last night? Much as I like being on stage, there are times when I do not want an audience."

"I, uh . . ." Linc paused, hammer aloft, waiting for my answer. I sent the message that he should strike.

He struck the ball but the hammer nearly bounced off the glass—and sent Linc sprawling back on his rear end.

I started to laugh but coughed to cover the sound.

"*What* is that made of?" he asked.

"Something not from this planet."

Linc looked like he wanted to contradict that statement, but instead said, "Are there a lot of things on earth that come from other planets?"

I avoided his eyes. When I'd been growing up in Putnam, I'd been on my own. There wasn't a person I could tell when I met someone who had died. I couldn't tell a child, "I'll make that heal faster," when I saw a bruise on her cheek. I couldn't tell a teacher that the man who lived next door to the school and raised dogs was actually a pedophile so I was going to do my best to get him out of town. There was no one to ask if I should do something and if so, how should I go about it? And there was no one to say, "Good job!" after I'd done something.

As a result of my lack of any true contact with people, I'd wasted a lot of my time and energy trying to do things I couldn't. When I met my husband I'd only recently left Putnam and I knew little about the power God had given me. I knew I could find things, but I hadn't stretched myself. In Putnam, I'd found rings and a couple of wandering two-year-olds, but I'd never had to deal with a kidnapping.

It was only after I met Adam and through him found my father, that I began to investigate what I could do. When a man held a gun on Adam and I felt for sure that he was going to kill Adam so he could take me, I found out that I could paralyze people. The paralysis lasted only as long as I could concentrate, but I could do it. In fact, I'd used it to— No, I wasn't going to think about the four people I'd had to kill. Yes, I knew better than anyone else that they were evil, but I still didn't want to kill them or anyone else. But I'd had to.

After the witches were dead, after Adam and I were married and we'd moved into a house with my father and Bo, my father began to work with me. His question was, What can my daughter do? Before we found each other, he'd spent years researching my ancestresses so he knew that each one had had different abilities. Some had more power, some less.

Since my father had studied many psychics, he knew how to test me.

We dispensed with the idiot card games right away. He soon found that I could make him choose the circle or the square or whatever when I wanted him to.

My husband didn't know—or I'm sure he would have protested—that my father and I went to places that were said to contain ghosts so I could talk to them. We didn't tell anyone, but some people from some churches called to ask me to cast out a few "demons." I had encountered several spirits that wanted only to cause harm. I managed to dispatch them.

Besides exorcisms and what the FBI asked me to do, my father and I tried to have some fun. We went to a few museums and his credentials got me into the basements so I could touch a few things and tell what I felt. I tried to solve a few mysteries about things like the Loch Ness Monster, the Abominable Snowman, and where Osama bin Laden was. I told my father who Deep Throat was and who had killed JFK.

He wrote every word I said down in his red leather journals, which he kept in a walk-in vault in the basement of the house.

Because of the years I'd spent with him and because of all the exploration, I'd seen some unusual things, such as a few things that had been put on earth by people from other planets.

When I took so long to answer, Linc said, "Forget it," and hit the glass ball with the hammer again.

He spent hours with the ball, just as I had done. When Linc's violence didn't work, and my mind had no effect on the ball, I told him that once my father and I had gone to a museum and on the way back we'd stopped for lunch in a cute little town and we'd passed an antiques shop. I'd felt a pull toward the shop so I said I wanted to go in. I'd never felt that way before so I was curious. I thought maybe it was one of those finds of a million-dollar painting that had a fifty-dollar price tag. What I found was a little ceramic man, about four inches high. He was in a bowl full of dirty, broken dishes and glasses. My father didn't show any surprise when I bought the object, and when I was outside, I said, "There's something inside it." When we got home, my father used a hammer to try to break it open but the ceramic didn't even crack. Frustrated, he looked at the object under a magnifying glass and thought he saw some markings on it. Since the little man was too dirty to be able to read, my father took it to the sink to wash it. The second the water touched the little statue, the outer covering dissolved.

"What was in it?" Linc asked.

"A key."

"A key to what?"

"I have no idea. Just a little key. Rather ordinary. I have it with me with the keys to my house and car. If you want to see it, I'll show it to you."

He looked at me. "You think the ceramic covering the key was from another planet?"

I wasn't talking to Devlin, or even to my father, and since I didn't want Linc to go running away from me in fear, I shrugged. "Who knows?" I said, looking away from him.

Based on my story, we dunked the ball in

water and when that didn't work, we went to the kitchen of the house, asked where the cleaning supplies were, then proceeded to rummage. I kept people away while Linc filled a big bucket with bottles of whatever chemicals were in the big old cupboard. Back at the Quarters again, we dumped ammonia, bleach, lye (which we'd found way in the back) and even floor polish on it. When Linc started polishing the ball and pretending he expected a genie to pop out, I laughed. He had an audience so he began putting on a show of making up three wishes. He was very funny, always changing his mind about the wishes he wanted, and I laughed hard.

After a while, he set the ball down under a tree and said, "I give up. Are you *sure* there's something inside there?"

"Positive."

"Hey! Maybe there's a magical, disappearing keyhole and your key—"

"Already tried it," I said, sighing. I really had tried everything I could think of to crack that ball open, but nothing had worked.

"What about the bills of sale?"

"No. They don't talk," I said, looking at the ball. When Linc was silent, I looked at him. "Oh. You mean, What did I find in the papers?" I handed him the one that listed Martin as the father.

Linc sat down on the bench beside me while he read it. I'm sure he put his shoulder against mine so I could feel what he did. When Linc touched the document with Martin's name on it, I knew they were related. When he and I had read the bills earlier I guess we'd been going too fast and maybe I'd been the one to handle Martin's bill so I'd missed the connection.

The bill was like all the others. It described a boy, about seven years old, very light-skinned, named Jedediah, trained in field work, who was for sale for eight hundred dollars. "Deceased" had been written in the mother's space, but the father was listed as Martin, without the dignity of a surname. On the back of the bill was handwritten "Sold to Charles Frazier in East Mesopotamia, Georgia," and the date.

For a few moments Linc held the paper and looked across the field that had once been full of cotton. "Field trained" the paper read. At just seven years old, the child had already been made to work in the fields.

"I'm sorry," I said to Linc.

He didn't answer but I knew he was imagining his own son having to work in the fields. "When I started this I just wanted to save my own child because he was connected to me. This was all about me, not him. But now I want to get him out of whatever he's in because of him, because *he* doesn't deserve this. If he has some sort of ability that someone wants to exploit, it's because I passed it to him from my grandmother."

Linc looked at me. "Darci, what can we do to find my son?"

"I don't know," I said honestly. "We can go to a couple of places, like the church and the site of the car wreck, but I feel that the answer is here in this house. That spirit, that man Devlin, makes me think that everything is tied up with my husband. I know that what's in there"—I nodded to the ball—"is necessary to finding Adam, but how is your son tied into this?"

I leaned my head against his shoulder and Linc put his arm around me as though I were his sister. Part of me was glad that his rampant sexual desire had been temporarily sated, but part of me missed the way he'd looked at me with red-hot lust.

We stayed like that for a few moments, then Linc moved to fish a piece of paper out of his pocket. It was his list of things Devlin had said we needed to do.

"We gave the slaves what they want," Linc said, "but now they're gone so how do we ask them anything?"

I didn't want to move, didn't want to think. I wanted to stay with my head against Linc's shoulder and feel the warmth of a human male next to me. If I closed my eyes and concentrated, maybe, for one second, I could believe that Linc was Adam.

"You don't have to have dark skin to be enslaved," I said, thinking about Adam and Bo—and myself. We didn't have a racial history of slavery but we were enslaved.

In the next moment, my eyes flew open and I saw that Linc was staring at me—and his thoughts were clear. Maybe all the dark slaves were gone but there'd been another slave in that house.

"Amelia," Linc whispered.

"Amelia," I answered.

LINC 🙵

🙵 *Chapter Fourteen*

We were going to talk to a ghost!

I like to think I'm a courageous person, but I followed Darci with such reluctance that I couldn't keep up with her short legs.

I had to work hard not to think Darci was the strangest person on earth, and for the thousandth time I wondered how her husband had dealt with her.

Last night had to be the strangest yet. Darci had gone crazy over some crystal ball so, like the gentleman I am, I said I'd help her get it. I risked my life to climb along a roof edge, then sneaked into the bedroom of a sleeping woman. I'd just unlocked the door for Darci when I looked back and there she was, awake. Ingrid was staring at me across a half-dark room, a question in her eyes.

So what was I supposed to do? Tell her the truth, that I was in the room to steal her crystal ball? That would get the cops called and get me splashed all over the newspapers in a way that wouldn't do my career any good. However, if I'd sneaked in the room to steal *her,* so to speak, that was okay. Did that make possessions more valuable than people?

Anyway, there wasn't anything else I could do but pretend I was after *her.* The truth was, though, that I figured she'd say no to me. In my lifetime I'd had only two women say no to me and they were Darci and her mother. But since they'd been the last two, I guess I thought my luck had changed.

It hadn't. By the time I got within a foot of the bed, I knew the woman wanted me in the worst way. I climbed into bed with her, let her undress me, and we began to make love.

I wanted to make love slowly, to take all night at it because who knew when I'd get laid again? Between Alanna's never being around, and Darci's medieval attachment to a guy who was probably dead, I wanted to make the evening last.

I didn't know the woman I was in bed with, but I knew she had some part in the whole strange thing I'd become involved in. I was sure Darci knew more than she was telling me, but I was reluctant to try to find out more.

As for the woman, the one time I tried to speak, she put her fingertips to my lips. We didn't exchange a word the entire evening. We just touched and licked and sucked. By the time the sun rose there wasn't an inch of her supple body that I didn't know.

At dawn she turned her back to me and went to sleep. No words spoken, just turned to her side and went to sleep. It was a dismissal. Her back was not an invitation to do that most intimate of gestures: cuddling. As though I were a stallion hired for the evening, she was through with me.

I got up, pulled on some of my clothes, left through the door, and went to my own room downstairs. I wanted to sleep for a couple of hours before the women started demanding I rub them down. There were only six of them but they each wanted an appointment every day. And each one wanted more than the hour allotted. "I have a pain right here," they'd whine, wanting me to spend an extra fifteen minutes on that area. I did it but I didn't like it.

However, the minute I put my head on my own pillow I was wide awake. Somewhere during the night I'd looked up to see Darci and that ghost playing "whose is biggest" with the wall to the room. Devlin, dressed up like some ancient Highlander, was leaning against the wall that was sometimes not there—which I can tell you looked pretty weird. He'd make the wall disappear, then Darci, concentrating so hard her eyes were down to slits, would make it reappear. Devlin looked like he was having fun, but Darci seemed to be working hard. No wonder she can't find my son, I thought, she doesn't have enough power.

When Darci saw me watching her, she was embarrassed, the ghost laughed, and the wall reappeared. Beneath me, the blonde woman didn't seem to be aware of anything that was going on, but I couldn't take that as a compliment. She was like a robot that had been programmed to give pleasure. If I hadn't been without female companionship for so long I wouldn't have gone to bed with her. To me, sex is better if there's a personal connection. Love makes it the best. Take Alanna, for instance. Or, maybe take Darci. She'd probably be fun in bed. Her little body could probably bend into some seriously interesting shapes, and what about that power of hers? She could read things that were in my mind. Could she put her visions and feeling into mine? If Darci and I had sex, could she make us feel both sides at once? I'd feel what she was feeling and she would feel what I did.

I lay in bed and thought about this for so long that someone knocked on my door and told me breakfast was being served in the dining room. Yawning, I got up, dressed, and thought about how I could ask Darci about her power as it related to sex. Subtly, of course.

After breakfast I was up to my elbows in too-soft white flesh. Maybe because I was feeling better I began to hint to each woman that I might be interested in her if she'd lose some weight and get a little muscle. At lunch Narcissa told me that they'd had to open the weight room because the women were demanding to use the equipment.

"Maybe you could give some lessons," she said.

Deliver me, I thought. Two-pound dumb-bells and showing women how to do shoulder presses was not something I wanted to do. However, it was great news to be told there was a weight room somewhere. I smiled at Narcissa. "I'll just let them watch me work out and hope that inspires them."

I canceled all my massage appointments so I could work out after lunch, but Darci wanted me to break that glass ball I'd helped her steal. I figured that would take all of two minutes, then I'd be free. The truth was that after I worked out I planned to pay another visit to Ingrid.

But breaking the ball proved to be impossible. Darci told me a bizarre story about alien substances, especially one that had been around a key, but I tried not to think about what she was saying. All I wanted to do was work out, then go to bed with a pretty woman.

I should have known that Darci would have other ideas. Talking to a ghost was on the very bottom of my list of fun things to do.

We paused outside the door to the room she said was Amelia's and according to Darci, Amelia was still in there. Still imprisoned, still waiting.

I was so nervous about what was behind the door that to lighten the mood I turned and started to walk away. Darci caught my shirt and pulled me back. I wanted her to laugh but she knew I was serious.

"Look," she said, "the truth is that I doubt if you'll be able to see anything. I've been around ghosts for years and only I could see them—and even then I couldn't see them."

"That makes sense," I said.

"I could see them inside my head. It's like in a dream. You can see the people in a dream clearly but no one else can. That's how I've always seen ghosts."

"Until this shape-guy, this Devlin."

"Right. Devlin is different. The point I'm trying to make is that you probably won't see any ghost. You'll just see a bare room while I'll see the ghost."

"If I won't see anything, why should I bother to go in there?"

When Darci hesitated in answering, I

knew she was trying to come up with a plausible lie, something I was to believe so she wouldn't have to tell me the truth. I'd learned some things about little Miss Darci. One was that she embarrassed easily and second was that she could see what was inside my head if I touched her. Maybe if I embarrassed her and distracted her, I could then ask her questions and get the truth. Why did I have to go with her to see this ghost? What did she know that she wasn't telling me?

Reaching out, I pulled her into my arms, her back to my front, and buried my face in her neck. I then began to go over last night in my mind, stroke by stroke, tongue on hot skin, groans, and especially the moment before the little death.

"Don't," Darci whispered, going limp in my arms. "Please don't."

I couldn't help myself, but the next second I was nuzzling her ear, and my head filled with visions of what I wanted to do to *her.*

If the door to the room hadn't opened and we hadn't nearly fallen inside, I don't know what would have happened. I'd meant to tease Darci into making her tell me the truth, but instead I'd—

Turning my head, I looked into the room. It was clean but it was exactly as it must have been in 1843, when Amelia Barrister had given birth to a half-black child. There were those snowman-shaped lamps with roses painted on them, crocheted doilies over every wooden table, and there were at least half a dozen little tables scattered around. There was a canopied bed along the wall on the right, the canopy draped with a long white crocheted cloth. On the left was a sitting area with a hard little couch and a couple of hard-looking chairs, their seats low to the floor. The wall facing us had several tall French doors. They were standing open and I could see beyond to a small, deep porch that was at the corner of the building. A person could sit on that porch and see but not be seen by the people below.

The only thing odd about the room— other than that it looked like a step back in time, that is—was that there was a woman wearing old-fashioned clothes sitting on a chair just beyond the doors, and whipping a crochet needle around and around a piece of thread. She looked so solid that I was sure she was real. Maybe she was someone we hadn't met, I thought. But then a breeze blew through the open doors, a couple of leaves blew in—and went right through the woman.

I tried to act brave. Humor under fire. "Tell me she's one of the guests I haven't met," I whispered to Darci.

" 'Fraid not," she whispered back. "That's two spirits in this house that people can see. That's a lot of energy. A lot of hatred."

The way she said this was as though she'd just seen a miracle, something wondrous and unique.

"I think we should—" I began, but the woman in the chair turned to me and smiled. She was very pretty, with blue eyes and dark blonde hair under a little lacy cap. I knew she wasn't real, was dead even, but I couldn't help thinking that, with the right makeup and good lighting, she could be a knockout. She had a little nose and beautiful, full lips. Her skin kind of glowed, but in a good way, not like a dead person's skin might glow.

I decided to leave.

"Martin," she said softly, "how good to see you. Come and sit by me."

You know how it is. A ghost holds out her hand to you and you want to go, but your feet freeze. I just stood there, unable to move.

Darci gave me a push on the back and since my feet were rooted to the floor, I almost fell.

"My goodness!" she said. "Did you hurt yourself?"

"Uh, no, I . . ."

"Come and sit down. We'll have some tea." She turned to Darci. "Penny, would you make us some tea?"

I had the satisfaction of seeing Darci look bewildered, as though asking, Now what do I do?

"Yes," I said loudly, "make us some tea . . . Penny."

I walked forward and took the seat across from Amelia's. If I hadn't seen a leaf blow through her I would have sworn she was real. She had on a dress that was so tight around the waist I could see the thread stretching in the seams. I knew she was

wearing a corset and if I were politically correct I'd think how unliberated she was, but
she had a prodigious bosom, a tiny waist,
and lots of hips under her gathered skirt. If
she was an example of my great-great-
great-grandfather's taste in women, I'd say
the men in our family hadn't changed much.

"How are you today?" I asked. Behind
her, Darci was pulling dishes from a cabinet
and I wondered if she'd make real tea. It
might be interesting to watch what happened when Amelia drank.

"I am well," she said, then rolled her eyes
back toward Darci. She was telling me that
she couldn't talk freely with Darci/Penny in
the room.

"Here, girl!" I said sharply to Darci. "Go
and fetch . . ." What? I wondered. "My
horse." Did Martin have a horse?

"Yes, masstah," Darci said, glared at me,
then left the room.

I looked at Amelia triumphantly, until I realized I'd isolated myself with a ghost.

The door had barely closed behind Darci
when Amelia came toward me. She half
floated, half walked. I was scared to death
until she touched me. I could feel her touch.

Darci'd said that the ghosts could manifest themselves because of strong energy, strong hatred. But when Amelia put her shapely body on my lap and slid her arms around my neck, I decided that strong *love* could also cause a ghost to appear.

Amelia put her lips on mine. At first I could barely feel them, but when I began to return her kiss, I could feel her lips more strongly. When I put my hand on that tiny waist of hers it was like touching air, sort of not there but there. As the kiss deepened, her body became more substantial.

When my tongue touched hers I was ready to see what interesting clothes she had on under that dress. My hand went to the top of the row of tiny buttons down the front of her dress. I had six of them unfastened before she pulled her mouth from mine.

"No, dearest," she said, her breath against my ear. "Not here and not now. Edward may return at any minute."

"No, he's with Jassy now so he'll take all afternoon."

As soon as I said it, I looked down at her in astonishment. Where had that come from? Please tell me a ghost wasn't taking over my body! Please.

"Yes, I know. Penny tells me everything. She delights in telling me all that Edward does with the women. Dearest," she said, putting her lips against mine. "We must be careful. Penny would tell Edward if she found out about us and he would . . ."

She buried her face in my neck. Maybe it was the corset—or maybe it was that she was dead—but she made me feel protective of her. And like I wanted her in bed with me more than I wanted to live. I unfastened two more buttons.

She laughed, a lovely sound that made me undo another button. "Behave now," she said. "I'll meet you tonight in the same place. Will you be there?"

I wanted her so much I was afraid I was going to start shaking like some high school kid. "With bells on," I said.

"With nothing on," she said so seductively that I grabbed at her as she got off my lap. "Not now," she whispered, then ran her hand between my legs in a way that made me catch my breath.

In the next second the door opened, Darci entered the room, and Amelia sat back in her chair, looking for all the world like an angel—except that the front of her dress was unbuttoned halfway down to her waist.

Darci stood close to us, her eyes wide in shock as she looked at Amelia's open dress, then at the front of my trousers. I crossed my legs and put a pillow on my lap.

"It is so warm in here," Amelia said as she began to fasten her dress. "Now, Martin," she said in a businesslike way, "what was it you wanted to talk to me about?"

"Jedediah," I said before I thought.

When she looked at me, her face was so full of anguish that it nearly took my breath away. Then, to my horror, she aged. She went from being young and beautiful to being an old, emaciated woman with all the misery of the world in her eyes, then she vanished. The room stayed the same, furnished like a Victorian movie set, the only difference being that Amelia was gone.

For a moment I sat still, staring at the empty chair, and feeling bereft, as though I'd lost someone very dear to me.

Darci plopped down in the chair where Amelia had been and I experienced culture shock. She had on jeans and a fuchsia-colored sweater. I felt disgusted by her attire. Women should wear skirts. Her waist was thick and straight; her hair was loose and slovenly and an unnatural color. And her face was painted like a cheap hussy's.

I felt this for just a second, then it was gone. I looked at Darci and she looked quite nice.

"You really are disgusting," she said matter-of-factly. "Last night was the woman who wanted to kill you, a few minutes ago you were all over me, and now you hit on a ghost." She looked pointedly between my legs.

"Back up. Who wanted to kill me? Other than in bed, that is."

Darci waved her hand in dismissal. "That doesn't matter. What did you get out of Amelia, other than what was inside her dress, that is."

"You sound jealous." I rubbed my hand over my face. "I really need to go to the gym for about three hours, maybe five." I started to get up but, yet again, Darci had paralyzed me. I couldn't move.

"What did she say?" Darci asked, her voice just a whisper because she had to concentrate so hard to hold me in place.

"Not a word until you release me," I said, my back teeth together.

Darci released me and I started to get up.

"Okay," she said, "I apologize. Deeply and sincerely, I apologize. I was jealous. I admit it. I've had a lifetime of ghosts talking only to me, then to have one dismiss me like a servant—"

"Slave," I said, still half out of my chair.

"Slave. Yes, like a slave. Well, it got to me. So what did you and Amelia, uh, talk about?"

"Was that a crack?"

"Just a little one. Please, Linc, tell me what was said."

I hesitated. "Why did you say I spent the night with a woman who wanted to kill me?"

"Ingrid was the woman who slipped into your house, opened the safe, and took the documents your agent gave you."

I sat back down. "She killed Barney?"

"Yes."

I leaned toward Darci. "I'm going to go work out long and hard, and afterward, you and I are going to have a secrets-sharing session. Got it?"

"Yeah. What did—?"

I stood up, looking down at Darci.

"Amelia is going to meet me tonight in our usual place. I leave it up to you to find out where that is. I'll see you at dinner." I left the room, shutting the door behind me.

DARCI ⟨⟩

⟨⟩ *Chapter Fifteen*

Research, I thought. I'd been sent off to do research. I'm sure Linc meant I was to go to the library at 13 Elms and search the books there, but I had my own plans, so I needed to keep Linc occupied elsewhere. When I'd been looking for Ingrid and putting my hands on the doors, I'd felt equipment inside one of the rooms. At first I thought it was the room for the cameras and microphones, but I'd already found out that that equipment was in a room just off the kitchen (and for the most part, unmanned), so what was in that room? When I glanced at Linc, I knew. It was workout equipment; all lightweight as befit the Barrister sisters' idea of ladylike behavior—and as befit the state of the old floors. Heavy weights would have crashed through the floor joists.

It hadn't taken much effort to give Linc the idea of encouraging the women to work out, which got Narcissa to unlock the door, which made Linc spend the afternoon in the gym. I knew he wanted to spend more time in bed with Ingrid, but she'd left that morning. Since the ornament I'd put in the bowling ball bag had no power, it was difficult to ascertain if she'd taken the bag with her, but I didn't think so.

Maybe I should have made an effort to follow the woman with my mind, but I didn't feel that she knew anything. Her aura was such a dull shade that I could see no passion in her. I'd seen people like her before. They were damaged. I didn't want to say soulless, but they were close. They felt nothing, not love or hate, not compassion or remorse. She could easily go to bed with Linc one day and kill him the next.

While I'd been near her I'd done my best to find out what was in her mind—not that I could read minds—but I saw little. I felt no remorse from her for having killed a man when she set fire to Linc's agent's office.

Whatever she'd done I knew that in the overall story, she wasn't important.

Anyway, I wanted to keep Linc busy for the afternoon so I could do some exploring. We still had the rental car we'd used to go to East Mesopotamia so I planned to use that.

That morning I'd talked to my daughter and my niece in Colorado. I missed them so very much! Their aunt Susan had found an old dollhouse in the attic, something made for the daughter of the original builder of the house. He'd been extremely wealthy and the dollhouse he'd commissioned in the 1890s had twenty-eight rooms on four floors. There were a dozen dolls with the house, each representing members of Kane Taggert's family, plus four servants.

"They have lots of clothes for them and we're playing with them nicely," my daughter said—and I knew from her tone that she'd done something she wasn't supposed to.

"Let me talk to Aunt Susan."

"What have they done?" I asked Susan.

"They seemed to have given the dolls life. I don't think it was a real life, with personalities and such, but the dolls were moving around in a rather lifelike way."

"Creep you out?"

"Like you can't believe," Susan said from her heart. "Mike was here so he got the girls to . . . to take off their spell. The problem was that they didn't know any other way to play with the dolls, but we taught them."

"Susan . . ." I began, but couldn't think of anything to say. I wanted to apologize and thank her at the same time.

"No problem," she said, obviously understanding what I wanted to say.

I did thank her profusely, hung up, then willed my father to call me. He and I had spent so much time together there was a channel between us that was so strong it was as though we had a telecable between us.

Dad called me minutes later. He was still on the trail of Boadicea's bag that had contained the mirror. So far, he hadn't found it but I felt that he would. I couldn't yet tell if he'd ever find the mirror but I hoped he would.

He asked about me and what I was doing, but I told him nothing. But then, there was nothing to tell. Linc and I had sent some slave ghosts away, and Linc had managed to create a sexual frenzy among all the women, both living and dead, but all in all, we hadn't made any progress in finding his son.

However, the reason I'd cleared the afternoon was so I could visit a few places without the distraction of Linc. The beauty of him, the sheer presence of him, distracted people from talking about what I wanted them to talk about, so I told my father I might have some news soon.

After I hung up, I went outside to the car. I'd been asking the other guests questions and had even pulled a few words out of a maid, so I'd found out where the oldest local church was, and where the woman who was supposed to be Lisa Henderson had crashed.

The first place I went was the crash site. As I'd known, it was at the bottom of a hill. I didn't know whether to be proud of myself or annoyed because I felt nothing more than I'd felt when I'd held the newspaper photo. I stepped into the tangle of growth at the base of the tree to see if any car parts, or anything at all, had been left behind.

Maybe if I touched something from the wreck I'd feel—

"Oh!" I said and jumped back. I'd put my hand on the tree to steady myself and had felt a jolt through my arm. The tree was very angry at having been rammed by a speeding car.

I drew back and looked at the tree. As Linc had said, it took a lot to discombobulate me, but this angry tree was doing it. As I stepped backward, I looked at the tree in alarm, half expecting it to start throwing apples at me—except that it was an oak tree.

When the tree stayed just a tree, I was relieved. However, I nearly ran back to the car, then took a moment to calm myself. As I turned the car around to get back on the road, I thought, Give me ghosts and dancing dolls, but let the trees be quiet!

I found the church I was looking for down a graveled lane. It was set in a little clearing, with a cemetery to the right and behind it. As I got out of the car I listened for a moment to the stillness of the place. There were so many spirits hovering that the birds made little noise. Quietly, I closed the door and walked toward the cemetery. What I hoped to find was Martin's gave, but I somehow doubted that Amelia's husband would have allowed the man to be buried in consecrated ground. I felt sure that Martin's grave was on the land surrounding 13 Elms, and unmarked.

As soon as I stepped inside the little white picket fence surrounding the cemetery, I was so bombarded by spirits that I put my arms over my face. It wasn't as though they would hurt me or that I feared them. It was just the sheer volume of them. It was as though they'd been marooned there for a hundred or so years and were dying to talk to someone. Since not many humans could hear them, they ran at me, eager for gossip and news.

"Have you seen my cousin?"

"I can't find my gold locket. My sister-in-law stole it. Can you get it back for me?"

"You have nice hair. Can I touch it?"

"Do you have children? I used to have children. Twelve of them, but six—"

"Ssssh," I said, drawing in my breath, closing my eyes and willing all of them to calm down. When I felt quiet around me, I opened my eyes. These weren't ghosts like Devlin and Amelia, but were the plain kind that only people like me can see. They were standing—floating, actually—all around me and looking at me with big eyes full of questions.

"Could I help you?"

"Ssssh!" I said sharply. "I told you—"

"I beg your pardon."

Turning, I saw a young man—an alive person—with blue eyes and dark blond hair. He was wearing a blue shirt with the distinctive collar of a minister. I'm sure I turned red down to my horrible black roots. "I'm sorry," I said, "I thought you were . . ." What could I say, that I thought he was one of the many ghosts? I gave him a weak smile. "I like old churches . . . and old cemeteries," I said. "I'm trying to find out some of the history of this area." He looked too young to have experienced any of the history himself.

He stood frowning for a moment, suspicious of my first reaction, but I managed to calm him down. He had an aura of blue with some red and a little bit of white in it. He was a man who liked peace, sometimes liked excitement, and was trying very hard to follow a righteous path. I liked him.

Smiling, he came toward me and offered his hand to shake. "Christopher Frazier," he said, which startled me.

"As in Charles Frazier?"

He smiled, showing perfect teeth—someone had spent a lot of money on those
teeth. "Sounds to me as though you already
know quite a bit about our local history."

I couldn't help returning his smile. "Just
bits. I know some of the slaves from 13
Elms were sold to Charles Frazier and took
his name. I met Pappa Al."

Reverend Frazier smiled broadly. "Wonderful man is Pappa Al. But fierce. You
wouldn't believe the battles he's had to win
to keep his school open. He's had trouble
making people believe that his 'Leaders of
the World' as he calls them need help. But
you didn't come here to talk about the
school, did you, Miss . . . ?"

"Mrs. Nicodemus," I said, hating the
name. I loved my husband's name of Montgomery and wanted to tell everyone that I
shared it.

"What can I help you with?"

"There was a slave uprising in 1843, at 13
Elms, and a man named Martin was
hanged. I want to find his grave and anything about him that I can."

"Sorry, but he wasn't buried here. Until

the 1920s, this was an all-white cemetery. Did you check the graves at 13 Elms?"

"Yes," I said. While he was talking I looked at the spirit forms floating around behind him. They were shaking their heads no, that they knew no one named Martin.

Dead end, I thought, but then thought of something he'd said. "You said 'local' history. Isn't East Mesopotamia, Georgia, where Charles Frazier lived a little far away to be 'local'?"

"The Barristers and Fraziers married into each other's families long ago. I believe it was before the Civil War, but I'm not sure when or who married whom. If you're interested in the family history, you should ask Henry."

"Who is he?"

"He lives just through there. See that little white house?"

I could see nothing through the trees. As I looked, Reverend Frazier put his hand on my arm and pointed, showing me the corner of a house. Instantly, I felt things about him. He'd done something when he was a child, something he considered very bad. To atone for it, he'd dedicated himself to God.

"You should forgive yourself," I said before I thought.

He looked startled for a moment, then laughed. "You and Henry will get along very well. He worked at 13 Elms for over fifty years, and he loves to talk about all the ghosts and goblins there."

"Me, too," I said, backing toward the house as fast as I could go and not flat-out run. Behind the reverend, I saw the spirits holding out their arms to me, imploring me to come back and socialize with them.

"What is wrong with this place?" I muttered. "Why are the spirits around here so unsettled? Why don't they have peace?" As soon as the question came to me, I thought, Devlin! Whoever and whatever that creature was, I was sure he was the cause of the unrest around here. For a second I imagined my father finding Aladdin's lamp. Somehow, I'd stuff Devlin inside and I'd take him out only when I needed him. But needed him for what? What could he do except make walls telescope in and out?

Thinking of peace, I knew I'd reached it when I was within twenty feet of the white house. It was tiny, square, with a small porch on the front. The little yard was surrounded by a white picket fence so exactly like the one around the cemetery I knew the same person had built both of them.

In front of the house was a garden of fragrant flowers: roses, stocks, honeysuckle. All of it was beautifully kept, not a weed in sight.

Sitting on the porch in a swing painted dark blue was an old, old man, African-American, at least ninety, if not a hundred. He was very thin so that his clean but worn clothes hung on him. His old hands were on an ivory-topped cane and he was looking directly at me. Only he wasn't seeing me because I knew that the eyes behind his dark glasses were totally blind.

"You have a presence about you," he said in a beautiful voice. If you heard it alone, you'd think he was about thirty and full of health, but I knew this man wouldn't live for more than two years, if that. He was going to be missed by a lot of people.

His aura was the most beautiful blue I'd ever seen and it stretched out around him for nearly three feet. I'd never seen anything like it. More than anything on earth I wanted to sit down beside him so my own purple-blue aura would mingle with his.

"What's your name?" he asked as I walked toward him.

"Darci Nicodemus," I said.

"I wasn't expecting anyone named Nicodemus."

I couldn't help laughing. "Use Darci then. May I sit by you, Mr. . . . ?"

"Just Henry. I won't take the name of a white master so it's just Henry."

"All right, Just Henry, may I sit by you?"

He chuckled as I sat down on the swing beside him. I didn't touch him but I was close enough to that aura of his that I could feel it. I closed my eyes and breathed of it, as though I could suck that delicious blue into my soul.

"Are you an old woman or just an old soul?"

"I don't know much about myself," I said, but didn't add that I wasn't interested. One thing I already knew about this man was that I could tell him anything. I felt that he knew a lot of secrets about a lot of people, and he'd take those secrets to his grave. "I'm trying to find a little boy, but people say he doesn't exist. He's the descendant of a slave who was hanged because he fathered a baby on the white mistress of 13 Elms. I feel the child is around here but I can't find him."

"Nothing ever leaves this place," Henry said. "Give me your hand and sit closer to me."

"Gladly," I said as I scooted across the swing and gave him my left hand.

"You're just a little bitty thing, aren't you?" he said, feeling my hand in his much larger one. I felt that he knew he wouldn't live much longer and he was almost ready. There was something he still wanted to do on earth but I had no idea what it was. "And you've known hunger. Is it hunger for food or hunger for . . . Is it somebody you hunger for?"

"My husband is missing. If I solve things here I think it will help me find him. What do you see in my hand? I want to know everything."

He rubbed my hand, lacing his old fingers with mine. His hands were worn from years of work and I was fascinated with the two skin colors and how good they looked together. I bet Martin and Amelia had looked like that, I thought, and I bet their son had been as beautiful as Linc.

I could have sat like that all day. I could

feel Henry's powerful aura blending with mine, calming me. He was doing for me what I did for others.

"Better?" he said after a while, and I knew what he meant. Was I calmer and not so agitated?

"Yes, much better," I said, feeling truly relaxed for the first time since . . . since my husband had disappeared.

"Now tell me everything from the beginning," he said, and I began.

If anyone had seen us on that old swing, sitting close together, holding hands, they would have thought we were lovers. I wondered if allowing auras to merge and mingle rated as adultery.

I told Henry a great deal and he figured out more. He was an old-fashioned soothsayer, a person gifted with second sight. He told me he'd been blind for about fifteen years, since he'd retired from 13 Elms.

I had so much I wanted to ask him that I didn't know where to begin. He'd known Narcissa and Delphia since they were children. "Not much good in those two," he said, smiling, "but there's worse. They like money. I don't know what they want it for, but they want it."

"Can you see Linc's child? He's close to here but I don't know where he is."

"Someone doesn't want him to be found, and you don't yet have the power to break through the hold."

"Yet?!" I leaped on the word. "How do I get more power?"

Henry chuckled, holding my hand tightly in his. "That's one of those things that hasn't been decided yet. There's a test—"

"Test," I muttered. Again some test I'd have to go through.

I could tell that Henry wasn't going to say any more so I decided to talk of something else. "What do you know of Amelia and Martin?"

Henry loosened his grip on my hand. "Are you thirsty? One of the neighbors made me a big pitcher of lemonade. I wonder—"

I jumped up and practically ran into the house. The faster I got the lemonade, the faster I'd get to hear the story. Once I was inside I slowed down. The house was small, cozy, very clean and perfectly tidy. It had a bedroom and a bath on one side and the other half of the house was a pretty kitchen open to a nice living room. I opened the old refrigerator and took out a pitcher of lemonade, then opened a cabinet and got out two glasses.

I didn't need psychic abilities to see Henry's life. He was loved by people, but apparently he wasn't fed by them. In the refrigerator was a roast chicken nearly picked clean, three apples, and a nearly empty carton of milk. In a cabinet over the sink was a half-empty box of cereal.

I took the lemonade, two apples, and a dull paring knife outside and sat down by Henry. I peeled the apples and handed him slices, and he chewed while he talked.

Unlike Delphia and Narcissa, Henry had once been a great reader, and since he'd lived in a small room at the back of the 13 Elms for most of the years he'd worked there, he'd had time to read, as he said, "Everything that had printing on it that was in that house." He was the one to organize all the old slave bills of sale. Between old diaries, boxes of old letters, a couple of local histories, and Henry's second sight, he'd been able to piece the story together.

Edward Barrister, owner of A Hundred Elms, as it was known then, had met the older man, Charles Frazier, at a sporting club in New Orleans.

"Gambling or girls?" I asked.

"Gambling," Henry said. The men became friends and Frazier gave Barrister an introduction to his son's family in Ohio. He hoped that Edward would marry his granddaughter, Amelia.

"Did Mr. Frazier know what kind of plantation Barrister had?"

"I don't know, but I'm not sure it would have made any difference to him. He knew from his cronies that Edward Barrister was financially secure so he hoped for a match. And of course he wanted his granddaughter to move back to Alabama to be near him."

I knew a lot of the rest of the story. Amelia Frazier had married Edward and gone to his slave breeding plantation in Alabama—and been sickened. Lonely, miserable, with her husband spending most of his evenings in the slave cabins, she'd fallen in love with the beautiful slave Martin and borne him a child.

What had happened to that child hit me. "Edward Barrister sold the child to his own grandfather," I said, aghast.

"Yes," Henry answered. "Barrister was angry that Charles Frazier had introduced him to a woman who'd go to bed with a darkie, so—"

"But Barrister was impregnating all of the slave women!"

Henry smiled. "The ultimate double standard."

I was quiet for a moment, cutting apple slices for Henry. "Do you know what happened to the child Jedediah?"

Henry smiled. "The plan backfired on Barrister because Charles Frazier, for all that he, too, bought and sold humans, wasn't full of hatred. He soon saw the child's intelligence and took him into the house. Frazier's youngest grandchild lived with him, a boy about Jed's age, so he had the children tutored together, a not uncommon practice in those days. When Jed grew to be a man he ran all the Frazier properties—and continued to run them after he was freed by the Emancipation Proclamation. Because of Jed's excellent management through very hard times, the Fraziers owned that land until they sold it in the 1920s."

"Jedediah should have inherited all of it," I said. "He was Charles Frazier's grandson."

I looked at Henry. "Did Frazier ever find out what happened to his granddaughter?"

"I'm sure he must have known. Gossip about a woman locked away in a room would have reached him. Between you and me, I think Frazier well knew who Jedediah was and bought him on purpose. He couldn't save his granddaughter because back then no one interfered between a husband and wife. Frazier must have known what a devil of a man he'd introduced his granddaughter to by then, so maybe Frazier allowed Barrister to think he was tricking him into buying his own half-white grandson.

"I like to think there was kindness behind Frazier educating the child and allowing him to manage the place."

I, too, liked to think the child born into such horror was, in the end, treated well.

"What do you think this child of Linc's has inherited?" I asked.

"Intelligence and his grandmother's power to heal."

Henry answered so quickly that I looked at him hard. I did my best to send him the message that he was to tell me everything he knew.

"You do have some power, don't you, child? Now stop that or you'll make my head ache. If you want to know what I know, all you have to do is ask."

"Sorry," I said, blinking, surprised but pleased that he knew what I could do, what I was doing. I decided there was a great deal more to this man than I originally thought. He was more than just a fortune-teller with a magnificent aura. "Would you please tell me what you know? Everything about everything?"

Henry talked; he loved to talk, but he told me little. As gently as I could, I tried to True Persuade him into talking about what I wanted to hear, but twice he told me to stop, and I marveled at his perception. He told me about his life at 13 Elms, and just when I was suppressing yawns, he started telling me about his second sight, so I perked up. I was always interested in hearing of other people's "special abilities." Since my own childhood had been so lonely, I thought maybe I should start a club, or at the very least a website. Was "weirdpeople.com" taken?

Henry could tell people's fortunes, which was something I couldn't do. Sometimes I

could see the future of a person, but it
mainly had to do with auras that were ab-
sent, weak, or missing pieces. I couldn't do
what Henry could and look at someone and
tell them they were going to meet a man
and find riches or some such.

". . . together," Henry said, then waited
for my reply.

I hadn't been listening carefully. "I,
uh . . ."

Henry smiled. "I was saying that you and
I have very different powers and wouldn't it
be nice to be able to merge them."

"Would it help me find my husband?"

"It would help you rule the world."

"That is *not* something I want to do," I
said emphatically. "Who is Devlin?"

Henry didn't answer right away and his
aura began to change shade; it began to
darken. I had no idea what that meant. People's auras change all the time, but it's always a superficial change. An angry person
with a red aura can take pills and relax and
a lot of blue comes into their aura, but the
foundation of it is still red. But I'd never
seen an aura darken as Henry's was doing.

After what seemed like a lot of time, he

said, "Devlin came to earth to accomplish a task."

I couldn't tell if he was lying or just leaving out masses of information. I decided that he was leaving out nearly everything, and he didn't want me to know what or why. I remembered that Devlin said he'd been around my daughter and my niece.

"What does Devlin have to do with me and how do I get the power to hold him in a room and how do I break into that crystal ball and remove what's in it and what and where is the Touch of God?"

All that made Henry laugh and when he did, his aura went back to that heavenly blue, and I must have pleased him because the size of his aura increased. By nature I wasn't an envious person but I envied Henry that big, beautiful aura.

"Ah," he said at last, "wouldn't it be wonderful if the little power I have could merge with what you have? I can see people's past and future, but you could change what I see."

I thought about that. What an interesting concept. "I could foresee that someone was about to get into a car and the car would crash, so I'd make the person stay home."

"Then they'd slip in the bathtub and die. No, I mean on a larger scale. Think big."

"The twin towers?" I asked, looking out at the garden and remembering that dreadful day.

"If you'd been able to see that that was going to happen, then you'd have been able to see what has come out of it and what will come out of it. You would have had to decide if you should stop it or not."

I wasn't sure, but I think he was telling me that he'd foreseen all of it. He'd foreseen what would happen and the results of all those deaths—and he'd decided to do nothing about it.

"No," I said. "I wouldn't want that much power. To have to make a decision like that . . . No, thank you."

Henry didn't answer and I wondered what he was seeing. Was he seeing that I was lying? Recently I'd thought that I'd do something for the devil if it would get my husband and sister-in-law back. But here I was saying I didn't want the ability to see the future and be able to change it.

I put my hand in his. "Will I find my husband?"

"You do know that this is all about you, don't you? It's not about your husband, but you."

I took my hand away and leaned back against the swing, no longer touching his aura. "Please tell me that the witch in Connecticut isn't still alive and that she's the one who's taken my husband. Tell me her spirit isn't still out there and she's still trying to get me so she can gain immortality."

Henry smiled. "Oh no, she's dead. She was of no importance, except to bring your powers to the surface. You couldn't very well have stayed in that little town in Kentucky forever and just worked on patching rocky marriages, now could you? You have bigger things to do."

I wasn't even startled that he knew so much about me when I'd told him little. Part of me wanted to say, "All I want is to take care of my husband and children," then flounce away dramatically, but I couldn't. If Adam hadn't been taken from me I would have been content to spend the rest of my life helping the FBI and traveling here and there to exorcize a few mean spirits. Was someone somewhere demanding more of me?

I pulled my knees up to my chest and wrapped my arms around my legs. I did what I could to pull my aura in so it wasn't touching Henry's. "If all that with the witch was about me, is the search for Linc's child about me, too?"

"Yes," he said softly.

"Test," I said, hating the word. I didn't want to be the cause of bad things happening to nice people. If someone wanted my power I'd give it to them, I thought. Just let me put my family back together.

Henry removed his dark glasses and turned to look at me. His eyes were sightless, but at the same time I felt that they saw everything. "Darci, we do not choose what we're given. No one would choose to have a birth defect, choose to lose a limb. All of these things are chosen for us and they're given to us for a reason."

As I looked into his old eyes, chills ran up my spine. My entire body broke into goose bumps. What he was saying was nothing I hadn't heard before and thought about many times. What was upsetting me was that I knew he'd voluntarily given up his sight. His blindness had not been caused by an illness or an accident. He had *chosen* to become blind.

"Why?" I whispered, knowing he'd understand my meaning.

"We all do what we need to," he said, giving me one of those nonanswers.

He turned away, put his dark glasses back on, and was silent.

What was *I* willing to sacrifice? he seemed to be asking me. I wanted to scream that I didn't want to give up anything. I wanted it *all.* I wanted my husband, my father, my sister-in-law, the two children. I wanted my beautiful house in Virginia. I wanted my beautiful *life.*

"We cannot choose," Henry said.

His words were a key that unlocked something inside me. I began to tell him how horrible my life had been since Adam had disappeared.

"There's something eating at you," he said, "gnawing away at your soul. You want to hide from it. Why?"

"That's because . . ." I didn't want to think about the injustice in my life, of what I'd been accused. "Have you heard of the

Hillbilly Honey?" I whispered, nearly choking on the name.

"I want you to tell me."

I did. It was difficult at first but, gradually,
I began to tell all of it. I told how I'd been
laughed at all over the world, then it had
been hinted that I'd had something to do
with my husband's disappearance. I told
him that I was a prisoner in my own house
and even my children had needed to be
sent away. At 13 Elms I'd had to work on
the guests to keep them from recognizing
me.

"Why do you want to find your husband?" he asked.

I wanted to say something sarcastic to
that, but I realized Henry was asking me
something besides the obvious. "Oh, you
mean, do I want him back so I can hide behind him?"

Henry nodded and I thought about what
he meant. For the year after my husband's
disappearance I'd hidden myself away
completely. Adam's friend from the FBI had
brought unsolved cases to me, but I'd ex-
pended little energy on them. My father had
encouraged me to seek out some haunted
houses, but I could never work up the en-

ergy to fight the reporters and the people who wanted to spit on me, so I'd stayed at home and hidden.

"You'll never accomplish anything with so much hate in your heart," Henry said.

I wanted to protest that I didn't have a heart full of hate, but I knew I did. When I looked into a mirror I could see my own aura and I could see little black flecks in it— and they were increasing. It was as though someone had used a shotgun on my aura and there were poisonous lead pellets in it.

I took a deep breath and pulled my legs tighter to my chest. "Henry, I want you to tell me my future."

He took a long time to answer. "Most people come to me, give me five dollars, and I tell them what they want to hear. She doesn't want to know her husband is cheating on her and that in eighteen months she'll be working two jobs and raising three kids by herself, while he's in another state having a great time. He doesn't want to know that two of their kids aren't his."

"Sex," I muttered. "It seems like the whole world has been reduced to sex."

"Darci, honey," Henry said in a slow

drawl, "far as I can tell, except for you and me, everybody's gettin' some."

He made me laugh so hard I forgot about my morbid thoughts—and I realized he was going to tell me nothing. I also realized that I wasn't sure he *could* see my future. I'd always been weird to so-called normal people, so I guess I was even weird to a fortune-teller.

When I saw Henry's aura begin to fade, I knew he was tired. It was time for me to leave. I stood up. "Could you at least tell me the time and place that Amelia and Martin used to meet?"

When he smiled at that, he knew I was acknowledging that he hadn't answered any of my questions.

"Twilight," he said. "Every night at twilight for over a hundred years, Amelia's spirit has gone to the big double-trunked elm by the river and waited for Martin. It's the tree where Martin was hanged and where his body is buried."

"Does his spirit meet hers?"

"No. Never. After his death, Martin stayed with their son. When he saw that the boy would be protected by his white grandfather, Martin's spirit left the earth."

"Poor woman," I said. "All those years of waiting for a man she'll never see again."

"Yes. Circumstances made Amelia a prisoner, but her death released her. She should have been free, but she chose to continue to be a prisoner."

"Subtlety is not your strong point, Just Henry," I said. He'd been comparing me to Amelia. I was choosing to imprison myself and maybe I was waiting for a man who'd never return.

Henry smiled but said nothing.

"May I kiss you?" I asked.

"Could I choose the body part?" he shot back.

"You dirty old man," I said, then kissed his forehead.

He put his hands on my cheeks and held my face in his palms. "Darci, you have been given a great gift, but you're not using it. The hate and anger inside you is becoming stronger than your gift. I've seen that you can use your mind to kill people. Now you're turning your powers inward. You're killing yourself."

I knew that what he was saying was true, and, in milder forms, I'd even thought what he was saying—but I didn't want to hear it out loud. I didn't know how to change my longing for my husband, and didn't know how to vanquish the hatred I felt at what had been done to me. If the media hadn't accused me of such horrible—and untrue— things I would have had the comfort of my daughter and niece even if my husband was missing.

Henry removed his hands from my face. "Hate is eating you up. I pity any witch or demon that gets near you now."

"I'd like to put that Devlin in a cage and make him answer my questions."

"Would I get a separate cage or the same one?"

"Separate," I shot back, wishing I could make him tell me what he knew. But I knew it was hopeless to try, so I said good-bye and walked back to the church. The spirits were there in force and they were calling to me to come and talk to them, but I kept walking. The pastor was nowhere in sight as I got into the rental car and pulled back onto the main road.

I was hungry so I stopped at a country restaurant. I loved the sound of the slam of the old screen door when I entered. It was a house that looked like most of the downstairs had been converted into a dining room. There was a swinging door that led into a kitchen but I could feel that a lot of the cooking was done outside on an old grill. I knew that upstairs were bedrooms and the living quarters of the woman who owned the place. There was a window into the kitchen and I could see a tall, stately black woman busy over her pots and pans. I could feel that she loved to cook but worried that she was going to have to close her little restaurant because she didn't have enough business. Had this been the woman Henry mentioned? The one who ended up having to support three kids alone? If so, had Henry directed me here? Had he concealed power as well as answers from me?

The young waitress (the owner's oldest daughter) came and I ordered chicken and dumplings, collards and glazed carrots. The order came minutes later and included two thick, fluffy biscuits and homemade applesauce.

As I ate, I looked about the place, at the other diners, all African-Americans, and I thought about Henry's nearly empty refrigerator. After I'd had some pecan pie, I paid, went outside, and walked around to the back of the house. As I'd willed her to be, the owner of the restaurant was sitting quietly and breaking green beans.

Quickly, I told her that I wanted to arrange for her to deliver three hot meals a day to Henry. As I'd assumed, she knew who I meant when I gave the single name "Henry."

To my surprise, she hesitated. I could see her aura (a nice green) leap up in flames so I knew she wanted the business. So why wasn't she talking money? Making a deal?

Instead, she was talking to me about the difficulty of transporting the food and keeping it hot.

"So buy some of those food warmer carriers," I said. "Like the pizza delivery guy uses. I'll pay for them."

"Maybe," she said, not looking up from her bowl of beans. "But it might be nice to cook the food there, at Henry's house."

I was trying to figure out what she wanted from me. To buy Henry a good set of pots and pans? Or did she want to close her restaurant and go cook for Henry? While I was thinking, the back door opened and a short, plump woman came out. She had an angry face, an angry aura, an angry voice.

"Onthelia," she said, ignoring me. "Today's biscuits were inedible, burned on the bottom and raw on the top. I cooked better biscuits when I was eight years old. And those—"

I concentrated so hard, my eyes started watering. Go away! I told her, and she did. She stopped her tirade mid-sentence and went back into the kitchen.

Onthelia looked at me as though she were drilling something into my head. "My mother-in-law. My husband ran off two years ago and left me with three kids and his mother. We would have been out on the street except for her. Her temper can curdle butter, but she is a great cook." Her brown eyes burned into mine. *"Great cook,"* she repeated, to make sure I got her meaning.

I thought about all my questions Henry had refused to answer. I felt a deep kinship with the man, but at the same time I wanted to scream because he hadn't confided in me. "How about five hundred a week plus groceries? Think your mother-in-law could put in a little vegetable garden at Henry's house?"

Onthelia nodded toward four large paper bags near my chair. I'd been concentrating so hard that I hadn't noticed them. They were all full of green beans. Hundreds of green beans. Maybe thousands.

"That's today's pick from my mother-in-law's garden."

Onthelia and I looked at each other and smiled in understanding.

"She's hired," I said.

"You ever need *anything*," she said, "you let me know," and we both laughed. She was getting rid of her bossy mother-in-law and I was getting someone to take care of Henry. Heaven knew the Montgomery family could afford five hundred a week for the short time that Henry had to live.

After we worked out the financial details, I called Adam's accountant and told him to send a check every month to Onthelia. I guessed she was going to tell her mother-in-law the salary was four hundred and fifty a week and keep fifty for her children. If she'd had to put up with that termagant for even a month, she deserved the money.

Onthelia and I shook hands on the deal and I left. When I was in the car I looked at myself in the sun visor mirror. I don't know what I'd been hoping: That one act of kindness would have taken the hatred out of me?

No, my aura hadn't changed. I'd had an adventurous afternoon, I'd received a message from a tree, been attacked by a bunch of lonely ghosts, and had met a man who was a kindred soul.

However, I didn't feel I was a millimeter closer to finding Linc's son.

Sighing, I drove back to 13 Elms to see if Linc had found out anything. As I drove, I thought of Onthelia's wonderful meal. Didn't I remember that Adam had said something about the Montgomerys and Taggerts opening a business in the South? Maybe this evening I'd give Michael Taggert a call and see if he knew of anyone anywhere who needed a cook.

LINC ⟨⟩

⟨⟩ *Chapter Sixteen*

Okay, so it was my ego. Ingrid and I had spent a night together, then I'd heard nothing from her. Except for Alanna—who often treated me like dirt so I was sure it was true love, ha ha—most women with whom I'd spent the night called me later. But Ingrid hadn't so much as spoken to me during, much less afterward.

When I went to the workout room, all six female guests followed me. It was a joke as a gym. The biggest dumbbells were fifteen pounds and only seventy-five pounds on the leg extension machine. I ended up doing donkey calf raises with Mrs. Hemmings sitting on my hips. After that all the women wanted attention so I ended up doing just what I swore I wouldn't do: be a personal trainer to the lot of them.

Somewhere in there I realized that Darci had set me up. She'd used her voodoo-witchcraft, whatever it was that she had, to get me out of her hair for the entire after-noon. I escaped from five-pound "beauty bells" (they were pink!) to look out the win-dow. Sure enough, the rental car was gone. *Our* rental car, the one *we* were supposed to go places in together.

Try as I might, I couldn't seem to break the spell Darci had put on me, so I stayed in the gym with the women until four P.M. I guess that's when Darci thought she'd re-turn because, all of a sudden, the women said they had to leave, and seconds later all the giggling stopped and I was alone in the room. I looked at the clock. Exactly four P.M. What had she done? Said I was to be re-leased from prison at four?

I pulled on my sweat suit over my skimpy workout clothes—yes, I'm guilty of "show-ing off"—and decided to search for Ingrid. It took three minutes before I was told that she'd left the grounds, luggage and all. One of the solemn-faced housekeepers told me. The woman acted as though each word she spoke would be deducted from her pay. She'd met me on my way up the stairs to the attic, and I could see that she meant to stay there until I went back to the slave quarters where I belonged.

With a warm smile—which had no effect on the woman—I went back down the stairs to step behind a potted palm out of her sight. I waited an entire three minutes, then headed back toward the stairs. When I got to the foot of the stairs I saw the house-keeper's cart. I couldn't believe what I was seeing, but there on the top was a set of keys. I could see the housekeeper inside a guest room, her back to me. I picked up the keys and glanced at them. It was a big ring with five little rings on it, one of the small rings labeled "attic." Crouching down so she wouldn't see me if she turned around, I removed the small ring of keys, then sprinted up the stairs.

That's one on Darci, I thought. Maybe when she returned from doing whatever she'd been doing for half the day, she wouldn't be the only one with news.

As quietly as I could, one by one, I opened all five doors on the attic floor. For the most part, the rooms were empty. One stored towels, sheets and bars of soap. I was glad to see I was no longer attracted to the lavender sachets.

I went to Ingrid's room last. I don't know what I was hoping for, that maybe she and her long, lean body were waiting for me in the bed? Slowly, I opened the door, but the bed had been made, and all traces of an occupant removed.

I knew I should leave the room. I needed to take a shower and I had to get ready for yet another dreary dinner, but instead, I walked to the window and looked out. The truth was, I was ready to quit this whole thing. Darci and I weren't making any progress in finding my son and, as interesting as meeting a bunch of ghosts was, my son was my main interest. Maybe hiring a PI would be better, I thought.

All in all, I was getting so frustrated I didn't want to continue. I thought about what I'd say to Darci tonight. It was great to have worked with her and I'd always love her for having helped me find my grandfather, but I needed to go back to L.A. and see if I could scare up some work. Maybe I could do some guest shots or—

I stopped my train of thought because I

saw a reflection in the glass. I was seeing something shiny catch the faded sunlight. Turning, I looked at the bed and saw nothing. I looked back at the glass and there it was again. Looking in the reflection, I counted rows of stripes on the bedspread, then I turned around, went to the bed and counted.

Being able to see the object in the reflection in the glass but not able to see it when I looked at it would have been something that, usually, I would have considered weird. But what was strange, eerie, and even frightening had changed for me in the last days. Truthfully, I didn't want to question how this object was being shown for fear I'd find out.

I moved the bedspread aside and there, caught between the fringe and a bedpost, was a little John Deere tractor. I'd had one just like it when I was a kid, given to me by a teacher as a reward for reading the most books. My parents had said it was a stupid award, with no educational value at all. It was the only toy I had that didn't try to teach me something. As a result, that little tractor had been my absolute favorite toy.

I didn't want to delve into the who of that

toy, as in who had snooped into my past to find out about my favorite toy. I just wanted to take it at face value. Someone—or some*thing*—was trying to give me a message.

I went to the window, the one I'd climbed through to get to Ingrid, and examined it. The window had been freshly painted, but I could still see the patched holes in the top and bottom. There were half-inch round holes spaced every four inches, and I knew they were holes from bars that had once been on it. This room had, until recently, had bars on the window.

I spent the next half hour examining the room but I found nothing else. Finally, I sat down on the window seat and looked at the tractor. Someone was trying to tell me something—and I knew what it was. Someone was reminding me that the child was real. He wasn't just "my son," just a couple of words. He was a real little boy. He had thoughts of his own and ambitions of his own, and he liked and disliked things in a way that was unique to him.

I ran my fingers over the little tractor and for a moment wished I were like Darci and could feel things. Had my son left the tractor wedged in the side of the bed in the hope that it would be found? By me? By his father? Did he know about me? Had his mother told him about me? Did he watch my TV show?

For a moment I smiled. I was a throwback to my grandfather, a grandstander if there ever was one. I imagined I was also like the slave Martin, who was so hot for a beautiful white woman that he loved her even though he knew what the consequence would be if he were caught.

If I was like my grandfather, maybe my son was like his grandfather, which would mean the child never got his nose out of a book. If I presented a child like that to my parents, would I at last please them? Wouldn't that be an irony? I thought.

Holding the tractor, I left the room, locked the door, and headed back downstairs. I put the ring of keys on the corner of the runner down the hall, as though it'd fallen and been caught.

I had about thirty minutes to shower, shave, and get ready for dinner. As I was rounding the corner, I saw two women heading toward me. It was Mrs. Hemmings, who was now in love with me after the donkey raises, and Sylvia Murchinson. She was older but extremely well-preserved. She was nice enough to me but she had a catty streak that made me want to run from her. I'd seen her do an impression of Narcissa that made me want to defend the woman. However, at the time, I'd been under Darci's spell of emasculation and I'd said, "Now, girls, pull your claws in." Sylvia, as she insisted everyone call her, had turned on me with a look that nearly singed my hair. If this weren't the twenty-first century I'm sure she would have made a racist remark. If it had been the nineteenth century, I thought she might have ordered me hanged—or at least sold.

I looked around for an escape route so the women wouldn't see me. At the end of the hall, near the big window seat, was a narrow door. Thankfully, it was unlocked and I stepped inside, practically right into a bucketful of dirty water with an even dirtier mop. With any luck, I thought, they'd go to their rooms, then I'd be free to leave the closet.

"Let's wait here for them," I heard Sylvia say. There was an open transom over the door and they must have sat down on the window seat.

I said a few curse words. I was trapped, with no escape route except past them. There was no dignified way I could explain why I'd been hiding inside a cleaning closet.

"That's her room, isn't it?" I heard Mrs. Hemmings say, and I knew she was talking about Darci. I no longer wanted to get out. I wanted to hear every word the women were about to say.

"Who *are* they?" Mrs. Hemmings asked. "Jason is the most beautiful creature on earth but he's the world's worst masseur. And according to Ingrid he's far, far from being gay."

"Didn't you know?" Sylvia said. "They're ghost hunters."

"They're what?"

"That's what Delphi thinks they are. She thinks they're writing a book about the ghosts in the area, but they don't want anyone to know about it, so they snoop around and think no one knows what they're up to. They used to get a lot of people like them here at 13 Elms."

"Are you saying they're reporters?
They're the last people we need here now."

"Don't worry. They're not interested in us.
They spend all their time in the slave cemetery and in the Quarters. And Delphi's sure
they're the ones who stole the papers from
the basement."

"She should call the police, or— Oh.
Right. No police."

"Delphi said they were just a bunch of,
rotting old papers worth nothing so it didn't
really matter. Anyway, as soon as they collect for this week, they're planning to sell
this place."

"But I thought—"

"That their ancestors were everything?
You can't heat this house, or cool it, and a
room upstairs has a ghost in it."

"There's no such thing as—"

"If you don't believe me, go have a look.
I'm sure Narcissa will give you the key. For
what you're paying, surely she won't charge
you to see the room of the infamous
Amelia."

"She's the ghost who's supposed to live
upstairs?"

"You don't know about this? Oh, but
that's right, this is your first time here. When

Delphi and Narcissa started, they tried to compete with other spas around the country but couldn't, so they decided to capitalize on their family ghost. They printed a brochure that told all about the woman who still inhabits an upstairs bedroom, and they said Delphia had a spirit guide, some half-naked Native American man. That's when they began to prohibit men and sex. Delphia wanted the women to lust after her phony spirit guide. Unfortunately, the brochure attracted a lot of freaks, and they still get them from time to time. That's why those two are here. They couldn't really turn them away for fear— Well, you know."

"Yes, I know. So tell me about the ghost."

"Back before the Civil War, an ancestor of Delphi and Narcissa did something to make her husband so angry he locked her in her bedroom. He didn't allow her out until they carried her to her grave, which was some forty years later. Delphi said that the reason this house survived the war is because Yankee soldiers heard her crying and thought she was already a ghost."

"Poor thing," Mrs. Hemmings said. "And her spirit is said to haunt the room?"

"Actually, there are two ghosts in the

room, the woman and a slave girl named Penny, who was incarcerated with the wife. The slave was paid by the master to report on everything his wife did—as if she could do anything while locked up. The two women hated each other, but lived together in one room for over forty years, although Narcissa said the slave girl could come and go to get food and empty the slop jar, that sort of thing.

"Narcissa says the woman and the slave girl are still in that room. I've not seen any ghosts, but I've seen the room and it's eerie. It's exactly the way it was in the 1800s when the man locked his wife inside. I mean exactly. Things in that room might be over a hundred years old but they look brand new. Narcissa said no one ever cleans in there but it's always spotless. 'Penny was an immaculate housekeeper,' " Sylvia said, sounding exactly like Narcissa.

"That poor, poor woman. Whatever is her spirit waiting for—if she does exist, that is? Why doesn't she . . . you know, go away?"

"Narcissa said Amelia's waiting for her dead child to come back to her."

"What?!"

"It seems that when her husband put her

inside the room she was pregnant and when the baby was born, it died. It's everyone's guess that the child wasn't the husband's. Considering the day and age, I guess it's good the kid didn't live."

"Truly awful."

"And what you're here for is less 'awful'?" Sylvia said.

"What I'm here for is justice. When that . . . that woman took my husband, she took everything I had in the world."

"Except the money."

"That was mine to begin with, and Daddy had made sure it was protected. This is about justice, not money."

"And you think your ex-husband will come back to you once his new wife is out of the way?"

"Of course he will. What's that look for?"

"I was just thinking that I've never been as young as you."

"Actually, I think I may be older than you are."

"I didn't mean literally." Sylvia laughed. "Let's go downstairs and see what's for dinner. If tonight is as bad as last night, let's go to a restaurant."

"Wait! What about you? What do you want from . . . from what he'll do?"

"Money. Just plain, old-fashioned money. If my rich old husband dies before the divorce is final, I get mega millions. If he's alive when it's final, I don't get a penny."

"That's not fair. You need a good lawyer. I can—"

"I signed a prenup. Had to to get him to marry me, but he was so old and unhealthy I thought he'd die in a year. He smokes three packs a day, drinks a bottle of whiskey, and has spent his life in a rage, but I've had to live with him for ten miserable years. What I can't understand is why he didn't die of a heart attack when he caught me in bed with the pool boy."

Mrs. Hemmings laughed. "You're awful. Come on, let's go."

I stayed in the closet for several minutes after the women left. It smelled bad in there and I was concerned that the other women would start coming upstairs, but I couldn't seem to move.

There was one sentence of what the women had said that screamed in my head: "What do you want from what he'll do?" Maybe I'd been around Darci for so long that I was beginning to feel things more than use my brain, but my heart knew that that sentence was about my son. I was clutching the little tractor in my hand so tightly my fingers were numb.

Suddenly, the door was flung open and there was Darci. "What in the world are you doing hiding in a broom closet?" she asked. "And what are you so happy about?"

"He's here," I said. "I know it."

DARCI ❧

❧ *Chapter Seventeen*

"I want to hear every word," I said as I
leaned against the wall. Linc was in the
shower in the men's bathroom down the
hall from his room. The door was open so
we could hear each other, and I did everything in my power to not think of his naked
body. I made a vow that if I ever helped
anyone else it would be a woman or a man
as old as Henry.

After I'd rescued Linc from his hiding
place in the cleaning closet (mists of his
aura had been drifting out through the transom) we'd gone back to the Quarters to
talk. We had just minutes before dinner so I
wanted to hear whatever it was he was so
excited about.

He'd asked me about my day, but I didn't

tell him about meeting Henry. I hadn't sorted that out in my own mind yet, so I could tell him nothing. To distract him, I told him about Amelia's nightly wait for Martin—who never came. And he told me that the women had said that Amelia was waiting for her child, so I told Linc what Henry had said happened to Martin's spirit, but I didn't tell where I got the information. I felt Linc's sadness at all of it, but like me, he knew love knew no color, race, or religion.

"We'll be there to meet her tonight," Linc said, and I agreed, but I cautioned him that he had to do what I said. I'd know what Amelia wanted.

"So tell me what you overheard from Sylvia and Mrs. Hemmings."

"Sylvia says Delphia and Narcissa think you're a spy," he said, then told me what he'd overheard the women say.

I smiled and silently congratulated myself. I'd done a good job of directing everyone away from the truth of what I wanted. "Promise you'll do what I say or I'll make sure Amelia isn't there tonight," I said to Linc.

"If she's been showing up at that tree for

a hundred plus years, how will you stop her?"

"I have ways. I need your promise. I don't want tonight messed up. No playing that I'm the slave she hates. Tell Amelia I'm your friend and must stay with you."

He promised he'd behave himself. Of course I wouldn't do anything like send Amelia away, but I didn't want Linc to know that. I just wanted to find out all we could from her, and when it came to ghosts, I had much more experience than he had.

Once we'd settled it between us about Amelia, he thrust a toy tractor into my hand and I became nearly as excited as Linc. Yes, it was his son's and yes it had been put there on purpose. Linc thought his son had put the toy in the room, but I knew this was the work of Devlin. The spirit wouldn't tell me outright where the boy was, but it looked as though he was going to eventually lead us to the child.

Under normal circumstances, if I'd held something owned by a person, I could have told where he was, but Devlin had put only what he wanted me to know in that toy. The child was well, was being taken care of, and he was being . . .

I rubbed the toy and tried to figure out what I was seeing. Stubborn. The child was being stubborn.

Stubborn about what? I wondered.

All that was important was that I knew Devlin was helping—slowly and in his own way, but he was helping. I had no doubt that Devlin had arranged for Linc to over-hear the women, and the spirit had made the women talk while sitting in the hallway near an open transom.

"Someone wanted me to meet Henry," I said.

"Did you say something?" Linc asked as he turned off the water.

"Just thinking out loud."

"So what do you think?" he asked. "Do you think the women were referring to my son?" He was standing in the bathroom door with only a white towel around his middle.

I was very glad he couldn't see auras because I'm sure mine must have looked like a fireworks explosion. It was a cliché but he looked better in person than on screen.

Able to see auras or not, he knew what the sight of his beautiful body did to

women. "How about a quickie before dinner?" he said, leering at me.

I laughed and that dispelled what could
have been an awkward moment between
us. Turning, I went down the hall to his bedroom. "Yes, I think they were talking about
your son. But I can't figure out what power
he has that these women want. Your grandmother was a healer but these women
seem to want someone killed. It doesn't
make sense."

Linc was pulling clothes out of a chest of
drawers. "Isn't it all the same?" he asked.
"Give sickness, take away sickness. Same
coin; two sides."

He'd said the words while holding socks
up to the light, but when he said it, we
knew. He looked at me and I looked at him,
and we knew.

Yes, the child could heal, but as Linc had
said, the opposite side of the coin was to
give sickness. Pappa Al had told us that he
and his wife had been offered a lot of
money to make rich people well. How much
more would they pay to make someone ill—
ill until they'd died?

Linc stood there in just his towel, holding

his socks aloft, one navy and one black, and stared at me. "No hit man," he said softly. "Nothing that could be traced back to them. No danger of being caught."

"Mrs. Hemmings wants her ex-husband's new wife dead so he'll return to her and Daddy's money."

"Sylvia wants her rich old husband to die before the divorce is final," he said.

"But your son is stubbornly holding out so the women are—"

"Waiting," Linc finished. "They're killing time by getting daily massages from the 'world's worst masseur,' and they're pretending to believe in fortune-telling done with a crystal ball someone found in the basement."

"Which just happens to hold something very powerful."

"But only you are weird enough to know that. Sorry. No offense."

"None taken." I began to pace the room, thinking about it all, seeing how it all made sense. "Maybe the child is being protected by Devlin," I said. "I don't think the boy has the power to block me from finding him, but maybe Devlin does."

"Who is he anyway?" Linc asked, stepping behind the closet door to get dressed. "And don't tell me that he's anybody he wants to be."

"I don't know," I said, putting my fists to my temples. "So much information is going round and round inside my head. Or maybe no information is in my head. Who started all this? Who told you your son was missing in the first place? I think you were given the note while you were near my mother so she'd see it and ask me to help you. From the beginning someone has wanted *me* involved in this. Was someone waiting for something to happen to pull me into this, or was your son kidnapped to make me come here?"

"If someone wanted you all he'd have had to do was call you and say, 'I have information about your husband.' "

I sat down on the edge of the bed. "That's true," I said.

Linc sat on the chair and began pulling on his socks. "So tell me, are we any closer to finding my son than we were ten minutes ago?"

I shook my head. "Not as far as I can tell."

I held up the little tractor. "He's safe. I can feel that. He's not in danger except—"

"Except for what?"

"Loneliness." I looked at Linc as understanding came to me. "They've taken his mother from him and they're telling him that if he doesn't do what they want, his mother will be killed—like the woman in the newspaper was." I stood up as I began to see things. "The woman who was in the car was a hitchhiker, a runaway. It was made to look like Lisa Henderson died so the child would have no legal guardian. The mother wasn't killed because they needed something to threaten him with. 'If you don't do what we want, your mother really will be killed,' that sort of thing."

"Who are 'they'?"

I stopped moving. "I don't know. Something powerful is blocking me from knowing. I thought it was the child but—"

"Whoa," Linc said. "The kid can heal and that's all. That's bad enough. I don't want him to be some little freak with so-called powers."

I opened my mouth to bawl Linc out. I'd been a child with power, and my daughter and niece were children of power. I took a deep, slow breath. Because of my abilities, I'd had a childhood of extreme isolation and loneliness, and my children had to be isolated from other children. Unfortunately, what Linc was saying was right.

"I don't think your son has enough power to be called a freak," I said, rubbing the tractor hard. "In fact I'm not sure he can do what it's believed he can do. I think these women will be charged millions of dollars, and if the people they want dead don't die, what can they do? Go to the police? Report the scam? They can't very well say they paid a child to kill someone."

Linc finished tying his shoes and stood up. He was wearing taupe cotton trousers and a loose-knit taupe sweater that molded itself over his pecs. It was Adam's sweater.

"Stop looking at me like that," Linc ordered, "and let's go to dinner."

As we walked together, he took my arm in his. "Quit thinking so hard. You know, today I was ready to give up on all this, but I think there's hope now."

I didn't feel optimistic. In fact, I was feeling like an idiot. Maybe I'd been spoiled in my life because it'd always been easy for me to figure things out. There weren't too many mysteries to me. I could feel a photo and tell whether the person was dead or alive, and I could usually tell where the person was. "Right now he's taking a shower with a woman who used to work for him," I'd once told my husband's FBI friend. They couldn't find the man but they easily found his former secretary—and he was with her.

But this little boy had me stumped. I knew it was for a reason and I knew that some "force" was doing it, but I didn't know who or why. I was sure that Henry and Devlin knew a great deal, but they weren't telling.

"Test." The word rolled round and round in my head. What test? When? Who was doing the testing? And, most of all, when it came, would I pass?

"Should I take Mrs. Hemmings?" Linc asked, meaning he'd sit by her at dinner and question her.

But he sounded so serious and so much like his detective alter ego that I couldn't help teasing him. *"Can* you take her? Are you big enough?"

Linc didn't smile. "Actually, I don't think I am."

I laughed and we entered the house smiling.

I didn't know the six women guests as well as Linc did. In fact, I had unwisely dismissed them as of little consequence. I'd seen that they were a cold, heartless lot, but I think I'd stereotyped them and left it at that. They were women with too much money and too much time and nothing to do with their lives.

As I took my place next to Sylvia at the table, I looked at the women anew. Each of them hated someone enough to pay a child to give that person a fatal illness.

I looked at Mrs. Hemmings down the table. It was easy to see that she'd once been pretty, but she wasn't anymore. She'd had too soft a life and it showed in her eyes and body. Her husband probably left her because he'd grown tired of her sense of entitlement. "Of course I should have anything I want," I could almost hear her say. "My daddy protects me."

Beside me was Sylvia Murchinson and of the women, I disliked her the most. Whereas the auras of the other women had redeeming qualities in them, Sylvia's did not. She was surrounded by the colors of sludge: gray-greens, murky browns, all swirled together with black. Sylvia Murchinson cared about no one on earth other than herself.

It wasn't easy to make myself smile at her and be friendly. I chatted with her and told her things that would confirm what she thought she knew about Linc and me. I told her I'd visited the local church that day and seen the cemetery. Over the second course, I lowered my voice and asked if she knew where a slave who'd led an uprising in 1843 was buried.

She was totally uninterested. If I didn't have my abilities, I think she would have picked up her plate and moved away. But I concentrated and made her stay where she was. Hers was a difficult mind to reach. She seemed to have made up her mind years ago and not all the True Persuasion in the world was going to change it.

I willed her to tell me about her husband. If I could get her to talk about her hatred of him perhaps she'd reveal too much. I also willed her to like me so she'd tell me as much as possible.

Finally, when we were served a plate of tough roast beef, she said, "I don't mean to insult you, but did you know that you look very much like the Hillbilly Honey?"

This was not where I wanted her to go. As I tried to cut the beef, I worked to turn her mind to other things.

"I'm glad you aren't the Hillbilly Honey because I was the one who told my husband to call her that."

I quit cutting but I didn't dare look up. "Did you?"

"Oh yes. My husband is Howard Murchinson, owner of the newspaper *Secrets Revealed.*"

"The tabloid," I said, barely able to breathe.

"Yes. 'Tabloid' has become a derogatory term but I don't mind it. You know, I never got any credit for anything I ever did for that man. Take the Hillbilly Honey, for instance. You know that book about her?"

"Yes," I managed to say.

"I was the one who got it published. The poor kid who wrote it was barely out of college and he'd sent his exposé of this weird Kentucky hillbilly to every publisher in New York but no one would publish it. They said it was libelous and even that it was trash. Finally, he sent it to my husband, who I can tell you never read a book in his life, but I did and I thought the book was great. What a gold digger she was! I told my husband he should publish it. I said, 'She's your kind, a real hillbilly honey.' You see, my husband was born in Tennessee.

"You know the rest. The book came out and made millions. Of course the Montgomery family sued. After all, they had to protect their name, but my husband was prepared for that. He'd cooked the books. The sales were double what he reported to the court so he paid the Montgomerys, but it was nothing to what that book earned."

She was laughing, pleased with what she'd accomplished. When she put her hand on my arm, I had to take deep breaths. I wanted to set fire to her hand, to her entire body. For real.

Oblivious, she kept talking, still under my spell of telling me secrets. "Then, when that woman's husband disappeared, it was I who said she probably killed him. I knew Howard had made a lot from the original book, but he'd also had to pay a lot, and he didn't like that. Howard doesn't like to lose.

And when the Montgomerys gave his money away to some charity, it was like they were saying his money wasn't good enough for them to touch. I can tell you that Howard was furious.

"He got all the Montgomerys back, though. Howard made the whole world believe the Hillbilly Honey had killed her husband. Oh! Look at the time. I have to go. Nice talking to you. Let's sit together every night. I rather like you. Maybe we'll be friends forever."

I watched her walk out of the room and, like a video, scenes played through my head. There was the misery that book had caused in my family. The Montgomerys blamed themselves for teasing me, but they'd done it with love, never animosity.

My children! I thought, including my niece with my daughter. They'd had to endure taunts and ridicule. They'd seen the woman spitting on me. They were now living away from their mother because of what this woman had done.

I looked at the back of Sylvia Murchinson's head as she left the dining room. I could kill her, I thought. Right now, I could make her brain explode and any investigation would say it was "natural causes." No one would ever know.

Somehow, I managed to keep my temper intact. I watched her until she left the room, then sat there, unable to eat anything.

LINC ⟨⟩

⟨⟩ *Chapter Eighteen*

I don't know what that catty Sylvia Murchin-son said to Darci, but it had a deep impact on her. Darci was sitting at the dinner table but it was as though she wasn't there. She ate nothing, spoke to no one.

When the long meal finally ended, the women gathered around me, issuing invitations that ranged from lewd to of such lone-liness they were frightening. I looked over their heads to Darci but she was still sitting at the table. The waitresses were clearing the dishes away around her, but Darci just sat, her hands in her lap, her eyes straight ahead.

As politely as I could, I pushed my way out of the encircling women and went to the table where I leaned across to Darci. "Could you get those vultures off of me?" I asked. "True Persuade them to go away."

Darci looked at me as though she'd never seen me before.

"What the hell did she do to you?" I muttered. The women were around me again, pulling on my arms and jabbering about what they wanted me to do with them and for them. They wanted me to go into town with them and go dancing. They wanted moonlight massages. They wanted skinny dipping in the pond.

As I looked at them I saw how much work Darci did when she kept the women away. Except for Darci, these creatures would have been all over me, the only male here, even if I'd slept inside a sarcophagus in the crypt.

But now Darci was keeping no one away. I put my hands on little Miss Burns's shoulders, picked her up, and moved her to one side so I could make a pathway. I went around the table, took Darci's hand and pulled. When she didn't move, I picked her up in my arms and carried her to the dining room door.

Turning back, I looked at the women and said that if any of them came near me tonight, she'd be taken off my massage list forever.

They were reluctant but they didn't follow me as I took Darci up to her room. Behind me, I heard hissing, and words such as, "Who does he think he is?" reached me, but they didn't follow.

Once in Darci's room, I wasn't sure what to do with her and wished I'd taken her outside to the Quarters. But it had rained the night before and I knew it was cool outside. The only thing I could think to do with Darci was to get her warm.

I put her in bed, removed her shoes, then wrapped the blankets around her, but she didn't respond.

"What happened?" I asked her. "Tell me what Sylvia said that's upset you."

Darci just lay there, staring up at the ceiling. If my words didn't get through to her, maybe my visions would, I thought. I put my hands on her upper arms and my forehead against hers as I sent images to her of her talking to me.

No response. Standing, I stuck my hands in my pockets and walked to the fireplace. Outside, I could hear voices. I opened the window and looked out. Through the trees I

could see the corner of the back terrace below. All the guests, with Delphia and Narcissa, were out there. I couldn't see them
for the thick foliage, but I could hear them,
could identify each voice. By now I could
have identified their headless bodies in a
morgue. They were laughing in an excited
way. "Wonder if they've been told that my
son has given in to their demands?" I said
out loud, hoping Darci would hear me
through her catatonic state. "My son is being threatened that his mother will be killed
if he doesn't use his powers to kill someone
for those women. Did they choose who got
to go first tonight?"

I knew my voice was as bitter as I felt.
Why did Darci have to choose tonight to go
into some sort of trance?

There was a light tap on the door. Angry, I
flung it open. "I told you that—" One of the
unsmiling female employees was standing
there, a tiny glass of the green liqueur on a
tray. Since there was only one, it was obvious that they didn't want me drinking the
laced stuff and falling asleep in Darci's
room.

I thanked the woman, took the tray, then
closed the door and locked it.

Maybe sleep would help her, I thought. I sat down on the bed beside Darci, pulled her up into my arms, and managed to get the drink into her. She made no response and I held her until she fell asleep.

Gently, I lay her down, got off the bed, then covered her.

Now what? I thought. Below me, I could no longer hear the voices so I was sure the women had been put into their nightly drug-induced stupor. I wondered if they realized what was being done to them—or had they agreed? I'd heard Sylvia Murchinson say she'd signed a prenup saying she'd receive nothing if her husband divorced her. In spite of knowing her penchant for "pool boys," she'd signed the agreement anyway. I could imagine that a woman like that would agree to being drugged and locked in at night if the end result was that she'd get "mega millions."

Turning, I looked at Darci on the bed, sound asleep, but frowning and restless. Whatever had been said to her had turned her mind upside down.

I had no doubt that what was said had something to do with her husband. I prayed that she hadn't been told that her husband was dead.

I looked at the setting sun and thought that, without Darci, I couldn't do much. If she couldn't find my son with all her powers, I couldn't—

Suddenly, I remembered what Darci and I had talked about before dinner: Amelia would be waiting in the twilight for Martin and her baby.

I left Darci's bedroom as fast as I could go, bounded down the stairs and ran out to the Quarters. I paused for a moment to remember exactly what Darci had said. "Double trunked elm tree by the edge of the river." The river was easy to find, about two hundred yards from the slave quarters. To the right was the road so the tree had to be to the left. I started running.

When I saw the tree, there was Amelia sitting on a bench that I doubted was actually there and doing her crochet.

Halting, I watched her for a moment and tried to compose myself. Every night for over a hundred years she'd gone to this spot and waited for my ancestor. It's where she'd met him when they were alive. She'd been safe at this time of day because her husband had been in the Quarters with the slave women.

I didn't want to think about that time. I just wanted to get my son, and Devlin had said a slave could help. If Amelia Barrister wasn't a slave, I didn't know who was.

"Hello," I said quietly so as not to startle her.

But she'd been waiting for Martin—who she thought I was—for about a hundred and twenty years so, yes, she was startled.

She dropped her crochet on the ground, put her hands over her face and began to cry. "You came," she said over and over. "You came."

I'd promised Darci I wouldn't do anything with the ghost without her there, but Darci was upstairs, drugged into sleep, and ghost or not, this pretty woman was in pain. I went to her, sat on the ground before her and put my head on her lap.

Amelia stopped crying and put her hands on my head, caressing my neck, running her fingertips over my face, memorizing and remembering.

So this is love, I thought, my hands on her legs through her heavy skirts. I kissed her fingertips as she touched my lips. This is love. The love wasn't coming from me but from her, and what I felt made me understand every song, every movie I'd ever seen. Until that moment I hadn't understood how anyone could, say, give up a great movie role to be with another human. I'd complained about Alanna choosing a movie over me but I'd understood.

What I hadn't understood until this moment was what people whined so much about. "I love her, man," I'd heard too often. And Darci! She had everything. She had money, beauty, power, but she was miserable because she didn't have the man she loved.

The love I felt coming from Amelia was enough to make me understand—and, more, it made me want that kind of love. It made me want to be part of what the rest of the world was experiencing—the lucky ones, that is. And I knew, without a doubt, that *this* was what that Shape-Changer had meant for me to remember, that love is all.

I don't know how long we stayed like that but, slowly, I began to come back to reality. What do I do now? I thought. The last time I saw Amelia I'd mentioned our son's—her son's—name and she'd disappeared. If

Darci were here she might know what to do,
but then Amelia believed Darci was the
slave sent to spy on her.

I took a breath and gave a prayer, asking
for help in knowing the right way. I took
Amelia's hands in mine. They were soft and
young and as solid as anyone's hands. I
could not, for the moment, believe she was
a ghost.

"I want you to listen to me," I said softly,
"and I don't want you to disappear again."

"Disappear," she said, smiling. "You do
say odd things."

I held her hands tighter. "How many times
have you come to this tree and Martin
hasn't been here?"

"A few," she said, smiling. "Edward keeps
you very busy."

"How many times?"

She stopped smiling. "More than a few.
Many, many times."

"Amelia," I said slowly, "the year is 2003
and—"

Her laugh cut me off. "How silly you are.
The world will end in the year 2000."

"People in our time thought that too,
but . . ." I didn't want to get off the subject.
"My name is Lincoln . . . Frazier, and I'm

from the twenty-first century and I'm a descendant of the child you and Martin had."

She started to fade; the information was too much for her to comprehend.

"Go ahead and fade away," I said, "but it could easily be another three hundred years before another of Martin's descendants shows up."

She came back into view, but she pulled her hands from mine. I could see she wanted me to move from the lover's position I was in, so I got up and sat by her on the bench.

"Who are you?" she asked.

I wanted my head back on her lap and I wanted her to look at me with the deep love she had for Martin. I reached out to touch her but she pulled away.

"Why are you here?" she asked.

"To give you peace. At least I think that's why I'm here with you. And to get your help, but I don't know how you can help me."

She sat in silence, looking at me with her beautiful blue eyes, and waited for me to continue. Where do I begin? I thought.

"Your father took care of your son," I blurted out, expecting her to start fading, but she didn't. When I saw the tiniest spark of interest in her eyes, I prayed I was on the right track. "Your father knew whose child he was. He couldn't save you and he couldn't save Martin, but he could save his grandson. He"—I tried not to choke over the word—"he bought the child and educated him with his other grandson. Does that sound like something your father would do?"

"Oh yes," she said, and there were tears in her eyes.

"Your father treated his grandson as his own." I hesitated before saying the name. "Jedediah ran your father's estates even after he was given freedom."

"Freedom?" she said, her eyes wide.

I reached out to take her hands but she wouldn't let me touch her. I wanted another second of feeling the love she'd given to Martin.

"Yes, freedom," I said. "Abraham Lincoln signed the Emancipation Proclamation about 1863, give or take a year or so."

"Lincoln," she said. "Like you."

I wasn't about to tell her it was a stage name. When I'd left home I'd wanted to disassociate myself so completely from my parents that I'd changed all of my name.

But for Amelia, I'd give her my real last name.

"And Martin?" she asked. "My Martin?"

I knew from her diary that she knew what had happened to Martin, but it looked as though, over the years, she'd blocked it out. I tried to tell her the truth about the man she loved because she needed to quit waiting to find peace. But I couldn't. I told myself this was the role of my life, the role that would make me win an Oscar over Russell Crowe, but, still, the words wouldn't come out of my mouth.

I'd never spent much time thinking about ghosts so I didn't know much about them—not that anyone except Darci did—but, even without being reminded of the grisly truth, it looked to me like Amelia was beginning to wake up. She took her eyes off mine and looked around her. She looked out at the river, staring at it for a moment.

"The river used to be much deeper," she said. "It was higher on the banks."

"Lots of people; lots of water used."

She nodded and I wondered if she'd ask me to tell her all about the wonders of the twenty-first century, but she didn't.

When she moved her head to look at the

tree, I wanted to tell her not to. I was afraid she'd see Martin hanging there.

She didn't look up at the branches, but kept her eyes on the double trunk. "Two trees were planted," she said, "but they grew together. There was a heavy rain and a boulder washed down the hill and pushed the trees together. No one got around to thinning them and eventually they grew into one. Martin and I said the trees were like us, that we weren't supposed to be together, but we were and we'd grown into one."

"Emmy," I said, reaching out to take her hands.

She put her warm, smooth hands in mine. "Only Martin called me Emmy."

I squeezed her hands and when I did I felt a softness in them, an insubstantial quality that made me know she was leaving. Not fading. Leaving. Going away forever.

"What do you want from me?" she asked.

"I need help in finding my son. He's here somewhere but we can't find him. He's your grandson, with a few greats added, that is." I wanted to make her smile.

Amelia didn't smile. "Martin? What did he do . . . afterward?" she asked.

"He stayed with your son for a while, then

he went away to wherever spirits go. Do you know where?"

She nodded once and her hands in mine grew transparent, there and not there.

"My son," I said, and the urgency I felt was in my voice.

"I will help you," she said. "I will wait and see what I can do to help you." With that she faded more, until there was nothing in my hands.

"Wait!" I called.

Instantly, she was there again, but not sitting beside me. She was standing a few feet away and she no longer looked like a living person. Now there was a light behind her and she looked like . . . well, like a ghost.

"Yes," she said, her voice sweet-sounding and faraway.

"I, uh, I wanted to ask you about Martin. Did he, well . . . did he look like me?"

The light behind her changed from pure white to a beautiful golden color. "No," she said. "Compared to him you are a plain man, and your body lacks muscle. Go now. I will help you."

With that she left and I was standing in darkness, smiling. To Amelia, the man she loved was the most beautiful person on earth. It had grown night while we'd been talking. I stumbled my way back to the Quarters, pulled off my sweater, shoes, and trousers, and climbed into bed in my under-wear. I hadn't had one of those lethal 13 Elms nightcaps, but I felt as though I'd had two of them.

As I drifted off to sleep, I thought that to-morrow I was going to hire some thugs to come in and take the whole place apart. If I had to, I'd remove every brick off that old house, take out every floorboard. I fell asleep before I could think anymore.

When I awoke it was all of a sudden and I was wide awake. I lay there for a moment, staring up at the ceiling, and thinking about Amelia. I remembered her hands and lips. I remembered my head on her lap and how good I felt when she touched me. I was wrong to have let her go. Wrong to have told her the truth so soon. I should have waited awhile, held her longer. Could I have made love to a ghost?

"Boy! You got to think of somethin' be-sides sex!"

I sat up so fast I banged my head against the wall. When I turned I saw an old man sitting in the chair on the other side of the room. He wore dark glasses and held an ivory-topped cane; he was blind.

"Who the hell are you?" I asked, rubbing my head.

"She didn't tell you about me?" he asked, chuckling. "No, she wouldn't."

I didn't have to ask who "she" was. No, Darci hadn't told me she'd met an old blind man who crept around in the middle of the night. "What do you want?" I asked.

"That house is on fire and unless you do something, they'll burn to death."

For a moment I was too shocked to move, then the words "fire" and "burn to death" hit me. I flung the covers back and opened the front door. I could only see part of the house through the trees, but it looked the same as always. I stared hard for two or three minutes. Nothing. No smoke, no flames, nothing.

Just in case the old man was telling the truth, I thought I'd better call the fire department. Better a false alarm than a fire, I thought.

I went back into the room and wasn't surprised to see that the old man was gone. "One of Darci's friends," I muttered and wondered if the old man had died a couple of hundred years ago. I pulled on a T-shirt, a pair of jeans, and stuck my bare feet into my already-tied sneakers, and opened my cell. I cursed when I saw the battery was dead. I'd forgotten to put it on the charger. I went down the hall where the pay phone was.

When I put in a quarter and there was no dial tone, I looked at the cord to the phone, followed it with my eyes up the wall, around the top of the doorway, then back to the floor—where it was cut. For a second I stood there staring at the severed telephone cord without comprehension.

It all hit me at once: Never, ever, had I let the battery on my phone die. My job depended on the telephone. I ran down the hall and toward the house. As I ran I looked at the house, and even though I could see nothing, I knew what was inside. My one and only concern was to get Darci out.

I jumped up to catch the top of the porch decoration, leaped onto the railing, then swung myself up to the roof. Within seconds I was at Darci's window. It was locked, of course. I stretched out on the roof and kicked in a pane. I didn't care if an alarm went off or who came running.

Inside her room, all was quiet. Everything was exactly as it had been when I'd left it. There was no smoke billowing under the door, no flames bursting through the wall. Everything was quiet and calm.

Except that Darci wasn't in her bed.

I checked the bathroom, the closet and under the bed. No Darci. If she were normal I'd have assumed she'd been kidnapped, but Darci was . . . Well, strange didn't quite cover it.

Something had happened to her at dinner that had traumatized her—and I had given her a drugged liqueur that had seemed to knock her out. Had it? Had she been faking it so she could go off without me to meet an old blind man who walked into my room in the middle of the night?

I decided I didn't know and didn't care. Whether she'd left on her own or been taken, I was going to find her. Enough was enough! If we were going to be partners— and she'd asked for my help in finding her husband—then I needed to know where she was at all times.

As I headed for the door, I pulled Darci's

sunhat off the wreath and looked directly into it. "Your house is on fire," I said, then replaced the hat.

The door was locked. Locked from the outside. Since the window had been locked from the inside, that meant she'd been— What? Abducted by ghosts? How about aliens who made little ceramic men that dis- solved in water?

No, she'd control *them.* I knew in my heart that whoever was holding my son was now holding Darci. I grabbed the fireplace poker, wedged it in the old door, and pulled. The door broke in seconds and I opened it.

Silence. There was nothing but silence in the house.

I walked down the hallway and tried the doorknobs. Each one was locked. If I had Darci's power I could have put my hand on the door and felt if there was someone—or something—inside, but I couldn't. Short of busting down all the doors, I didn't know if they were empty or not.

At the end of the hall, at the foot of the stairs, was Amelia's room. I couldn't resist opening the door. Moonlight shone in through the French doors in the far wall and the hall light shone behind me. It was

enough that I could see the room: filthy, un-
cleaned since Amelia died over a hundred
years ago. It was as though her body'd
been carried out, the door closed, and not
opened again until now.

And there, lying on the floor, was Darci.
She had on some long white robe, her
hands crossed over her breast. She looked
like a sacrificial virgin in a bad B movie.

With my heart pounding in my throat, I
ran to her and picked her up. Until I touched
her, I didn't realize I'd expected her body to
be cold. When she was warm to my touch I
almost cried with joy. As I picked her up in
my arms and pulled her to me, I sat down
on the filthy old floor, putting my back
against a wall. I'd played a cop in too many
episodes to trust my back to an open door.

"Darci," I said, smoothing her hair back
from her face. I kissed her forehead, then
her cheek, then her chin. My lips hovered
over hers.

"Don't even think about it," she whispered when my lips started to touch hers.

"You're alive!" I said.

"Did you think I was dead? Were you going to kiss a *dead* person?"

"I was going to run off with one this evening," I said as Darci got off my lap. She was rubbing her head and blinking a lot.

"What dead person did you want to run away with?" She looked at me sharply. "You didn't see Amelia by yourself, did you?"

I wasn't going to let her get out of telling me about herself. "Would you mind telling me what happened to you at dinner, and why you aren't in your own bed now, and who's the old blind man in my room?"

"Henry went to see you?"

She'd avoided all my questions. Before I could say another word, her eyes opened wide, the last of the sleep out of them. "This house is on fire."

"That's what Henry said."

"He told you this house is on fire, but all you're doing is sitting here?" She got up but then had a dizzy spell and grabbed on to me.

"Darci, you're in no shape to deal with this. I want you to go downstairs and get out of this house immediately. Get in the rental car, find a telephone and call—"

I stopped because she was running out the door. "The women are still in their rooms asleep," she said.

I ran after her. "Their doors are locked,

and where's the fire now?" As soon as I said it, I knew. I could smell the unmistakable odor of smoke. It came from upstairs in the attic.

"Open the doors and get the women out," Darci ordered as she put her foot on the bottom stair.

I caught her arm. "No, you don't. You don't go anywhere without me."

"Someone's up there. I have to get her out." Her voice was urgent. "Linc! Let me go!"

I didn't release her. I meant it when I said she wasn't going anywhere without me. She looked at my hand and made it burn. I held on. The burn grew worse. I didn't let up. My eyes watered; my knees grew weak; my stomach clenched. But I didn't let go. I'd come to know Darci Montgomery and I knew that she wouldn't continue giving pain to a good guy, to me.

I was right. The fire in my hand stopped as abruptly as it had started and I'd not let go of her arm.

"I have to—" she began, but then she turned away from the stairs and ran down the hall, me right behind her.

I knew what she wanted. I held on to her

arm as I kicked open the nearest door. Mrs. Hemmings was sound asleep in her bed. "Help me search for her cell phone," I said, and two seconds later Darci had it. Moments later I'd called the fire department.

"They're on their way," Darci said as she ran out the door toward the stairs up. "They'll be okay. I see no death around the women."

I ran up the stairs after Darci and stopped her just as she was about to open the door to the room where I'd spent the night with Ingrid, where I'd found my son's toy. "It's hot," I yelled. "Don't touch that door."

"But how—?" Darci asked, meaning, How do we get into the room?

I wanted to ask her who was in there that was so worth saving, but I didn't. We'd lost too much time already to talk about anything.

The door to the next room wasn't hot, so I turned the knob and it opened and we went in. For now, the fire was on the other side of the wall. My guess was that the fire was at the end toward the door, so maybe the other end of the room near the windows was free of fire. Maybe there was enough air in that end of the room that a person would still be alive.

But how to get into the room? If I went out the window in this room, across the roof, and into the next window, it would take too long.

My thoughts had taken only seconds to reach the conclusion that there was only one way to get into that room quickly. Darci had to do what she'd done the night I'd been with Ingrid: She was going to have to use her mind to open the wall.

I couldn't waste my time with words that took too long to say, so I put my hands on Darci's shoulders, her back to my front, and in an instant I sent the image to her that she had to open that wall.

"But I can't do that by myself. I need—"

I tightened my grip on her shoulders. We didn't have time for this "I can't" garbage.

I knew I couldn't help her, but maybe my presence would give her support. I pulled her closer to me and my hands dug into her shoulders until I was sure I was hurting her.

I could feel the tension in her body. She became as stiff as steel. "Come on, Darci baby, you can do it," I said, and her body tightened even more. "Where the hell are you, Devlin?" I said through my teeth.

I felt more than heard his laughter, then when I looked at the wall, I saw the flowers in the wallpaper become eyes. They crinkled up in laughter. I shook my head to clear it, never letting go of Darci's shoulders. I looked back at the wallpaper, the eyes blinked twice, then changed back to flowers. As far as I could tell, Devlin the Shape-Changer was here and he'd changed himself into wallpaper.

I conjured up an image that told Darci Devlin was here helping her and did what I could to send it to her. I didn't want her to know he was playing tricks with the wallpaper, so I sent her the vision that he was standing behind me, looking normal, his strong hands on my shoulders.

I don't know if I had anything to do with it or not, but the wall began to open. When the wall was open only about a foot high, I felt Darci move under my hands. She was planning to wriggle through that space all by herself—without me. She had the advantage on me that she had unbelievable mind powers, but I was a lot bigger and a lot stronger than she was. I knew she could paralyze me or give me a headache, but I also knew that she couldn't do two things at once.

I wouldn't release her shoulders and I sent her a vision of my going through the wall with her. I felt her tense, as though she wanted to argue with me, but I guess she decided not to waste time. She concentrated more and the wall opened wider. Seconds later, we were on our bellies and snaking into the room.

It was Sylvia Murchinson on the floor, passed out from the smoke. Fire licked around the door. It wasn't too big and too hot, yet. Holding my breath, I grabbed bedclothes and began to hit the fire.

Behind me, Darci was over Sylvia, and at one point I saw Darci giving the woman mouth-to-mouth. The second Darci had turned her attention elsewhere, the hole in the wall closed, which was good because an increase in oxygen would have fanned the flames.

As soon as the fire was out, coughing and choking, I opened the door, then I ran to the window, unlocked it and pushed it open. I took a few deep breaths, then looked down at Darci. She was leaning against the window seat, breathing the clean air. Opening the wall had taken a lot out of her.

Beside her, still on the floor, but now opening her eyes, was Sylvia. It looked as though Darci had saved the woman's life.

As Sylvia began to come to her senses, she reached out to Darci, but Darci pulled her arm back, not letting the older woman touch her.

I remembered that it was Sylvia who'd talked to Darci at dinner and afterward Darci had been catatonic. Yet Darci had saved this woman's life. She may have saved her life, even given her mouth-to-mouth, but Darci wasn't allowing the woman to touch her.

"Let's get out of here," I said. Since Sylvia wasn't in any shape to walk, I picked her up and ran for the open door, pausing to look back at Darci. She was getting up but she was having difficulty. My inclination was to drop Sylvia and go get Darci, but my conscience wouldn't let me.

"Go to my room," Darci said, sounding like a hundred-year-old woman. "He's in the basement now, lighting fires there." Before I could speak, she said, "Get everyone out of the house. I can hold him, but I can't hold the fire."

Opening the wall had exhausted her, but she still had to paralyze a man in the basement.

With Sylvia in my arms, I ran down the stairs, and by the time I got to the bottom the woman was stroking my arms and neck, running her hands over my chest. I smelled booze and I wondered if she'd been on the floor in the room as much from being drunk as from smoke inhalation.

"You rescued me," she said. "You saved my life. I felt your kiss and I knew—"

"Darci saved you, not me," I said and was sickened by her.

At that Sylvia gave a little laugh, which sent her coughing. We were in Darci's bedroom now, so I dropped the woman on the bed and went to the doorway. I was going to get Darci, but Sylvia's words halted me.

"That proves she isn't the Hillbilly Honey."

Turning, I stared at the woman on the bed. "What does that mean?"

"Last night I told her it was me who coined the phrase and that I got my husband to publish the book about her. If it was

her, she would have let me die." She
seemed to think this was a great joke.

"Murchinson," I said, realizing who Sylvia
was. "Howard Murchinson, the owner of the
tabloid."

"One and the same."

"And you—" I couldn't think more about
what she'd just told me, and if she said another word I might kill her. I had to leave the
room. Darci was at the head of the stairs,
sitting there, her eyes glazed. I knew she
was using her powers to hold the man in
the basement. I didn't want to break her
concentration but I did want to get her
downstairs closer to me.

I picked her up, carried her downstairs,
and put her on a chair in the hallway. As far
as I could tell she never broke her concentration.

I looked at the long corridor full of locked
doors. How did I open the doors in a hurry?
I didn't have time to break them all down.

I went back to Darci's bedroom. Sylvia
had pulled the coverlet around her and was
peacefully sleeping. It wasn't easy to tamp
down my hatred of her. What she'd done to
Darci— No! I couldn't think about that now.

"Get up," I said, pulling her out of bed.

"I'm tired. I want to sleep."

I leaned over her. "You get up and you help me get the other women out or so help me God I'll toss you out that window."

She blinked at me a couple of times and looked as though she was going to protest, but she got out of bed.

"Do you know where keys to the rooms are?"

"Yeah, but why do you need them?" she asked, yawning.

I shoved her shoulder and pushed her toward the doorway. I wanted to ask her a lot of questions about the room upstairs and why she'd been locked inside with a fire. I wanted to ask about who was in the basement, but I didn't have time.

Sylvia walked ahead of me with the air of a martyr, of someone being persecuted unjustly. "I should be in a hospital, you know," she said. "I should—" She stopped when she saw Darci sitting on a chair in the hall. I had to admit that Darci looked almost as strange as she was. She was wearing a long white robe with a gold belt and little gold sandals. She was sitting utterly rigidly and her eyes were narrow slits.

"What is her problem?" Sylvia asked, as though she and I were friends.

"There's a fire in the basement," I said calmly, "and if you don't hurry up we're all going to burn to death."

Without a word, Sylvia turned on her heel and started for the down staircase. If there was a fire she was going to get herself out and the rest of us be damned.

I pulled her back, said, "Keys," then gave her another push that let her know I meant business.

There was a portrait halfway down the hall. She grasped the frame, pulled hard, and it opened to reveal a rack full of numbered room keys.

I shoved a handful at Sylvia. "Open the doors," I said as I grabbed the rest of them.

"I don't know why you're so mad at *me,*" she said, moving down the hall. "I'm the victim. I'm innocent in all of this. I was just paying for a service."

I didn't have the time or inclination to discuss philosophy with her. She didn't know I knew as much as I did. What I really knew was that my son couldn't have been exploited if it weren't for people like her. "Sylvia?" I said.

"Yes, Jason," she answered, smiling at me.

"Don't leave this house until the last person is out." I didn't say any more because I knew she got my meaning.

I went into Mrs. Hemmings's unlocked room first to wake her and tell her to get out, but the woman was so hard asleep I couldn't wake her. I ran to the rooms of four other women but I couldn't wake any of them. There was no way I had time to carry each of them down the stairs and out of the house.

I met Sylvia in the center of the hallway. "Two are asleep, Delphia and Narcissa are gone," she said.

Darci, I thought. Only Darci could wake the women and get them out in time. But if she did that she'd have to release the person in the basement. Where oh where was the fire department?

"Get a cell phone," I ordered Sylvia. "Call the fire department again *and* the police."

"The police?"

I gave her a look and she disappeared down the hall. I could smell the smoke now. The fire was eating up roomfuls of old trash in the basement.

"Darci," I said, touching her shoulder and sending her a vision of the urgency of needing to save the drugged women.

She came out of her trance instantly. When she tried to stand, she nearly fell, but I caught her and the next second she was running from room to room. She put her hand on each woman's forehead and the woman woke in a panic. Darci seemed to have filled them with the adrenaline of fear because they instantly jumped out of bed and started running for the stairs.

I was too busy with Darci to give Sylvia any thought, but I assumed that since I didn't see her she'd disobeyed me and run downstairs and outside to safety.

When Darci and I reached the end of the hall, she said Narcissa and Delphia were already outside.

"Let's go!" I shouted, grabbed Darci's hand and started running for the stairs, but halfway down, she wrenched away from me and began running up again. I caught her in her room. She was opening the window seat and withdrawing the bowling-ball bag. The crystal ball was inside.

I grabbed her hand, but when I turned, I

looked into the eyes of my agent Barney. Had his ghost come to help us?

Since I was holding Darci's hand she felt what I was thinking.

"He's real," she said.

My head reeled with thoughts. Barney was the only one who'd known my son was mine. He'd known my real name so it would have been an easy matter to find out about my grandmother's abilities. And Barney had been the first to read the PI's reports about my son. Suddenly I was sure I'd been given false reports.

I glanced at Darci. She'd known a man had been killed in the fire in my agent's office, and she'd known that Ingrid hadn't meant to kill anyone. What Darci hadn't known was that the man who'd burned to death hadn't been my agent but some other man.

Barney had a gun, which he pointed at me. "Do it again, missy, and I'll kill him."

I assumed the "it" was Darci's paralyzing of him. However, I guess he'd had enough experience with Darci's abilities to know that her paralysis was gradual. When she'd done it to me I'd been tying her shoe. She'd paralyzed my body before it spread to my

hands. That meant that if she began paralyzing Barney he'd have time to pull the trig-
ger.

He looked Darci up and down. "With a
mind like yours and my talents we could
have made a fortune. But you already married one, didn't you? Too bad you have to
die with him."

I started to move away from Darci. It was
a trick we'd used in my show, to put distance between the victims, but Darci held
on to my hand. She seemed to want to see
what I was thinking.

I want to get him talking, I sent to her. I
want to get him to tell me where my son is.

"So, Barney," I said, releasing Darci's
hand and moving toward the fireplace.
There was a poker there. Behind him, the
door was open and I could see smoke coming from downstairs. It wouldn't be long
now before we saw flames. "How ya been,
Barney?"

Barney gave a one-sided grin. "I always
did like your sense of humor, kid. So why
didn't you tell me you had a grandmother
who could make people sick? Give 'em a
disease?"

"I didn't know she could," I said, still

moving, taking Barney's gunsight with me and away from Darci. She was standing there, silent, staring, that big crystal ball in its bag hanging by her side. I wished I could will her to run as soon as I got Barney's back to her.

"So how'd you pull this off?" I asked, smiling at Barney like we were old friends.

"Easy. You were always so easy to fool. You cared about gettin' in bed with that two-timin' girlfriend of yours and actin' and that's all. You left the rest up to me. I had a PI find out about that kid of yours. His mother moved him around so much because the kid could heal people. Like somethin' out of the Bible. Little kid would fall on the playground and your kid would put his hands on the kid's heart and the brat would get up and run away."

"So you decided to make money off him," I said.

"Oh yeah. Lots of money. I just had to figure out how. It wasn't until your kid's mother got a job here and I checked out the Barrister sisters that I got some ideas. Those two are into every scam goin'. There isn't a con artist on earth who couldn't take lessons from them."

I was inching closer to the fireplace. Darci was just standing there, now nearly at Barney's back, and she was doing nothing. Her eyes weren't narrowed so she wasn't doing one of her voodoo spells. Instead she was just staring.

I don't know why her lack of spell-casting was so scary, but it was terrifying me.

"So where's my son?" I asked.

"Damned if I know."

"You faked your death to get him so where is he?" Maybe I was an idiot but Barney's gun scared me much less than Darci's staring did. Maybe it was because I'd faced so many guns—fake, but they looked the same—in my acting, but he didn't frighten me at all.

Barney shrugged. "I needed to get out. I have a problem with gambling so there were some people who wanted my kneecaps." He laughed as though this was a very funny and very original joke. "So I got cute little Ingrid to help me out. I used some old wino for the body and stuck my dentures in him."

"And my son?" I was inches away from the poker now and I began to wonder what I was going to do with it. Throw it?

"It took me a while to figure out what to do with the kid. I couldn't see myself runnin' a healin' parlor." Again he laughed at his own joke. "It was Delphia that found out the kid could make people sick. She hated kids but she had trouble gettin' employees to stay on account of the ghosts and all, so she kept the kid's mother on in spite of him."

Again, he paused to laugh. "One day the kid was doin' somethin' bad and rotten, like all kids, and she threatened him with dis-memberment or somethin' unless he stopped. He said he hated her and that he was gonna make her sick. That night she spent throwin' up and in the can, and the next day she was sneezin' and blowin'. Lit-tle Lisa went to Delphia and apologized for her son and that afternoon Delphia was fine. Never felt better.

"She and her sister were just startin' to figure out how to make money off the kid when I showed up for my yearly visit to wherever the kid was. I'm Uncle Barney to him."

His story made me feel naive and self-centered and oblivious. All this had been going on for years and I'd known nothing about it. I'd received a piece of paper every year from Barney about my son and I'd thrown it into a safe and not even read it carefully.

"Who sent the note saying my son was missing?" I asked.

"You got me on that one," Barney said.

He started to say more but, suddenly, everything happened at once. Maybe because of what was going on in the room I didn't hear the sirens of the fire department. The first I knew of them was when the front door opened and men started shouting, "Is anyone in here?"

The fire, contained until the front door opened, rushed up from the basement windows and licked into the windows of Darci's bedroom.

Somebody screamed, Barney shot, and I felt something hit me. I looked down at my chest. There was a hole right where my heart was. The next thing I knew I was looking down at my body and there was light all around me. I saw men grab Barney, and I saw Darci kneeling over me. I felt her trying to pull me back into my body, but the heart was no longer beating in that body so I couldn't get back into it. I really wanted to

go toward the light but Darci wouldn't let
me. I tried to touch her, to tell her to let me
go, but I could see that she wasn't listening.
Let me go! I tried to send to her, but she
wouldn't release me. I gave up trying to reason with her. All I could do was hang around
and wait until she saw that she had to let
me go.

DARCI ⟨⟨⟨

⟨⟨ *Chapter Nineteen*

Linc was dead.

The second that man, that Barney, appeared, Linc's aura disappeared, so I knew that Linc was going to die and there was nothing I could do to stop it. I didn't know the details of how it was going to happen, so I couldn't work to prevent it. If I paralyzed Barney that might cause him to shoot Linc. If I ran, that might cause him to shoot Linc. There was nothing I could do except stand there and watch—and prepare. I could prepare for what I knew was about to happen.

I had connections to some people nearby so I put out a psychic SOS. I wanted to be ready when the time came. Maybe . . . I thought. Maybe there was something that could be done *after* Linc was dead.

I hurried the firemen into the room. They took Barney away and I kept them from seeing that Linc had been shot. I made them leave a stretcher leaning against the wall.

Behind the firemen came the pastor, Christopher Frazier, Onthelia, and her big fourteen-year-old daughter. I'd had to put them all into a trance to get them to walk into a burning building.

Without a word, without being aware of what they were doing, they picked up the stretcher, rolled Linc's body onto it and carried him downstairs. The fire was all around us now but I couldn't take my eyes off Linc. I clutched the bowling-ball bag to my chest and concentrated with all my might. I had to control the three people carrying the stretcher, had to keep Linc's spirit from leaving the earth; I had to keep all the people outside away from us, and most of all, I had to get Linc's child to meet us at the double elm.

Amelia was helping with that. She'd been behind Linc the whole time Barney had been holding a gun to him. I don't know what Linc had said to her, but she felt she owed him.

They carried the stretcher to the tree, set it on the ground, then Christopher, Onthelia, and her daughter left. Once they were out of sight, I released them. They'd not remember what they'd done.

I turned to the people standing under the tree. There was Lisa Henderson, and the moment I saw her, information came flooding into my mind. I hadn't been able to find her because she had no real connection to Linc. To be able to find someone I must have something that's close to them. When I looked at her I saw that she'd been incarcerated in a small, isolated house owned by Delphia and Narcissa. The women had left her alone there, drugged senseless, for days. When Barney had arrived just hours ago, he'd awakened her and hit her to make her tell him where her son was.

Lisa had taken all the blows, but never told him anything about her son, not past or present. I knew that her son was her life.

Barney, in his rage at having his plans thwarted, hadn't bothered to secure Lisa very well when he'd left. He'd wanted to kill her but he thought he might need her with the child in the future. All he'd wanted was to get to 13 Elms and set fire to the house.

He wanted no one, meaning all the women guests, around to talk about his failed scheme. When he'd found a half-drunk Sylvia snooping upstairs, he'd set fire to the room and locked her in.

After Barney left, Lisa had escaped her bonds, crawled out a window, and started running. Whoever had directed her son to go to the double-trunked tree had told her where to go.

Turning, I saw a little boy. He looked like Linc, just with lighter coloring. He was the child of my dreams. The child who would help me find my husband.

What I knew about him was that he'd been protected. While I had been at the church, he'd been there, taken care of by the pastor and his wife, who'd had no idea the child was being sought. When I was with Pappa Al, I'd felt someone in the church, but the feeling had gone away, had been taken from me.

For a moment, I marveled at the power it had taken to hide the child from me. Had Devlin done it? Had he told the child to leave his hiding place and come to us?

No, I thought, and suddenly knew that Devlin was a tool, like the Mirror of Nos-

tradamus was a tool. Devlin was a tool being used by a very, very powerful human.

Who? I wondered. I was certain I'd never
met anyone with such power, but then I'd
been fooled in Connecticut so maybe
someone else had fooled me.

I looked at Lisa Henderson. She was
holding her son's hand in both her own,
protectively, and when she saw me, she put
herself between the child and me. But the
boy, tall for his age, stepped forward. I saw
that he was an old man in a child's body.
He'd been through so much in his short life
and already he knew a lot. Instinctively, he
felt the psychic kinship between the two of
us.

The child and I said nothing to each
other. We had understanding beyond
words. He knelt on his father's left side, by
his heart. When Amelia appeared at Linc's
head I heard Lisa gasp at seeing a ghost,
but the boy didn't so much as look. He can
do things besides heal, I thought.

I knelt on the other side of Linc, my white
robe pouring out around me. Narcissa had
put the robe on me. She knew that Delphia
had meant to kill me—as ordered by Barney—and putting me in a shroud so I'd be

wearing white when I met my Maker was her idea of kindness. But Devlin had awakened me and led me to Amelia's room. Devlin had taken away a lot of the drug from my body, but I was still sleepy so I'd stretched out on the floor and slept lightly.

I looked across Linc's lifeless body at the boy, then set the bag I was clutching to the ground and unzipped it. I knew something had happened inside the bag in the last hour, but I didn't know what. Whereas it had once been heavy with the big glass ball, now the bag weighed little.

When I opened the bag, a white light came out. It was a beautiful, warm light that soon grew larger and larger, until it made a circle of light around the old tree. There, hanging on the tree was a man, a thick noose around his neck, his neck broken. It was Martin, and he looked like a darker-skinned Linc. To my left I heard a little moan of anguish from Amelia, but she didn't leave her place at Linc's head.

As I watched, the man opened his eyes, straightened his neck, the rope disappeared, and he stepped to the ground. His eyes were only on Amelia as he walked to Linc's feet.

Martin nodded as he put his hands on Linc's ankles, signaling that he was ready. Amelia put her hands on the sides of Linc's head, and his son placed both his hands on his father's still heart. The child nodded at me.

I reached into the bag, and withdrew a little white glass ball. It was about the size of a golf ball and it was the most wonderful object I'd ever held. A Touch of God, it had been called and when I touched it, I finally had some of the answers I'd been looking for.

I suddenly knew that the object I held was old beyond understanding. God had given the angels a touch from His fingertip. Each angel blew on the touch, then enclosed the touch and their breath in what looked to be glass. I knew that the ball was indestructible.

I also knew that I was allowed to have this object because I'd passed a test. I had known what Sylvia Murchinson had done to me and my family, but I'd saved her life anyway.

I held the beautiful, warm ball in my left hand, the one closest to my heart, then held out my right hand to the child. He put his left hand under mine, and we clasped right hands across Linc's body.

The boy and I looked into each other's eyes. He didn't have to tell me that he'd never done this before. He'd cured a few ailments, and he'd made many injuries heal faster, but he'd never come close to raising someone from the dead.

What I knew was what Linc had said, that healing and giving illness were two sides of the same coin. In Connecticut I had killed four people. If I could use my power to kill, I felt sure I could use it to give life.

I looked at Linc's son and nodded to him. We were to begin.

Closing my eyes, I concentrated. Only once before, when I'd been led into a sacrificial chamber, children in cages, ready to be used, had I concentrated as I did over Linc's body.

I could feel energy coming from Amelia, from Martin, from the child, and most of all from the ball. I prayed. I concentrated. I prayed.

As though I too had died, I felt my spirit leave my body. I looked down on the four of us kneeling over Linc's body, the child's

mother in the background, afraid but praying with us.

My spirit floated into the light, the Death
Light, and there I found Linc. He'd gone farther in than I thought he had.

Oh, but it was pleasant there! There was
no heavy body, no pain, no tears, no worries, just sweet sensations. I looked down
at my body and I could see my earthly misery. I could feel every tear I'd shed and
every tear I would shed.

Linc's spirit was before me. He reached
out to touch me and, like always, I could
feel his thoughts. When he was with Amelia
he'd felt love, real, true, deep love, and he
knew he didn't have that kind of love on
earth. His message to me was that he was
willing to leave. Whether he went alone or
with me was my choice.

I looked back at my miserable earthly self
and I was tempted. Oh, so very, very
tempted.

But then I looked at the child still kneeling
by Linc's body and I knew that he could
come to love Linc greatly. The child *needed*
Linc. I looked at the mother. She was sitting
on the bench, scared nearly witless. She
was a simple woman who'd just wanted to

have a movie star's child. The son she'd received was out of her capacity to deal with. She too needed Linc, I thought with surprise.

I looked back at Martin and Amelia, both bodiless. Someday, I thought, my husband and I will be like them. And there were two little girls who needed me desperately. They shouldn't have to live with someone who was "creeped out" by them no matter how well they meant. And they didn't need a mother who was frightened enough of the Sylvia Murchinsons of the world to hide from them.

I looked at Linc and he smiled. He knew my decision. Like Amelia had loved her Martin, enough to wait for him for a hundred years, I was going to wait for the man I loved. Forever.

I smiled back at Linc, we clasped hands, and we returned to earth.

EPILOGUE 🍃

Henry laughed when he saw Linc's body gasp and come back to life. In the human world he was a blind old man, but in the spirit world he was young and could see everything. It was a choice he'd made long ago. Human sight took away too much from his inner visions, so he'd given it up.

"She passed," he said to Devlin.

"So far," Devlin said, "but she understands little." He'd changed himself into a fat old man and was eating a bag of kettle corn. "I'm not sure she'll succeed."

"She will!" Henry said so forcibly that the corn spilled.

Devlin changed himself into a Viking, as though ready to do battle.

"Would you stop that!" Henry said.

"You conjured me so I am what you wanted."

"I must have used a wrong ingredient somewhere."

Devlin smiled, his weapons disappeared, he took off his horned helmet, and he sat down on a fur-covered chair. "If you're such an inept wizard why leave your power to anyone?"

Henry didn't bother to answer the rhetorical question. "I think she's the one but she needs—"

"More temptation?"

Henry smiled in memory. "She did well with that woman, didn't she? She could have killed her but she blew her own breath into her. Oh! Look at this." He looked down through the mists to the scene below.

Thirteen Elms was no more. The house had burned down, and the slave quarters as well. The land was covered with fire trucks, police cars, and people.

Smiling, Henry watched as Barney, Delphia and Narcissa were taken away in handcuffs. Henry pointed a finger and a headlight caught Sylvia sneaking away into the forest, a large tote bag clutched to her. Startled by the light, she dropped the bag and out fell jewelry. While Darci and Linc had been waking the women up, Sylvia had been emptying jewelry boxes.

Smiling even more broadly, Henry watched the police take Sylvia away. The women claimed their jewelry, but when they finished, lying on the ground was a little gold watch. It was the watch Adam had given Darci before they were married. "She'll want that," Henry said. "Make sure she finds it."

"Yes, sir!" Devlin said and changed himself into a handsome soldier, with six stars on his collar.

Henry kept smiling. "Even you can't annoy me tonight. I feel in my heart she's going to prove worthy."

"If you give her your power plus what she has . . ."

"I know," Henry said. "That's why I'm being careful. If she has her own small power and—"

"Your very large power—"

"Plus three magic objects—"

"There are twelve of them."

"She has two of them already," Henry said. "And a key."

"She has only one object," Devlin said. "She has the Touch of God. It can—"

"I know very well what it can do, but she needs to find out. She has a second object, but she doesn't know she has it." He looked into the mists and there was an object that looked like a little birdcage, only the bars were made of string. Inside the cage was a rock.

At the sight, Devlin disappeared in a cloud of blue smoke.

Henry laughed again. "Come back, old friend. He's asleep. He can't harm you."

Just the head of a man appeared—a head wearing a spiked steel helmet. "Does she know . . . ?

"Nothing. She found him when she was just a child—or, as you know, he found her. She was lonely so they used to talk. Her mother thought the child was strange enough without talking to a rock, so she told her daughter she'd thrown away her 'pet.' "

"But the mother kept . . . him?"

"Yes. He's in Putnam, Kentucky, at the back of a closet. Darci needs to find him again, don't you think?"

"I think you're giving too much power to

one lowly human. With all this she'll be able to—"

"Change the world," Henry said, smiling.

Devlin transformed into an old man with a long gray beard and a coarse white robe. "She'll be able to change *history!*"

"Yes, she will," Henry said, then looked down through the mists. Darci and the child were on either side of Linc and helping him to walk. As they made their way through the forest, she halted for a moment to pick up her beloved watch that Sylvia had dropped. In the pocket of her robe was the little glasslike ball.

"Thanks," Linc said to Darci, and since he was touching her, she knew he meant thanks for finding his son.

"Couldn't have done it without you," she said, smiling up at him.

The mist closed and Henry looked back at Devlin.

"How much does she know?" Devlin asked.

"Not much now but she'll figure it out. She already knows someone hid the child but she doesn't yet know who. We have to plan her next test."

"The one with more . . . temptation?"

"More of everything."

"In Putnam, near . . . him?"

"No, not yet. She needs to learn some things first." Henry looked hard at Devlin. "As for you, no more wallpaper!"

Devlin just laughed.